OF ARMS I SING

by
Joseph J. Bohnaker

Sunstone Press
Santa Fe, New Mexico

This book is dedicated to the memory of Dr. Philip Gallagher, recent member of the English Department, University of Texas — El Paso. I hope that in some small way, this modest book will do justice to the memory of Phil's literary genius and dedication to the art of teaching.

This book is based on data gathered from many fine historical works. Several specific extracts from archival data are used which should be acknowledged: (1) The poem on page 3 and monologue on page 159 are based on G. Espinosa's translation of Villagra's poem, *Historia de la Nueva Mexico* (Quivira Society - 1933); (2) The letter by Fray Escalona on page 150 appears in Hammond & Rey's *Don Juan de Oñate Colonizer of New Mexico* (University of New Mexico Press - 1953); (3) The report on pages 60-61 by Castaño de Sosa appears in M. Cohen's *The Martyr* (Jewish Publications of America - 1973); (4) The map on page 14 appears in P.J. Blackwell's *Silver Mining and Society in Colonial Mexico* (Cambridge University Press - 1971).

Library of Congress Cataloging in Publication Data:

Bohnaker, Joseph J., 1935-
  Of arms I sing / Joseph J. Bohnaker -- 1st ed.
    p.   cm.
ISBN: 0-86534-136-2 : $10.95
  1. New Mexico--History--To 1848--Fiction. 2. Oñate, Juan de, fl. 1595-1622--Fiction. 3. Villagriá, Gaspar Pérez de, d. 1620--Fiction. 4. Pueblo Indians--Fiction. I. Title.
PS3552-05217034 1989
813'.54--dc20   89-34611
                                                             CIP

Published in 1990 by SUNSTONE PRESS
              Post Office Box 2321
              Santa Fe, NM 87504-2321 / USA

HISTORIA
de
La NUEVA MEXICO

Of Arms I sing, and of that heroic son.
Of his wondrous deeds and of his victories
won.
Of his prudence and his valor shown when,
Scorning the hate and envy of his fellow men,
Unmindful of the dangers that beset his way,
Performed deeds most heroic in his day.

I sing of the glory of that mighty band,
Who nobly strive in that far distant land,
The world's most hidden regions they defy.
"Plus Ultra" is their ever battle cry.
Onward they press, nothing they will not dare,
Mid force of arms and deeds of valor rare.
To write the annals of such heroic men,
Well needs the efforts of a mightier pen.

> *Stanza I, Canto I.*
> *Captain Gaspar de Villagrá*
> *(1610)*

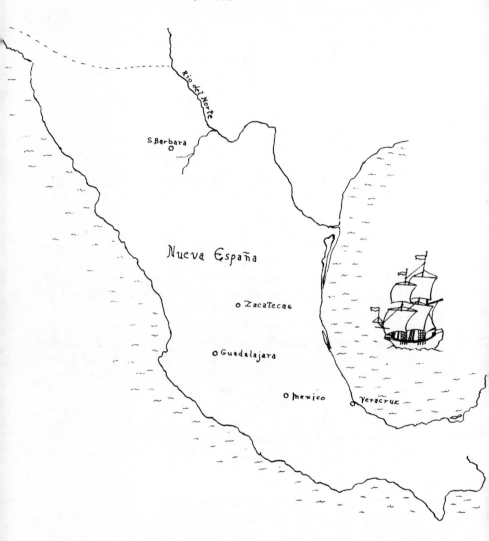

Nueva Mexico

Rio del Norte

S.Barbara
O

Nueva España

o Zacatecas

O Guadalajara

O Mexico   Veracruz

PREFACE

In 1598 at a point 1200 miles north of Mexico City, Don Juan de Oñate and his followers peered for the first time across the spring-swollen waters of the Rio del Norte. The brown, turbulent stream formed the final dividing line between the old civilization they were leaving behind in New Spain and the vague and mysterious Indian Pueblo cultures to the north.

Crossing the boundary would be the ultimate challenge and they hesitated for one final communion with the soul of their homeland. Here, close to a place to become El Paso, Texas, they spent several days gathering strength for the trials ahead, ever reluctant to leave their foothold in the past.

In this band of rugged pioneers were people from every walk of life; soldier-colonists who had been ranchers or craftsmen or workers in the mines and on the ranches of New Spain, or citizen of cities in Portugal, Castile and Aragon, of Zacatecas, Mexico and Guadalajara. They were served by dark-skinned slaves from every point of the globe. Amongst these soldiers, slaves, and servants moved the dauntless Franciscans who would walk the entire distance between Mexico City and their ultimate destination and the women and children whose support and suffering is mostly unrecorded.

They had been led to this place by the indomitable Oñate, citizen of Zacatecas. In the face of adversity and jealous opposition, he had brought this band safely to a boundary between two worlds and would go on to establish the roots of the first permanent settlement in the American West.

For Oñate, it was the fulfillment of the impossible dream. Many years had been spent in Mexico and Zacatecas pleading with the viceroy and king and maneuvering with government officials for the privilege of becoming the governor and captain-general of the unconquered territory known as New Mexico. There was fierce competition for this privilege. It offered prestige and power and the contenders were soon caught up in the tumultuous politics of New Spain and danced dangerously around the entanglement of evil spread by the infamous Inquisition. But the position of "Conquistador" had been greatly changed in the almost one hundred years since the magic days of Cortes and the conquering of the Aztecs, and such an appointment no longer meant the same thing. Those who gained this position could not rule a conquered territory with unbridled freedom and decree their own laws and punishments over the native populations. But this did not dim Oñate's vision of glory and adventure. Through dogged determination and wealth, he won the coveted post. While his perseverence was remarkable, it seem that later his judgement was questioned and before his ends could be achieved much internal strife divided his group into warring factions.

In the end, many of his followers turned against him. The reasons were many but dissension was largely due to the great poverty of the regions where they settled and the even greater dissatisfaction of certain friars. Several letters were written to the viceroy accusing Don Juan of grievous imcompetence and cruelty while governor of New Mexico. These letters appear to be half-truths and are mostly opinions of the disgruntled friars. But the letters were ignored by viceroy and king at the time of their writing. It wasn't until after the death of Philip II and the appointment of a new viceroy that the letters received attention. Some thirteen years after writing, the enemies of Oñate saw that the letters culminated in his trial and conviction. These very letters have been drawn upon time and again by historians in portraying a view of Don Juan. Thus has be passed into history.

Fortunately, several valiant captains, including a soldier-poet, Gaspar de Villagfa, remained loyal and became Don Juan's strongest supporters. An epic poem was written by Villagfa to celebrate Oñate's exploits and today this poem provide a meaningful view of the author, Don Juan, and those times and events. Villagfa was determined to bring their exploits to light through a classical form similar to Virgil's *Aeneid* and in so doing, his praise of Oñate is unstinting and his sense of drama acute.

Shortly before all this occurred, the sprawling Spanish Empire had stretched to its limits. The citizens of Castile were reeling under a system of improvident planning brought about by the government's foreign adventures. The colonies fared somewhat better than the old country and many sought passage to the New World.

But affairs for the Americas were strictly governed by the mother country under the "Council of the Indies". In reality, all was under the control of the dark prince, Philip II. This moody monarch was also a master bureaucrat and his fastidious requirements for paperwork permeated every facet of government. Every move and appointment in the New World was written in a legalistic, bureacratic language that could easily put modern governments to shame. To carry out the conquest of New Mexico required that a voluminous contract be made between the royal government and the privileged subject to be selected, detailing every item to be considered. In addition, any gains made from such contracts were taxed by the crown which demanded a Royal Fifth, sorely needed to fill the princely purse at home.

To make matters more difficult for the colonies, it was also a time of high tension between Catholic Spain and the "heretics" of England. This tension came about mostly because of a bitter quarrel between Philip II and Queen Elizabeth. The final, humiliating results for Phillip were the death of Catholic Mary and the destruction of the grand Spanish fleet. Black with despair, he turned with renewed vigor to the opiate of religion and the demonic instruments of the Inquisition. This river of religious bile reached every portal in New Spain and embraced the leading citizens in its poisonous flood. Strict religious upbringing, medieval superstitions and plain fear caused the people to acquiesce to the demands of the Holy Office and the strong treatment meted out to the New World Jews.

But not everyone gave in to the fearful demands of the Inquisition. On the question of "tainted persons" there was serious dissension within the ranks of the church. Certain leading Franciscans disregarded the rules of the Holy Office and one Franciscan commissary-general, Fray Pedro Oroz, openly declared its wicked punishments as misguided and unnecessary. Such temerity was not unusual amongst these Franciscans as they did fierce battle with each other for control of the order and maneuvered for political power with the royal office. While these few were also deeply imbued with faith, they remained a small but stabilizing influence against the Inquisition, going so far, in some cases, as to actually protect convicted Jews.

The temerity of the Franciscans was only equaled by the bravery of the "Christianized" Jews. Also known as conversos, New Christians, and the most derogatory of all, marranos, the Spanish Jews suffered for their faith at the hands of the Holy Office. Created in its modern form in 1483 by the infamous Tomas de Torquemado, this office was distinguised by the most flagrant violations of the basic principles of justice and humanity every witnessed up to that time. The aim of the Inquisition being to protect the faith from a relapse into the laws of the Old Testament, an attempt was made to stamp out every vestige of Judaism and Mohammedism. Thus, all Jews were forced to convert to Christianity or to suffer expulsion from Spain with the forfeiture of all their possessions. Many chose to stay and convert, but later found themselves still hounded by the Inquisition, looking to root out every last trace of Jewish practice. It was true that most of the converted Jews were not converted at all and practiced Judaism whenever they could. It was in this group that the Holy Office reaped its most grisly harvest. Many were burned alive and otherwise tortured and accordingly, many Jews sought refuge in the New World hoping to escape the terrors at home. Although forbidden to migrate, many *New Christians* managed to slip aboard ships bound for New Spain through bribery and deception.

It wasn't long before the Holy Office realized this and established itself in Mexico City. The New World Jews were once more menaced at every turn by the zealous souls who carried out the dark mission of the Holy Office.

Inquisitional terror did not extend directly to the natives of New Spain and many were the holy and royal orders demanding reform in the colonial system which abused the indigenous peoples. In this matter, the Church and State were unified against the secular citizens of New Spain. Bitterness arose between the Spaniards from the old country who supported Church and State and the citizens of New Spain who saw their lives threatened by such reforms. On the wild frontiers of New Spain, the settlers had encountered fierce nomadic tribes, quite unlike the sedentary civilizations found earlier in Mexico. Ruthless in their methods of warring and given to committing barbaric cruelties with captives, these tribes, known as the Chichimecas, threatened the encroaching settlements and soon had the citizens locked in a bloody life and death struggle.

In the forefront of this fierce struggle was the town of Zacatecas. Founded in the middle of the sixteenth century, the town grew from a crude frontier outpost to a rich silver mining center in spite of the Indian threat. The leading citizens thrived in this environment and soon became well known as Indian fighters and military leaders. It was here that Oñate gained the wealth and power that eventually led to his appointment as conqueror of New Mexico. It was also here that captured Indians were used as slaves, forced to work in the mines under the most brutal conditions, often resulting in death.

The soldiers fighting against the Indians were little more than brigands. To make matters worse, they were paid no salaries, received little training and were, at best, only supplied with arms and armor. They were dependent on selling captured Indians as slaves which only led to further Indian raids in retaliation. As this state of affairs became more heated and bloody in the 1580s, leaders with even the vaguest of military backgrounds and the desire for military service were in much demand. For many such men, battling the Indians was a romatic adventure in spite of the great risk. It was a time when many Europeans lived in knightly fantasies and some, such as Villagfa, had a literary bent as well and pursued adventures energetically. But, while military commissions helped satisfy the fulfillment of knightly dreams, it was a haphazard career at best. There were few, if any, regular military or naval units in New Spain and most military forces were under the control of local noblemen or other influential citizens. These military units were little more than civilian defense units and seemed ill prepared for real battle. The terms "captain" and "general" were only deferential titles and signified little in terms of real military expereince.

Commissions were readily available to men of means, however, since officers were expected to recruit and train their own men and, except for cannon, supply arms, horses and armor. The royal and provincial governments paid little or nothing but did supply priests and cannon and offered titles and privileges to those who would carry the Spanish banner.

The Pueblo Indians of New Mexico and Arizona were remotely aware of the political cauldron to the south. They had been visited several times in the mid-sixteenth century by the strange, bearded men from Mexico and both sides had suffered in the encounter. When the first major expedition arrived at Hawikuh in 1540, they were greeted by a hostile Zuni nation and several of Coronado's soldiers were killed. Coronado himself was sorely wounded. Yet, the Pueblos were seemingly possessed by a fatal curiosity about these people and their strange animals and implements and, on several later occasions, allowed them to move in amongst them with no immediate attempts at resistance or defense. At first the two cultures skirted each other warily, bound by curiosity and perhaps hoping for a serious accommodation without further bloodshed. But as the Spaniards secured their tentative foothold, they became bold and their claims for sovereignty and missionary zeal to convert the natives led to inevitable clashes which were often fatal for the Indians and sometimes for the invaders.

One such clash resulted in the death of three Franciscans who had set out determined to plant the cross permanently in New Mexico. Inspired by stories of great settlements, Fray Agustin Rodriguez led a missionary expedition to New Mexico in 1581. He was accompanied by Father Juan de Santa Maria, Father Francisco Lopez and a military escort led by a red-bearded captain known as Chamuscado.

Unable to understand the close communion between the dry land, the boundless sky and the natural spiritual needs of the pueblo culture, the friars were at first treated cautiously, but then, when they confronted the native priests and gods of the Pueblos, the treatment changed to suspicion and hostility and finally resulted in the death of Father Santa Maria.

Being greatly outnumbered, Chamuscado wisely decided to return to New Spain, but he was unable to convince the others. They stayed behind to carry out their missionary work, electing to remain alone and unprotected amongst the Pueblo people. A short time later they too were killed, although their fate remained a mystery for some time.

Seventeen years later, Oñate's expedition carried this same missionary zeal and claim of sovereignty with them certified by royal contract with Philip II and endorsed by the Holy Mother Church. It was not unusual, under these circumstances, that the new settlers should feel that it was their right and destiny to rule in the land. To this end, they held officious ceremonies whereby the Pueblos unknowingly swore obedience to the crown and were from that time considered subjects of the realm. In addition, the friars were once more determined in their zeal to Christianize the "savages" and it was in this missionary act of conversion, more than anything else, that antagonism arose between the two groups. Their judgement marred by ignorance of the native culture, the friars would not tolerate any heathen practices and the Pueblos suffered deeply when deprived of their native and natural spiritual needs.

Finally, in a move that hastened the end of the ever decaying relationship, the new governor demanded tribute from the Pueblos based on their status as subjects of the Spanish crown. This further infuriated the recalcitrant pueblos and culminated in the bloody battle of Aćoma in the year 1599.

It was in this battle that the captains and soldiers put their fledgling combat skills to the test. While it was true that the Pueblos lacked firearms and armor, it was also true that they were, when given the need, warriors of the first order quite capable with bow and war club, and the Aćomans were well fortified on their lofty rock fortress. It was here that the two cultures finally put each other to a deadly test. The blood of Aćoma has washed down through the ages forever coloring the faded images of these first Southwest pioneers.

Finally, while this is a historical novel, no claim is made on history or historical accuracy. The historical persons presented here are dramatized as I imagined they would have lived and loved and died. Also, as a help for the reader, a glossary of terms can be found at the back of the book.

Joseph J. Bohnaker
El Paso, Texas 1989

BOOK I

*" . . . The man to be selected should be
the best man for the task, not necessarily
the person with the finest character, or
the most full of charity . . . "*

Aristotle

1

I am not a handsome man. My head is bald in the manner of the friars, which seems ridiculous now, but was even more so in my early years, and my face is aligned under my large nose and around my thick lips in a permanent scowl. I am dark like a Moor and of low stature, almost to the point of being dwarfish. Because of these deformities, women of class are usually repelled by my approach. I have learned to accept this and perhaps it has much to do with my adverturing and foolishness. Thus I found it incredible that on that night, so many years ago, the beautiful Indian maid, Doña Inez, made certain efforts to catch my attention. As I try to recapture my memories about the great Conquest and set them down for all to read, she stands out as a torch in the blackest of nights.

It is difficult to think of these things without great pain, a lance of bitterness piercing my soul. The great Conquest which began with love and enthusiasm for the Holy Mother Church and His Royal Majesty, and was carried out with unrelenting devotion to Duty and to God despite the many hardships and blood-soaked encounters with the bestial inhabitants of those savage lands has ended for all of us in dismal apprehensions. I sit here in this sunless cell in Seville and wonder what force drove us and still drives others to undertake such hazardous and unrewarding adventures. There are those among my accusers who claim that we are filled with the vice for gold and indeed we are now scorned, not only by the vile heretics of England, but also by our own clergy, for all of our wondrous exploits in New Spain and New Mexico. We are accused of murder, rape, disobeying the King's orders (God forbid!) and other sinful things too painful to mention. But of all these charges, as I shall soon show here, we stand guiltless before God and King. If we suffer from any vice, it is only the infirmity of the noble heart that seeks recognition from his fellow man and, at least for myself, an insatiable desire to quest for the unknown. But I disgress.

Next month I shall again be allowed to petition for exoneration but it is difficult to gain the ear of this new monarch. In any event I shall set down here the whole truth about the Conquest, to the best of my memory.

Although time has dimmed my powers of recollection, it seems like only yesterday when, on that fateful day in San Filipe, I broke the seal on the envelope from Don Juan.

"Dear Captain Villagfa," the invitation read. "I am happy to learn of your safe arrival from Seville. You will, of course, move to our garrison here in Zacatecas as soon a possible. Please be advised that on the night of the 21st, I will host a dinner party. It will be our pleasure to have your company. You will meet many people important to our enterprise." It was signed "Don Juan de Oñate."

The general had sent the invitation allowing me just sufficient time to secure leave and travel the 50 or so leagues between the post at San Filipe and the town of Zacatecas. Although I had arrived in New Spain several months earlier, I was still unsettled by the extraordinary precautions that were required of travelers in those regions. I, then a captain in the king's service, had to be provided an escort of four soldiers armed with muskets and lances.

"It is for your own safety," the captain who delivered the invitation said. "Besides, there are many scoundrels here about who would force you to pay dearly for an escort. It's the law, you know." He smiled, and turning to leave continued, "I wish you a pleasant journey. These men are capable and will serve you well."

I set out with the sergeant and three soldiers. Military outposts were everywhere along the route although I was told by my fellow officers that the local militias manning them were a sad lot. The soldiers (if such misfits could be so called) were unpaid, untrained and filthy. Due to their great poverty, the captains said, they were forced to loot in the countryside which often let to further villainies such as murder and rape. God's joke! The people needed those filthy beggars to keep their scalps in place and yet were in great danger of losing their horses or their wives, and if ill-fortune should be their lot, their lives into the bargain.

I remember well the heavy traffic we encountered during those days on the road connecting the high civilization of Mexico with the wild frontier at Zacatecas. The dreams of Conquest and commerce given root by the noble marquis, Hernan Cortes, were spreading northward with great speed. Large, two-wheeled carts filled with barrels of silver ore or quicksilver were driven with disregard for life or limb by native muleteers who bellowed unceasingly at their charges. At a point not too distant from my post, the road joined another coming up from the city of Guadalajara. Here we saw streams of Indians afoot carrying heavy baskets loaded with ore. They shuffled back and forth between Guadalajara, Mexico, and Zacatecas with a rapid and peculiarly flatfooted gait, their legs stiff and bodies bent like broken sticks. Amongst these carts and carriers were private coaches handled by wild coachmen, pulled by magnificent horses, and itinerants and soldiers of every description.

The spirit of New Spain and the rewards of Conquest were all here and I was glad then to be part of that world and away from the dismal prospects of my own beloved country.

The soldiers sent by Don Juan were followed by an Indian servant and a scruffy burro hauling my hampers. I asked the sergeant riding next to me about the armed guards everywhere. He glared at me suspiciously. Although he wore a pikeman's pot and a soldier's metal breast plate over a doublet he looked wild and dirty.

It's the scummy Chichimecas," he replied. "The bloody heathen are everywhere." He resumed his glum silence which I decided not to break again.

The problem with the Chichimeca Indians was on everyone's tongue, but I had thought the threat was far north of Zacatecas in a wild land known as *tierra de guerra*. I would soon discover that I was mistaken.

We completed the journey, as I recall, without incident and upon reaching the main road into Zacatecas, the soldiers took their leave, leaving me with the Indian and the burro.

Zacatecas, I had been told, was a coarse frontier mining town rich with silver, recently commissioned as a royal city by His Majesty. The town rested on a high desert plateau, cradled between canyon walls that grew into low, uninspiring mountains. Approaching the southern limits, I could see flat-roofed block houses flanking the narrow road within a harquebus shot. The buildings had gun slits and two iron halfdoors on each side. They would hold several men armed with harquebuses and several small cannons and perhaps even a larger brass falcon. It was a formidable defense, set up, I later learned to prevent a siege by the Indians such as was carried out a few years before.

We proceeded slowly up the main road where the soldiers had left us. The air was thin and cold and clouds piled up on the mountain tops like snow-capped peaks, reflecting the later afternoon sun. The road was lined with low, mud-colored huts which seemed to be falling back into the earth

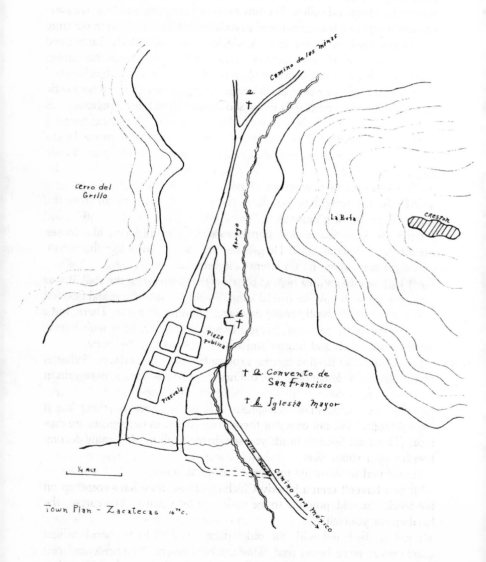

Town Plan - Zacatecas 16ᵗʰ c.

and a dry mountain stream bed wondered among them. I could see dark shapes flitting in the cold shadows cast by the overhanging canyon walls. The shapes seemed to emerge and then disappear into the earth and I was glad there was still light enough to approach the city.

Shortly thereupon we passed over a sturdy bridge of large timbers crossing the dry stream bed. A cold wind swept down from an open plaza. I dismounted and put on a leather doublet lined with deer skin. The Indian remained barefoot and sullen. The town seemed to spring to life as we passed a district of fine houses made of peculiar reddish stone, then into a large square occupied by many Indians, Africans and Spaniards. Large-eyed Tlaxcalan children swarmed around us as we moved through the square. They were begging and selling trinkets of bone and straw. Sellers hawked their goods from canvassed stalls and I stopped to examine the exotic wares. One stall I visted sold gems and artifacts from those regions.

"A beautiful piece," the hawk-eyed shopkeeper said as I examined a stone knife. "Obsidion," he continued, "used by the Chichimecas to cut the heart out of the poor devils they catch." He flashed an evil grin. "While they are still alive."

"This knife seems new to me," I said.

"Ah, that's a rare knife you have there, sire. Came straight from the hands of the fiendish heathen . . ."

I put the knife down and started to leave. "Would you like to see something . . . special, sire?" He grabbed my arm. I didn't like this scoundrel, but I was driven by an intense curiosity.

He led me into an area behind the canvas at the rear of the stall. It was dark and I groped until he fired a lamp. As the light came up and flooded the small room, a ghastly scene emerged from the darkness. There, but a few thumbs from my nose, hung a braided rope, threaded with human skulls, dried hands and fingers and what I took to be a leg bone.

I jumped back, startled by the grotesque object before me. "What is that . . . thing?" I demanded. The old man flashed the same sinister grin in the lamplight.

"Why, it's a Chichimec' war-girdle. You haven't seen anything like it have you, sire? We get many of these prizes when those beggars are captured. Those are Spanish heads you see there, I'll allow. T'is a fine decoration for your room, sire."

He wanted to show me more but I asked to leave.

"If you haven't seen a bloody Chichimeca yet, they have some up on the block," he said, pointing to the middle of the square. "You can see the heathen for yourself."

I left his tent and with the old Indian I walked to the stock where Chichimecas were being sold. There were soldiers, merchants and one man who seemed to be in charge. He was holding a savage-looking Indian by the arm.

". . . One Gauchichil Indian," I heard him say, "age 25 with a stripe from the hair of the forehead to the lip below the nose, three stripes on the chin and two each eye to the temples, legally convicted of participating in murder and robbery and sentenced to 20 years of slavery . . ."

The merchants were bidding on the savages of which there seemed to be eight.

"Fifty pesos," the man next to me said.

In quick succession I heard "60 pesos," "70 pesos," and the bidding stopped at 85 pesos. The fettered Indian was then forced off the block onto the ground where he sat in the dust. A young, naked female Gauchachil with stripes on her face and body was next on the blocks.

"What are done with these savages?" I asked the man next to me.

He looked at me suspiciously, eyeing my courtly clothes. "Why it's all legal, you see. Those soldiers there are selling these Indians captured while raiding hereabouts . . ."

"What would you do with one if you won the bid?" I asked.

"I buy here in Zacatecas and then sell them in Mexico or Gaudalajara. Some of the men here are from the mining haciendas. Use them in the mines, they do." He looked me in the eye, "All legal you know. They have all been convicted and sentenced."

The Indian now being sold looked fierce indeed. Even in utter nakedness they portrayed a savagery that caused my soul to shudder when I thought of the war-girdle I had seen moments before. Their bodies were striped and covered with all manner of barbaric tattoes and many hideous scars, such that their lack of clothes almost went unnoticed.

I left the place and moved towards an area where a great commotion was occurring. Benches had been placed in a circle and in the middle, a wild-eyed dancer with hair that reached to his fingertips, whirled crazily to a monotonous drum and shrill flutes played by lethargic Indians.

The old Indian accompanying me seemed to come to life when he saw the dance; a faint trace of a smile crossed his face. Tantalizing odors drifted around the square and drew me to a stand where whole goats were roasting on spits. I threw a few coins to the vendor and he ripped off a chunk of the blackened meat for me and the Indian. We followed the dancer for a while and then moved on, passing a blind beggar with one leg. He looked like a filthy English pirate. Later, we passed a large wagon from the back of which a doctor was selling cures. Finally we reached a small cathedral and exited the square gaining the Franciscan monastery at the north end. Here was a mine-works with ugly sheds and black earth heaps and large apparatus reflecting the now disappearing sun. The Indian pointed to a road to the west and we traveled until reaching a large house built of fine stone.

The Indian grunted and signaled for me to dismount. He pulled a bellrope and presently another Indian came trotting down the long path from the house. I walked up to the entrance, my horse and burro being led in another direction. The building loomed large and foreboding in the fading light. Don Juan appeared and greeted me as a returning son.

"Don Gaspar Perez de Villagrá," he said in grave and stately tones, "welcome to the very noble and loyal city of Zacatecas," and he gave me the customary embrace.

2

Despair grows like a chancre in my heart. This cell is cold and forbidding, although I know the Andalusian sun blazes outside. What has happened to me and my country? Since I have returned to Spain I have seen sons of noble men now turned into filthy beggars and beggars turned into murderous thieves. Clergy and aristocrats are vegetating in decay. Taxes are ruinous and it seems that collectors and constables are everywhere. Does the king know this?

And why am I being detained? Does the viceroy and Franciscan community of Mexico have the right to reach across the great ocean and have me jailed? I am, as well, suffering a great poverty. Only small sums, yea, insignificant amounts, arrive from my epic poem, which is now all but forgotten.

The viceroy's letter arrived last week. I find the whole affair incredible. How they have persecuted us! The viceregal court finds us guilty of crimes of cruelty, murder and negligence during the Conquest. I have also learned that Don Juan was charged with immoral conduct. But alas, it is the Holy Office which has detained me. My convictions include failing to allow two deserters to confess before execution. I will certainly refute this charge and other with ample demonstrations of my love for the Holy Catholic Faith.

But it is in the recounting of the Conquest in as detailed a manner as possible and without falsehood that I shall gain exoneration by the king. And thus I return to that evening in Zacatecas:

After refreshing myself from the hardships of the journey, I was invited to join Don Juan in a large room, walled by dark stone on the main floor. A great fire blazed and the firelight illuminated a large black cross. Overhead, a huge wood and iron candelabra flickered as the light of day disappeared from the rose-glass windows. Everything in New Spain seemed massive and crude and here in Zacatecas one could feel the difference between the strained culture within the pink walls of this city and the savage surrounding land outside. I felt so in this room, resplendent with old world trappings, yet primitive and savage at the same time.

After another effusive greeting and much questioning about my family and friends in Castile and my recent journeys, Don Juan led me to the fireplace.

"This is Dona Inez," he said. I was startled to see a savage beauty sitting in a tall chair facing the fire. Flickering light reddened her bronze cheeks and sprang from her large black eyes. I bowed and she lowered her eyes in response. She answered my greeting with an oddly accented Castillian, one I had not heard before.

"She is of the New Mexican people from the Pueblo San Cristobal," he said. "She was brought to New Spain as a child by the expedition of Espejo. She speaks a fair Castillian, several tongues from her own land and now understands Nuhuatl, the Mexican tongue. She has told us much about her land."

Her beauty was remarkable. Through most of the conversation, she kept silent, gazing into the fire, except, from time to time, I found her gaze curiously directed towards me.

"Don Gaspar, what news do you bring from His Majesty and the Council of the Indies?"

I did not like answering this question. Although I had been at the court of Philip, times had been difficult and most of my petitions had been stopped by lowly functionaries who were paid by the aristocracy. Thus, I was only privy to undistinguished rumors.

"The royal decree was issued long ago." he continued, "and no one has yet been selected?"

"The king and council are not satisfied that Espejo, or for that matter, any of the other petitioners can lead such an enterprise," I answered with what I knew to be true. "There's much jealously and innuendo about the court such that all are cast in a bad light. Urdiñola seemed for a while to be the favorite but is now accused of murdering his wife. I fear, sir, that your petition has received little favor for the moment."

Don Juan nodded, "As I thought. But now we must press this matter with the viceroy. I have plans that will eliminate those who cry out against me. You, sir, are part of those plans."

I noticed that Don Juan was becoming agitated, as his voice trembled and issued forth in bitter tones.

"This war with the savages has been costly," he continued. "My father died poor because he put everything into raising militias. And now I fear the same will be my fate, unless . . . As you can see, the Conquest is important to me."

I knew Don Juan to be one of the wealthiest men in all of New Spain. He owned estancias with large herds of cattle and sheep. More important, he owned the largest silver mines in Zacatecas, Cusco and San Luis Potosi.

He could see the question on my face.

"Mining operations are expensive." he continued. "Can you understand what it takes to feed a hundred slaves? A hundred mules? Horses? To buy barrels of quick-silver? The mines produce much wealth but the veins have thinned-out and the Chichimecas have forced our operations to almost a stand still. Expenses now easily exceed income." He paced uneasily in front of the fireplace.

"This is why I sent for you, Don Gaspar. I must work for the king's favor on my petition for the Conquest. You will be very useful to me in that respect. In the meanwhile, I also need a soldier of your experience to help eliminate this threat from the Chichimecas. Unless the mines are profitable, there will be no money to finance the expedition . . ."

During the previous year, while on a trip to Seville, Don Juan had offered me a post on the Conquest which I had readily accepted. When he later had sent the letter to Seville asking me to report to New Spain immediately "concerning matters related to the Conquest" I understood little about the state of affairs so recently related to me. I was, of course, delighted.

We toasted with a goblet of excellent wine which Don Juan told me was imported from Asturias, his father's homeland. Doña Inez did not drink but rather toasted the occasion merely by smiling. It was rare to have a woman present on such an occasion and I wondered as we drank, why Don Juan had allowed her this opportunity. I found myself making a concious effort not to look at her.

We finish the wine, which was cupped in beautifully wrought silver goblets. An Indian servant promptly filled them again and I restrained myself to sip the pleasant but heady draught slowly.

"As to the dinner this evening, I have invited many guests important to our success. Some are friends and others are . . .well, let's say it is in our best interest to know what they are thinking. My two nephews will be here, Juan and Vicente de Zaldivar. They are active in our campaign against the Chichimecas. You will get to know them well."

He rested his hand on the high mantle over the fireplace and gazed into the flames. They illuminated a serious, lined countenance not unhandsome, an iron-colored beard and a full head of hair. His black velvet doublet and grey breeches fit perfectly on his robust frame. He was tall and I envied the respect commanded by his appearance. I felt, as always, much diminished by my stature.

Dona Inez got up to leave the room at Don Juan's whispered request. I watched her until she disappeared. Her eyes seemed to have a life of their own and I felt that she was trying to tell me something.

Excitement stirred within me and I felt intrigued by this exotic beauty.

My thoughts were swept away by the intruding voice of Don Juan, ". . . she will be invaluable to the Conquest. I hope soon she will be my consort . . my wife is dead. She was the daughter of the village war chief, when Espejo took her from her people. Nevertheless, she has always been treated as free.

Putting aside my thoughts about Dona Inez I questioned him further on matters concerning the Conquest.

"My brother, Don Alonzo, is on his way to Don Philip's court to represent my interests with the Council of the Indies. We are preparing the ground for our seed, which I tell you, shall be sown."

I asked him about the petition of a certain Juan de Lomas. I knew this de Lomas to be a rich man who presently had the ear of the Mexican viceroy. I had heard in Seville that de Lomas was to get the highest considerations as Adelantado of the Conquest.

Don Juan grimaced at my question and slammed his fist on the table. "His petition will be consumed in his bowels when I stick it between his buttocks!"

I remained silent in face of this outburst.

"But we are getting ahead of ourselves," he said, the flash of anger dissipated. "A certain friar, Father Pedro Oroz, will be dining with us tonight. Much depends on our success with this Religious, who seems to be my sworn enemy, He is cunning and must be handled carefully . . ."

I didn't understand, I knew little about Franciscans and the idea of a cunning Franciscan seemed strange.

"Aren't the Franciscans known for their denunciation of all wordly goods and pleasures?" I asked.

"Let me explain," he said. "As my captian, you must be clear on these points which are of extreme political importance. While there are many things about the Religious in this new world which you must become familiar with, my main concern at the moment is the relationship between us, the Religious and the Chichimecas. Foremost is that the Franciscans are dedicated to Christianizing the savages as you must already know. What you may not know is that they are also dedicated to protecting these inhuman beasts from us! And this Oroz is the champion of the Indians. As the former leader of the Franciscans and now, as adviser to the new commisary-general, he has done much damage to our campaign to eradicate these vermin!"

The fire had diminished considerably and a noticeable chill invaded the room. I drew my cloak about me while the Indian servant replenished our cups which had been emptied but little.

"Oroz cries that we brutalize the captives by making them slaves and that we work them to death in the mines. Of course, they say this is why they cannot Christianize the savages and why we suffer such cruel tortures at their hands. It's more likely, as I'm sure you will find out for yourself, that the Franciscans themselves are corrupted by their own power at court. Their influence has filtered into the viceroy's office as well as Don Philip's court. The so-called *New Laws*, which they were so determined to create have been the ruination of us here on the frontiers. We are painted by these friars as cruel and greedy exploiters of a simple native people. Nothing could be more absurd."

I mentioned the remark that the sergeant who had accompanied me to Zacatecas had made, "And he seemed exceptionally unfriendly, even though he was a Spaniard. But I did notice the exceptional precautions being taken by all I observed."

"Yes, you see, the Chichimecas threaten the entier region. As for the sergeant, he probably could see by your dress that you were a recent arrival from Spain. He is a *Criollo*. You will soon understand the differences between us, *Criollo* and Spaniards. I can easily see, as you stand here, that you are not one of us." He pointed to my suit of clothes. "This difference is even more plain to see among the Franciscans. The *Criollo* friars rail against those from Spain like barnyard cocks dueling over a hen. Oroz is fully caught up in this war and therefore has many enemies amongst his own order." A smile passed over his face. "You too will feel this for a while, but as you learn the way of New Spain you will become more and more like us. We can more easily affect the dress and habits of Spaniards than you can of us. And while we, too, claim our Spanish ancestry, we are at the same time proud of our new country and feel obligated to live our own way."

I felt obliged to ask him a question: "Is it true? I mean that which Oroz claims about slaves being worked to death? I saw many being sold today in the square."

He gave me a peculiar glance, "We can no longer take Indians as slaves unless the friars approve first that the Indians were captured because of their own hostilities against us. I can assure you that under Oroz's administration, this approval has been impossible to obtain!"

At that time I knew little about the conditions of slavery in New Spain, except for those few I had seen that day or as livery men or servants. On the question of slavery, I was and still am, inclined toward the Aristotelian view that it is a natural state, that men by nature are not equal, and that some persons were naturally meant to be slaves and would be of little value to the world as anything else. And when hostilities arise, I find myself unsympathetic toward the conquered. The very nature of war is such that it cannot be otherwise than cruel and hard. Conquered people, forced to serve as slaves, have no rights to be otherwise, even if they are not natural slaves.

". . . We need more slaves," Don Juan continued, "but, more to the point, this is the only way we have of paying the regulars serving in the militia. Without slaves, they receive no pay. Do you know that a good slave can bring two hundred gold pesos in Mexico? That will keep a militia man for up to half a year . . . damn Oroz anyway! You know he is the main obstacle against my selection as Adelantado!"

3

The general sat at the head of a long table. Doña Catalina de Salazar y Oñate, the general's mother, sat on his right. She had me seated to her right, which I took was a position of honor. She was the hostess at the pleasure of her son but ruled the occasion as if she were the general himself. Indian and mulatto servants and black slaves scurried in and out of the great room, passing under the watchful eyes of portraits of Oñate and Salazar ancestors, pious saints and, above all, the king himself. They carried silver trays filled with fowl and meats of every variety: capons and guinea hens and great turkeys and pigeons and quail, veal and mutton all stacked in marvelous arrays. The servants were controlled by the clap of Doña Catalina's hands. Her dress was of green silk with a white parmentiere. With her large thin nose and piled hair, she was easily distinguished from the rest.

"I am so happy to finally meet the great Captain Villagŕa," she said in a high-pitched, scratchy voice. "Your illustrious ancestors are well known at court." She smiled and laid a bony hand on mine. "Have you met Doña Inez?" She was sitting across the table from me.

"Yes, I had the pleasure earlier today," I replied.

"Isn't she a beauty, though? She is from the savages in New Mexico, you know." Her lip curled as she said the last words.

Doña Inez smiled, "We are honored by your presence, Captain. Will you remain here?"

"I believe so," I replied. "I have been commissioned by Don Juan." I nodded to Don Juan.

"You must take good care of him," Doña Catalina said. "It's not often we get such distinguished visitors."

"Of course," Don Juan said to his mother, "he shall be well cared for. You will see that he is given a servant won't you, mother? A nice Chichimec girl perhaps? Or one of your handsome Tarascan women?" He laughed as I squirmed uneasily at these words.

At the other end of the table sat Father Pedro Oroz, the same friar Don Juan had earlier described in such bitter tones. A slight, thin man, he had white hair and a thin, white beard. To his right sat a Dominican, a certain Father Alonzo Marquez, wearing a mink-collared cape over his black robes. I learned that this Marquez was an official of the Holy Office of the Inquisition just recently established in New Spain. The Dominican was considerably younger than the Franciscan and seemed to defer to him during conversation. I also learned that Don Juan was friendly with this Inquisitor.

Doña Inez remained silent. As we progressed through dinner I could see that she was a small person, as dark as I, with a beautiful full mouth. She was wearing a plain white shift with a cloak in the Mexican manner. I learned later that she refused to imitate Iberian manners or dress. The other guests were dressed in the latest fashions, which included dress armor of silver plate, engraved with every sort of flourish; rose and green colored suits of Holland cloth with white silk stockings; ladies in plush velvet dresses of every design and color and certain men from the Ibarra and Zaldivar clans who dress in the frontier fashion with large sombreros and deerskin suits, fringed and decorated. It was quite different from the traditional black found around King Philip's court and worn by all the nobles of the old country. Such dress as was seen here would have been shocking in Spain. I began to understand Don Juan's earlier remarks about the differnces between Creoles and Spaniards and I vowed to obtained some new clothes to replace my black suit.

Babble ruled the table. Most of the guests were clucking away in that barbaric tongue of the Basques which vied with the more soothing Castillian and the strange Indian language spoken by the servants. The African Negroes, who, I learned, has been captured from the villainous Hawkins' fleet some years back, spoke broken English. While the conversation was animated, it was polite and reminiscent of courtly affairs at home. Eating habits were very different. The people fell on the food like a great hunger gnawed at them. The servants could not keep up with delivering fresh food and clearing the table and floor of bones of bird and beast which were flung about the room with abandon. Even the Religious fell prey to this wanton behavior and everyone swilled wine from great cups which were constantly filled by the servants. Strangely, I found this impressive.

When the meal was finished and the women retired the conversation became more restrained. Don Juan, in dramatic tones, spoke to Father Oroz:

"Dear Father, your presence here tonight is a great honor, as you know. With the aid of Our Lord and his Blessed Mother and through the assistance of your holy friars, children of Saint Francis, salvation shall come to this savage land. But you must come up here to the frontier more often to familiarize yourself with the savage conditions . . ."

The priest wearily tossed his head, "I know, Don Juan, that you and I very often are on opposite sides of this affair. Yet, I think I know well enough about the conditions of which you speak."

Don Juan smiled slightly. "Then you know of the disappearance of your brother in Christ, Father Andres de la Puebla?"

The priest seemed startled. "We sent Father Andres to Zacatecas some years back because of his advanced age. I am told by the Custos that he is very dedicated and his work with the Indians has been most impressive."

Don Juan nodded, "Yes, and such work must be done because it is the will of God. But did you know that this holy brother desired to go to New Mexico to be a confessor to those savages? He is much taken by the deaths of the three friars led thither by Chamuscado."

Oroz seemed uneasy, "I see nothing strange with that. He and many other friars desire the conversion of those lands to the Holy Faith. I myself would cry out for such a chance."

"Yes, he is innocent of any wrong doing, replied Don Juan, "But he made Doña Inez a spiritual daughter. Last week he bid farewell to her and Zacatecas. He said he had seen a vision of his death and was going forth to confess the bloody Chichimecas!"

"I . . . didn't know," the priest replied.

Don Juan slammed the table with his fist. "Give us permission, good Father, and with God's aid I will find him before the Chichimecas tear his heart out. But to raise a troop I must be allowed to take captives."

"I cannot," the priest replied angrily. "You know I cannot go along with your attempts to enslave the Indian population."

"Don't you understand that many of our people have been tortured and cruelly murdered by these savages?" he replied. "You must grant permission!"

"They are under Satan's spell which must be broken. Killing them or making slaves of them will do no good and is against the will of God."

"They are the children of Satan!"

Silence fell over the table. The Inquisitor twisted his mink collar and then whispered to Father Oroz. If caution was advised it was not heeded.

"I thank you for your offer to help Father Andres," said the priest, "but let me remind you of the legality of your request. Archbishop Contreras has agreed that the New Laws as given by the Crown are just and should be enforced. The native Indian population should be delivered from the villianies of your spoils system. They must be given just payment for their work, including laboring in the mines and war against the Chichimecas must be halted for good. Now, these are the thing you are asking me to go against in favor of rescuing a Religious." The priest ended on a firm note and seemed satisfied. He took a long draught from the wine cup. Several of the guests nodded cautious agreement with the priest. Don Juan stared stonily in my direction.

"It seems, Father," said Don Juan, "that you are more concerned for the welfare of these . . . heathen . . . than you are for our, or your own, safety . . ."

"Yes . . . and it must be so!" he answered quickly. "We are servants of the Lord and have receive his salvation. As servants of God we must convert the unbelieving ones to the faith of Christ. My brothers, such as Father

Andres, have such zeal in their heart for the salvation of souls that they do not spare their lives and regard hunger, thirst and fatigue as blessings. Cruel torments cause them no fear. On the contrary, they welcome death with joy if it results in converting one single soul to God. This is why I cannot agree to your request."

Perceiving that he could not convince Father Oroz, Don Juan shrugged and turned to the others around the table and fell to discussing the intricacies of mining silver and the Chichimeca raids which were still very severe. Juan de Zaldivar, a short man with a black beard, related a tale concerning a certain rancher who lived some 20 leagues to the north who had recently lost his wife and children during a raid and had discovered their mutilated bodies some days later.

It was feared that this particular tribe was keeping the heads and other body parts as trophies which they wore slung about their waists. They had a particular fondness for Spanish females and children. I thought of the war-girdle I had seen that very day.

As the conversation continued along these lines I perceived that Father Oroz looked awry on such course fare and in short order he and the Inquisitor took their leave. Don Juan's tactics had failed. The priest was even more firm in his resolve than before.

When they had left, the men loudly agreed that the Franciscans were a villianous lot, given to consorting with women and great bouts of drinking in the friaries. Juan de Zaldivar recounted a tale concerning Father Oroz and the friary at Tlatelcolco where it was said that he and several other friars had entertained the viceroy's wife and entourage for several weeks in a continuous orgy of the flesh. I found these statements questionable at best, yet almost every one to a man agreed with Zaldivar and had yet another tale of his own. They become more and more sordid, ranging from accusations of turning the friaries into bordellos to those of incest and pederasty.

When most of the guests had taken leave, Father Marquez reappeared and held a private council with Don Juan. The general then called me, Juan and Vicente de Zaldivar and the priest together.

"Gentlemen, I believe I have something noteworthy to relate. As you may know, the Holy Office has already questioned Father Oroz about his conduct concerning problems between the Creole and Spanish friars. In this respect, Oroz has made some great enemies in his own camp." Don Juan, who had been standing, was forced to sit as the wine took hold. He was becoming difficult to understand.

"But now hear me for the best," he continued. "Oroz has taken under his charge a certain Jew called Josephus, a marrano who has the real name of Luis de Carvajal. He is, by chance, the nephew of the governor of Nuevo Leon. It seems that the Franciscans have given free reign to this scum during sentence of service at the friary in Tlatelcolco. If I know Oroz he will give us the opportunity to rid us of him for good. Even a Franciscan must answer for such things." Don Juan looked at me. "You, my dear Spanish friend, will be very useful, when the time arrives. You see, Oroz is a man of literary tastes and judgment and of many languages and is very scholarly. Since you are of similar learnings and taste, you have cause for seeking a more intimate relationship with the friar. It will be easy . . ."

4

The next morning I awoke with severe head pains from the previous night's draughts. Daylight came thinly through a narrow window in my bedroom even though I sensed it was late. I opened the window and saw that my room, which was high from the ground, faced a dark granite cliff which stood me in a deep shadow. A wild-looking servant brought water for washing and fresh clothes from my hamper. After I had finished dressing a knock sounded and another hooded servant brought a tray of food. Before I realized, the door was pushed halfway closed and to my great surprise I saw that the servant was Doña Inez. She quickly put down the tray and asked me in her odd Castillian to forgive her boldness and not send her away.

I sat down at my tray, thanked her and took a sip of the steaming chocolate beverage which I had come to like. I didn't know what else to do. She stood by the door watching me like an animal ready to spring for cover.

Regardless of her savage ancestry, I could see she was a woman of breeding. Her nose was fine and straight and both her hands and feet were small and delicate. Her skin was smooth and while dusky, she was fairer than any savage from those parts. Her hair was long and as fine as silk and a glorious black. Although I perceived in her glances something suspicious and untamed and there remained an element of fear in her restless countenance, I decided to take part in whatever she was up to.

"Why," I asked, "are you here?"

"Don Gaspar, I have known of your coming for a time now," she said. "Don Juan speaks of you and your family. As I am a spiritual daughter of Father Oroz, he too speaks of your arrival. A friar wrote to him about you from your land . . ."

She asked permission to sit.

"I beg of you . . . do all you can, in God's eye, to rescue Father Puebla. I know what will happen to him if the wild ones have their way. He is old and not of full mind . . . that would save him, but his cry against the devil's way will anger the wild ones . . ."

She was out of the room and gone before I could respond. I was puzzled by the visit although I understood her concern for Father Puebla. I felt there was more to it; that it had been a chance occasion to speak with me about something other than the rescue of the friar.

I finished my meal, which was as lavish with meats and fowl as the night before, and tried to understand the events of the preceeding evening. There had been a sense of adventure in the air, an excitement about this Conquest that had our blood hot for adventure. I found the politics of New Spain to be even more complicated than at home. Here, it seemed, every problem was compounded by birth status. The Creoles were fierce in their determination to limit rule in New Spain to what they decided was good for crown and country. They were angry at the meddling from the Council of the Indies and the Franciscans in their affairs. It was odd that it seemed to the Indian that we were all Spanish and they feared and hated us all. Yet, we were splintered by jealousies and estrangements and were as diverse and divided as any group could be.

I found that Don Juan's optimism concerning his award as *Adelantado,* was found on the fact that his old friend, Juan de Velasco, Count of Santiago, had recently been appointed as the viceroy of New Spain, replacing Zuñiga, who had supported the position of the Franciscans. Velasco and Don Juan were friends from boyhood and their fathers had been friends before that and very active in crushing Indian revolts.

Later that morning I was escorted by Don Juan to see the mines at Zacatecas. The machinery and apparatus, mostly mule-driven on the surface, rumbled and caused the very earth to shake. The apparatus were great stone ore crushers that made a fearsome noise as teams of mules blindly circled the great gear-works. All this industry laid a great pall of dust over that end of the city, mixed with the black smoke from charcoal fires.

I found that Chichimeca and negro slaves were employed in the heavy labor although there were some Tarascans who worked for wages. The ore was hauled up from the deep pits in baskets or leather sacks slung on their backs and the work was strenuous. A good slave needed great care if he was to survive such rigors, as most did not. At my insistance we entered a mine and I found the descent into the black hole fearsome. The ladders seemed weak and shaky and I wondered how the miners managed to haul the heavy loads up such contrivances. The place smelled of urine and the buring oil used to illuminate the rough passageways and smoke and dust drew tears from my eyes. As we worked ourselves down to lower and lower levels, water could be heard seeping through the walls. Don Juan was proud of this structure which, he claimed, was one of the deepest mines in the New World. In each passageway there were dark naked forms huddled in shadows, our flickering lamps catching pale reflections of yellow eyes. They seemed to be part of the dark walls and malodorous smells that eminated from that region. What I remember most from that journey into darkness was how good it felt to be on the surface and in the sunlight again. It was a sobering prelude to my adventures in the New World and it was some time before I could again see in the strong light.

At that point it was not easy to see the dark path down which I would be led by the Inquisition and the Conquest. As in the mine, I could only sense the shadowy figures acting out their ultimate roles.

We retired to the general's quarters where he detailed a strategy for eliminating Oroz that left my blood cold.

BOOK II

*"... We must say that every evil,
in some way, has a cause. For evil
is the deficiency of good that is a
birthright ..."*

St. Thomas Aquinas

1

For the most part, I've finished outlining the events leading up to the Conquest. I must remember all that took place. I was again this day brought before the Holy Office for a hearing. I found myself unable to recall everything, yet the Inquisitors insisted that I do so. They are interested in my connections with Father Oroz and the Carvajals. I must be careful on these points and relate only the truth. They will not tell me why I am being detained or what charges, if any, I must answer. The executions seem to be unrelated to what concerns the examiners. Fear is spreading through my bones. The Inquisitors are skilled in ways of raising this fear. The examinations are repetitive, searching for inconsistency in the telling. I should learn more as questions are asked. In answer to *my* question, they said it was not possible to say when I might be set free.

I was told that I would be moving from this cell, part of the municipal jail, to the Fortress in Triana. I fear more intense interrogations will be my lot, but let me continue with my relation.

My stay in Zacatecas was prolonged. It was Don Juan's plan first to search for the wandering priest. Should we be successful, it would force Oroz to abate his attack on Don Juan. Several days elapsed before we were sent in search of Father Puebla. Meanwhile, I found a residence close to the Franciscan convent and had my goods and livestock transferred from San Felipe.

I saw Doña Inez frequently in the convent library and she continued to plead for the rescue of Father Puebla.

"I fear he has a need to die," she said. "It is something of these religious I do not understand. Many of them want so much to die for God."

"Yes. They are so devout that martyrdom seems natural to them," I said. "The perfect end of their earthly existence."

She was looking through one of the library shelves. "Is death so natural to your people? My people have no such feeling. Death is a great mystery to us and not so desired, even by priests." She pulled a manuscript from the shelf and sat on the bench next to me. "Here is a book Father Oroz is writing. It is about cures for sickness and wounds. I am helping him with this work."

I examined the beautifully hand-lettered pages. They were on thin, delicate parchment and were decorated with detailed drawings of plants.

"I still have some knowledge of the ways of my people and it is this that Father Oroz is putting down on this paper." She looked out the library windows. "When do you think you will be able to search for him?"

"Soon. Don Juan is still asking Father Oroz for permission. But, I think we should leave soon."

In the course of these visits I learned much about her, her people and her desire to return to them. She seemed a strong Christian, having been raised in the monastery at Tlatelolco under the strict eye of Father Oroz. Perhaps she could be of much assistance in the Conquest to any friars bent on the conversion of those heathen peoples.

We met frequently in the monstery garden back of the small library established by Father Oroz. She told me of her culture as she remembered it. She described the dances and songs that accompanied the seasonal changes, and the rituals of the Turquoise, Flint and Squash societies. She spoke of strange gods and the black rituals of the heathen with regard to killing the enemy and wild progenation ceremonies.

She confided in me about her relations with Don Juan.

"I am not his woman," she said when I boldly asked if she intended to marry. "I am devoted only to the love of God."

I tried to discern her status in the Oñate household. "Have you lived here in Zacatecas long?"

"I was sent here from Tlatelolco one year past," she said, "Don Juan wrote a letter to the viceroy asking for my services. He wanted to learn the tongue of my people and about our land."

"Are you happy here?" I asked.

"I have taught Don Juan all I know. He does not learn easily, but I respect him. He is not able to sit long enough to learn much . . ." She paused and folding her hands, said a short prayer. "Yes, I am happy. But I want to return to Tlatelolco and Don Juan will not let me. I pray for this always."

I asked her if she knew about the Chichimecas.

"The wild ones. They are evil and kill for pleasure. They attack us to steal our food and animals. We must always guard against such people."

"Will the friars be able to change the wild ones and bring peace?" I asked her.

"No. The friars do not know the wild ones. They cannot be changed by kindness. I agree with Don Juan on this matter."

In mid-February we set out in search of the wayward priest. Father Oroz agreed to the expedition, Don Juan agreed not to take captives. We left Zacatecas before dawn heading towards San Martin, some 40 leagues to the north.

The moon loomed on the horizon as I pointed my horse toward the unknown. We were a meager troop: five militia and twice that number of Tarascan auxiliaries, who were, at that time, the only Indians allowed to mount horses and carry bows. Juan de Zaldivar commanded the small force. We moved through the town at two abreast and took the northwest road at the point where it divided. All was still at that early hour and the sound of horses' hooves and the jangle and creak of armor and cannon made an eerie spectre of our troop in the moonlight. Our destination that first day was Fresnillo, a mining outpost with a small frontier fort.

Leaving the town limits, we encountered many wild beasts that howled with such fierceness as to set our horses on edge. The Chichimecas imitated these beasts when signaling during an attack and we proceeded warily through the darkness.

The first streaks of dawn broke across a desolate and treeless plain. The countryside appeared grey and arid much like the plains of Castile at that time of year, but lacking the comforted feeling of any intervening civilization. Naked mountains stood guard over stands of thorny, stunted brush called mesquite and many varieties of cactus.

"The heathern live off these infernal plants. Can you believe it?" Zaldivar said as we passed through a field thick with the plants. He pulled some dried pods from a bush as he passed nearby. "These are mesquite beans. The Chichimecas are very fond of these." He handed them to me. I examined the brown dried pods, swollen with a kind of bean inside.

"Are they tasty?" I asked.

"No. None can eat them except these heathen. They are not any different than the beasts they live with. Let me show you something else." He dismounted and, using his dagger, he cut a large fruit-like growth from a formidable looking cactus. "They eat this too," he said as he handed the barbaric-looking fruit to me. It was full of vicious thorns and after some painful jabs I dropped the wicked morsel to the ground.

I wondered how such a thing could be eaten but did not ask. "Maybe it explains their fearsome temperment," I said.

"There are vicious snakes here about as thick as your wrist with dry rattles on their tails," he continued. "The venom is fatal. They find this a great delicacy, too."

He had piqued my curiosity, "What else do they eat?"

"Lizards, worms, wolves, rabbits, anything they can kill or capture. They are particularly fond of Spanish horse."

I patted the neck of my noble steed and kept a close eye on our flanks.

When we reached Fresnillo, the presidio was in a state of excitement. The commandant, Captain Bustamante, told us that San Martin had been attacked the evening before and he expected an attack at Fresnillo any moment.

"It was the Moriscanos," he told us. "They are the worst ones hereabouts. I expect they'll be here shortly. Best if you rest your horses now."

"Have you seen an old friar hereabouts?" Zaldivar asked.

"No. Why do you ask?"

"We are searching for a Father de la Puebla. He set out a few weeks back to convert the Chichimecas."

"No, I haven't seen him. But ask my men and the Indians. They may have seen or heard of him. I doubt if he's still alive."

The presidio was a small adobe fort built low and shaped by many connecting rooms into a large square with an opening at one end. The stables stood at one end and I led my horse there to water and rest. He was a fine black horse of excellent breeding and character, and after he was unsaddled I rubbed him down. My simple labors were interrupted by a rough voice. "Sire, that's a fine horse you have."

I looked around and saw the zambo servant of Juan de Zaldivar. Before I could reply, he continued. "If I were master and had a hundred mares, I would trade them all for your mount."

"Yes," I replied, flattered by his enthusiasm, "you won't find one in all of New Spain as fine. I brought him from the great Estancias at Seville."

He stepped closer and examined my mount. "Yes, as fair as any I've seen." He stroked the horse with pleasure.

It was bold of him to approach me so, yet I knew it was not my place to be in the stables. He was a stout man with black eyes that flashed like the devil's, set around an aquiline nose. He was dressed in a bright colored coat and breeches.

"I see you have no servant, sir. If you are of a mind, I, Luis Bautista, can be of assistance to you. I can arrange things for you as I am well placed in these parts."

I declined his offer and feeling uneasy with his increasing boldness, I turned my mount over to a stable hand and set out to find Zaldivar. He was in a great state of excitement when I found him. He had news about the possible movements of Father Puebla. Borrowing two mounts and an escort from Captain Bustamante, we started for the silver mines just above Fresnillo. As we rode, Zaldivar explained that one of the soldiers had heard of a friar visiting the Indians at the mines most recently. Perhaps it was Father Puebla.

We passed the square where a large, remarkable ash tree stood surrounded by a fence. The tree was said to have sprouted by itself and was nourished by a nearby spring. The small town had a wild, unkempt appearance. Only Indians could be seen in the plaza. No fountain blessed this square, no stone paved the dry dust.

Mining haciendas stood at the north end of the village at the base of a hill. Each hacienda looked like every other: long, ugly sheds and storerooms, stables and corrals filled with mules, and miserable adobe huts for workers. Each had a mill for crushing ore and they rumbled as loudly as they had in Zacatecas.

The black and grey dust gave the place a forlorn look. The Indian workers were black with the dirt and grime of mining, without face, bent under the leather sacks of ore.

We dismounted and I followed Zaldivar into one of the mining shacks. A ragged mixed-blood greeted us with a snarl, although he showed deference to our rank.

"No," he said, after being questioned by Zaldivar. "I have not seen the friar and it is not possible to question the workers; I cannot stop production here, *Your Graces.*"

Zaldivar's breast plate and *morrion* helmet gave his dark face and pointed beard a menacing air. As he listened to the insolent reply, his eyes flashed. He slapped the table with his open hand and at the same time drew his sword and before I could react, he had the point jabbed into the man's breast bone, pinning him to the wall.

"Son of a whore," Zaldivar said, "do not tell me what I can do."

The man trembled and I noticed blood was staining his shirt front. He begged for mercy and agreed to tell us all he knew. Zaldivar lowered the sword. The dazed foreman sat down.

"Yes," he said, "I have seen the friar. He made us promise not to tell . . ."

"As I thought. How long ago?" Zaldivar demanded.

The man thought for a moment. "Three weeks," he said.

"And where did he go?"

"I don't know . . ." Zaldivar made a move to lift the sword.

"I think . . . it was Nombre de Dios. Yes. I think so. Nombre de Dios."

2

"Nombre de Dios is 20 leagues to the northeast," Bustamante explained later that evening. "There is a presidio in San Martin, but only two men are left. The attack took three men from us. They captured all the slaves and laborers and the wife of Alonzo Enriquez. She was in town at the time of the attack. Unfortunately, Enriquez is in Mexico on business."

Zaldivar was greatly agitated by the news, as was I. An Indian servant brought a large bowl of rabbit stew, flat bread and wine. We fell silently to eating. I remember that excellent stew because it was laced with fiery Mexican condiments of which I was not yet fond. With our fingers we retrieved pieces of tough, stringy rabbit from the stew.

"I apologize for the meager fare," our host said. But we were satisfied; even the condiments failed to stem my appetite and I devoured the somewhat painful fare.

We thanked him and washed down the food with the rough wine.

"I have a plan of action," Bustamante said. He was a thin, pale man from Aragon and his high forehead glistened in the lamplight. Grey streaked his black hair and beard.

"Doña Francesca is a beautiful woman," he continued. "There is a chance the Chichimecas will not kill her, at least not for a while. They keep prize captives alive for some time. But then . . . I'm afraid her . . . light hair will be prized by some chief . . . " He turned to a black crucifix on the wall and made the sign of the cross. "With your force, coupled with mine, we can prepare a trap for the savages and try for a rescue . . . I believe they will attack here soon."

Zaldivar was numb with fury. He wanted to set out immediately but Bustamante dissuaded him of such a foolhardy adventure. "they are like devil cats," he said. "They see in the dark."

He finished outlining his plan and we agreed to support him. Following his instructions, we gathered our troops and hid well above the settlement in the mine's rocky outcroppings. With straining eyes, we searched the dim pool of light surrounding the fire kept lit by the Indians through the night. A brass petronel loaded with chain shot menaced the main stable where the mules and horses were kept. The firelight played dimly on the Indians, horses and mules and created ghostly shadows everywhere.

They never came. By morning we decided to carry the war to the savages and set out on a back trail through the countryside. We traveled throughout the day. Finally, Bustamante led us to a suspected hideout. They had fled just a few hours before. The Indian scout turned up the grisly remains of a murdered Indian. He told us that at least two people traveling with the group were not Indians. We prayed we would be able to save them.

We marched north for severals days. The savages seemed to be increasing the distance between us even though they were on foot. The scouts estimated that there were at least 50 warriors and as many captives. We were then at 15 soldiers, more or less regulars, and as many mounted auxiliary Tarascans. The Tarascans were armed with bows and arrows as they used this weapon with great skill in close bombat. Clubs were slung to their waists.

Three of the soldiers carried a harquebus, strapped to the rear of their saddles. These weapons were powerful and the savages were greatly afraid of them but they were difficult to bring to bear quickly. The remaining soldiers carried muskets, swords and spiked clubs called Morning Stars. I carried pistol, dagger and long sword. We were well armored with mail and plate, except the auxiliaries who wore thick leather vests. Two mules pulled the cannon on which we were greatly dependent. A small two wheeled *carreta* carried the supplies and ammunition.

It was this diminishing pile of logistics which eventually forced us to turn to San Martin to resupply but the town proved to be in sore shape. No residents could be found and most of the buildings were burned. The few soldiers remaining at the presidio were greatly relieved at our arrival and immediately joined us. They said that most of the Indian miners had fled or were captured by the savages.

"Did you see Doña Francesca?" I asked.

"Oh yes sir. She was here staying at the chapel. Such a beautiful woman. Lovely blond hair."

I asked if they had seen her taken by the Chichimecas.

"No sir. We were counting souls in the mines when the attack occured. Part of our regular duty."

"Are you certain she was captured? Couldn't she have fled with some of the others?" I asked.

"Not likely, sir. God I would pray that though. But you see sir, she was staying at the little room in the chapel and that is right where the bloody heathen struck. As if they knew she was there."

We found few supplies in that abandoned settlement and we were forced to halt for some time. There was little feed left for the horses and winter pastures were dry. We needed maize but the Chichimecas had burned the granaries. By nightfall we had gathered only a few hatsful of maize which was only enough to sustain us for a day in garrison. It was not sufficient for the pursuit so we decided to continue searching for supplies.

Indian scouts, sent out by the commandant to hunt game, returned with rabbits and a dog-like wolf called a coyote. The had also found a wild cow, much to our relief.

The following day passed in searching for more grain and resting the animals. While the day had been warm, the evening turned cool and a light breeze chilled our bones. A pale moon floated over the broad valley streaked by thin black clouds. The Tarascan horsemen were returning from hunting and seemed ghostly apparitions as they rode into the camp.

"Eeeeeeiiiiii!! Eeeeeeiiiiii!!" A wild, blood-curdling cry cut through the camp.

Stark naked and painted yellow, striped with black and white, they fell on us like demons from hell. Grimacing and screaming with great ferocity, they seemed unaware of any threat from our quarter. Arrows flew like rain into our midst. In an instant I saw one protruding from Bustamante's mouth and the back of his neck. He looked at me with wild eyes and clutched his throat. A terrific blow on my arm almost threw me over. I turned quickly, drawing my sword in a clean arc, lopping off the head of the savage. Blood spurted from the neck stump. The savage stood there with club still poised to strike again.

"Santiago !" I heard Zaldivar cry and then saw him in the firelight swinging his sword in every direction, scattering savages. This encouraged the troop and they recovered from the first shock. I ordered the harquebus and cannon pointed in the direction of the savages attack and after the first fusillade the siege ended as quickly as it had started. The Chichimecas melted into the night, carrying their dead with us in hot pursuit.

Zaldivar called a halt when we had passed the town limits. We were too vulnerable in the darkness. Retreating to the camp, he ordered the cannon and harquebus into position facing the direction in which the Chichimecas had fled.

"Fire!" he yelled.

The fusillade cracked the night air, spitting flame and smoke into the darkness.

"Reload," he ordered. The barrels were stoked with shot and caps inserted.

"Fire!" he yelled. Again, the night resounded with a mightly roar.

Zaldivar was plainly in a fury as I noticed he was easily put into.

"I believe they have fled!" I shouted to Zaldivar as he ordered us to reload once more. He pierced me with a crazed look. "These vermin never flee!" he screamed. "I would that their blood flow like rivers."

He kept this senseless maneuver up for some time and the tactic worked. The savages did not return. We kept a close guard through the night.

Two Spaniards were dead, including the unfortunate Bustamante. Four Tarascans had been killed and almost everyone was wounded. I was stunned by the power of the fragile-looking arrows. Many horses were down for good. In the firelight, I saw that I had been sprayed with blood and in the aftermath of the struggle I had to vomit. The balance of the night was spent dressing wounds and butchering the dead horses. Later, sleep came fitfully as I held the image of those bestial savages with girdles of skulls and bones and painted, hideous faces.

The next morning we resumed the pursuit. Our diminished force looked impotent and sad under a sky darkened by sheets of leaden clouds. We could not retreat. The woman and the friar were possibly still alive. We now had plenty of horse meat to eat even if that loss slowed us greatly.

Some leagues to the north of San Martin we discovered several wounded Tabasco Indians and a soldier from San Martin, more dead than alive. They had been top-scalped and some were emasculated with great bloody holes where their privy parts should have been. The soldier seemed able to talk. His wounds were grievous but he had yet some life.

"Ay, they killed the woman," he said when we asked, "two nights past. She was stripped and tied to a rock. The scum raped her until she screamed with pain. The bestial women encouraged their men and beat her then. She screamed much, but later, only groaned and finally was quiet. Then they scalped her the long way." He indicated how they had pulled the scalp from the back of the neck and lifted off her face with it. "It's a great prize for them — long yellow hair. They cut off her privy parts . . . and head and . . . smeared their bodies with her blood"

Man is such a fool. He secretly believes, hope against hope, that the best will happen, that such hideous things are not possible, even while he says there is little or no hope. He is lying; his heart is ever hopeful; full of hope and that deepest secret of all: that God would not let this happen, that God would save. This is the lie he lives with.

It was not a time for words. Bitter tears mingled with the dreary rain and blood-soaked mud. The forlorn Indians and this young soldier were dying before us and we knelt and prayed and salved their vicious wounds as well as we could. There was little that could be done.

"What is your name?" I asked the dying soldier.

"Pedro . . . Armendariz." I lifted the bleeding, scalped head from the mud and cradled him in my arms.

"There is no priest here," I said.

"There is . . . with the savages . . . he gave me final confession . . ." I held him for some time there in the rain, until he died.

We continued north for three more days, in low spirits, the rain relentless, making everything unbearable. Finally we found Father Puebla.

His body hung by the feet in an oak tree. He was naked and his upper and lower leg bones had been removed, cleanly, as if by a butcher. The bloody head stump protruded grotesquely from between the compressed shoulders. His privy parts were missing and his skin hung in great bloody shreds. He had been whipped to death.

The shock was more than we could stand. We cut the body down and covered it with a cloak but none could bear to go near those dreadful remains for some time. We sat silently in the rain each trying to comprehend, in his own way, what meaning could be found in this bestial violence. Finally, with emotion choking my words. I spoke to Zaldivar:

"Jesus Lord . . . .God. Is God with him?"

"Crucifed Christ," he said.

"Can it be? Is this what he wanted? Did God give him this?"

"Yes . . . he wanted this . . .God . . . I don't know," Zaldivar's eyes were glazed.

We wrapped the remains in a cloth and tied the grisly bundle to a mule. Zaldivar asked me to return to Zacatecas with the remains and the other dead and wounded. He would stay with two soldiers and four Tarascans, the mules and the cannon. He intended to pursue and punish the devils, foraging off the desolate countryside. I tried to dissuade him from this foolish plan. Our force was totally spent. But he was not moved, and he said he would meet me in 14 days in San Martin.

It was a time to remember. Zaldivar's heart was black with hate. My own was heavy with the events of those past days and I cursed the dark skies as we set out on our return journey. We took leave with a paucity of supplies, leaving everything we could with Zaldivar's little band. I embraced him heartily and said goodbye to the others. I feared I would not see them again.

The ride back was wearying. As I rode, I pondered in silence these past events which had scarred my soul. Were these acts of violence controlled by the devil as Father Oroz had said? Was it possible to believe that such cruelty was involuntary? To disagree with Oroz was to conclude the opposite. But the savages could be considered accountable only if their acts were voluntary. Father Oroz, then, would have to conclude that this recent outrage perpetrated by the Chichimecas was neither just or unjust, because it was not voluntary. But I could not believe that the Chichimecas committed such violence in ignorance. God! It seems to me that such cruelty is not natural and is born in lust, according to some fierce passion twisting in the breast of the savages. Can a sensible being commit such bestial acts? I think not. If the devil's work is to be found I think it will be found in this lust for blood, the lust that drives even civilized men to acts of bestiality and crime.

3

Our arrival in Zacatecas was met with great wonderment and painful grief. We were starving. The armor had rubbed our protruding bones raw so we abandoned it at Fresnillo. My own hunger had subsided several days prior to our arrival into a blind numbness as though I had drunk hemlock. Although we had searched for the woman's body after leaving

Zaldivar's troop, we were not successful. The friars were stunned by the news of Father de la Puebla and Doña Enriquez. Many priests had been killed by the Indians but none had suffered such brutal mutilations.

Father de la Puebla was buried quickly so no one could see the remains. Later, the friars proclaimed with great faith that as the body was buried, a miracle occured: it was made whole again and gave off a sweet fragrance and a smile played across the restored face of Father de la Puebla. Such simple faith is of great wonderment and mystery to me.

A messenger was dispatched to Mexico to inform the unfortunate Alonzo Enriquez of the death of his wife. A mass was held for the victims, including the Tabasco Indians.

"Now, it can be seen that they are truly possessed by the demons of hell," Father Oroz said during the service. "Their human element has succumbed to the dark animal soul of Satan." But while he steadfastly maintained this position, he quietly agreed that punishment was needed "to drive the devil out of them" and he signed the order allowing that band of devils knowns as the Moriscanos to be arrested and punished according to law or to be sold as slaves. It was a small victory for Don Juan.

After the burial, I spoke with Doña Inez in the nave of the friary and tried to explain what had happened. She was greatly disturbed by the death of Father Puebla and the story that the dying soldier had told us about Doña Enriquez.

As I related the incidents one after the other, I became aware of the smoking lamps and burning incense still fragrant from the solemn mass and the eerie, dim light filtering through the glazed cloth window high over our heads. The light penetrated the nave and illuminated a rough circle on the wall behind her.

"I am afraid now," she said in a strange accent I had not heard her use before. "There is too much killing." Her words were strange and those that were Castillian sounded like the crude Indian tongues. She was in a state of great agitation.

"Your people took me away. They killed my father who was cacique. After, I was taken by the Castillos. They hurt me as you say this woman was hurt by the wild ones . . ."

I was appalled by this accusation against my own kind.

"I was unharmed, but my spirit fled. Father Puebla helped me when I came here. I was made spiritual daughter. He did much to ease my sorrow and show me the Great Lord."

"Why did they kill your father?"

"He was cacique."

"But he must have threatened the Castillos." I found myself using this strange word to describe my countrymen.

"It was . . . They found him wearing the cross of Father Juan." Juan was one of the three priests killed on the Chamuscado expedition some years back.

"Father Juan was killed," she said, "by a shaman in my village. Men who known about spirits, chaiani, told that the priests were evil witches. One night they spied Father Juan talking with the Great Bear in heaven. The spirit men said this was bad magic, a sick one would soon die. The next day a sick man was found dead. My father called council and decided that Great Bear was offended by the evil priest. The Religious were ordered to leave, but they refused. Because of this, the shaman were sent out to kill the Religious . . . after the Castillos left. The priest's clothes, a cross on a chain and scalp were brought back to my village. They did these thing because they believed the Religious were evil . . ."

"Incredible," I said.

"I was a child. My people believed in their way, like you believe in your way," she pointed to the altar.

"Later, when the Castillos came again, my uncle told me this story. My father was hung when they found him wearing the cross. You see, he thought wearing the cross would please the Castillos . . . We cannot understand your ways. This killing will never end until death rules the land." A tear glistened on her cheek.

At that moment, Father Oroz entered the church. Doña Inez greeted him with great reverence and then quickly left. I asked Father Oroz if he knew the story she had related to me.

"Oh yes, it was a time of sadness for her. I demanded the names from Espejo . . . those who had raped her. I was furious with him for not punishing those swine. Then he told me the following story:

"When his force arrived at this village, they found girls who were just reaching child bearing years. Doña Inez was among them. These people have the heathen custom of having their young girls roam about naked until they have been married. The Spaniards, of course, were raised to great passion by this sight of nubile charms and when they found the belongings of Father Juan, a fight broke out and blood was spilled on both sides. In the heat of this battle, some of the men found the naked girls hiding in a house . . . and well . . . it happened." He adjusted his cloak. "But come, let's take some comfort from this sad day and renew your wasted bones."

4

Soon we regained our strength. My arm was bound in a sling, as the savage's blow had broken it. Don Juan left for Mexico to argue for a full military effort, a war of fire and blood, against the Chichimecas, armed with the agreement of Father Oroz for the capture of the Moriscanos. He ordered me to raise another force to rejoin Zaldivar at San Martin. I was occupied for many days finding fresh horses and men and logistics to support this effort. Merchants were unwilling to supply us on Don Juan's account since it was known about Zacatecas that mining had been halted at San Martin, Fresnillo and San Luis Potosi. These merchants were short-sighted men, God's word, since failure of our mission would have exposed Zacatecas to siege again. But it was impossible to argue with them so we secured only a minimum of provisions.

We followed the same trails back to Fresnillo which was abandoned since the presidio was no longer manned. We then went directly to San Martin and arrived at the time we had agreed to. We found Zaldivar badly wounded, a lone survivor, waiting for us. I wondered how many of these provincial town would die if these attacks kept up. I was glad to see him even though he was more dead than alive. He told me the story of his ordeal:

"Several days after you left, we caught up with those devils. They were camped in a valley unconcerned with any threat from our quarter. We positioned the cannon on a hill and I took three horsemen around their opposite side. When the cannon began firing, we attacked and killed many savages. The cannon did much to diminish their strength. But so many . . . there were so many and eventually we were overrun. Everyone fought bravely and to the death. I had taken many arrows when my horse was struck, staggered and fell into a deep arroyo." He stopped and asked for water.

"I blacked out," he continued. "When I awoke I was amazed to be alive. It took some time to convince myself of this. My horse lay on top of me, but a large rock next to my chest had kept me from being crushed. The savages were not to be seen. I pulled myself from under the horse. Those arrows, as you can see, had caused much loss of blood. I was weak and delirious but somehow through some great miracle, I made my way back here."

His wounds were indeed grievous — some had started to putrefy and run with pus. He had extracted several arrows but several still remained in his body. Miraculously, they had not punctured any vital parts. I worked with a Tarascan who knew about surgery and medication and we cut the remaining arrows from his tortured body. The operations were painful and it showed in his eyes as we cut away dead flesh and cleaned the wounds. Zaldivar had great strength and we found courage as he refused to cry out. The Tarascan boiled water and with herbs that he drew from his saddle bag, he made a dressing and salved the wounds.

Within a few days Zaldivar recovered to a remarkable degree. The herbs erased all signs of infection and seemed to have restored much of his stamina. But he was still weak and I insited that he return to Zacatecas for treament by a physician. Reluctantly he agreed and I sent him back with an escort.

We searched the regions for days that blended into each other and then into weeks without finding further signs of the savages. They had, it seemed, become part of the landscape. Bitter with disappointment, I ordered the troop back to Zacatecas. I longed to see civilization again and especially Doña Inez and I wondered if Don Juan would still pursue the downfall of the ancient friar and the Jew.

BOOK III

"Evil, as such, cannot be desired."
St. Thomas Aquinas

1

I have not always supported the punishments meted out by the Holy Office. They have been accused of great injustice and inhumanity towards those condemned; and these accusations, sadly, are true. Yet, I must support this determination to root out the seeds of heresy. There are amongst us those who would destroy the Holy Faith by turning many against it. I have witnessed such things myself, as I shall soon relate. I have already made these depositions in Mexico but shall do so again to convince the Holy Office of my faithfulness and steadfast, if sometimes reluctant, support of the tribunal.

I have been moved to the fortress in Triana. This black edifice strikes such terror in the hearts of men that I now fear for my life. But of course, I am being foolish. There is no reason to have this fear. We are housed in the deepest vaults without the light of day. I, most fortunately, have been separated from those heretics who would destroy the faith and have some privilege of contract with persons outside. These very pages are given over to my sister's husband, a Dominican priest, every day for safekeeping. I would not make all known, if only to protect the names of those I admired in New Spain.

Last week, I was again summoned for questioning. I sat before the Inquistors and found myself, once more, filled with fear. They seemed possessed; their eyes penetrated to the depths of my soul. It was as if they already knew everything I was going to say: everything I held as thoughts private to myself. The dark living presence behind the table possessed a terrible power beyond mortal comprehension and surely could divine the truth. I was afraid to tell, but yet even more so not to. It was such that I felt they hoped to hear of my most secret lusts and other odious weaknesses of faith.

The room was dark and lit only by smoking torches. My interrogators sat behind a curtain of darkness and I saw only their eyes which glowed in the flickering light.

A scribe sat at one end of the long table. I dimly perceived a wooden contraption at one side of the table; I took it to be a type of torture rack.

The head Inquisitor questioned me about my stay in Mexico: "When did you first enter New Spain?"

I thought carefully before answering, but in the silence between question and answer the scratching of the scribe's quill almost drove me mad. It too seemed to be part of the interrogation. "It was . . . in the year of our Lord 1588," I said with a quaver in my voice. "A sad year for us and our great prince," I hastily added.

"On what ship did you travel to New Spain?"

". . . I believe it was . . . the Santa Cruz? I am not sure it was so long ago. I remember that noble galleon returned to our beloved country and took part in the great sea battle. I believe she was sunk."

The interrogator pointed to a paper in front of him and fell to whispering to the assistants flanking him.

"Good. Your memory . . . shall we say, is getting better. Now, whom did you meet with while traveling on this ship?"

I began to tremble. How could I remember such facts? What papers were they examining? Why were they able to reduce a battle-seasoned warrior to such a cowardly show?

"I . . . can't remember." The quill continued scratching in the gloomy silence. "I . . . wait. Yes. There was one. An Alonzo de Cordoba. Yes. He was surely on that ship?"

Again they murmured and examined papers.

"Captain, can you explain why there is no record of your journey? Why can't we find any trace of your journey?"

"I . . . I don't know. It was that year and I believe it was that ship. Why is this important to you? If I knew exactly what you want I could be of more assistance." I swallowed as I forced the cowardly fear from my brain.

They continued to question me in this fashion, asking inane questions and never answering any request I made.

When I left the room I was wet with fear. Yet they did not threaten me with violence or any coercion; such is the force that penetrates the mind with the subtle tongue of the serpent. Fear stems from our own guilt and weaknesses.

Now, safe in the seclusion of my cell, I continue my account of events in New Spain.

2

The viceroy would not agree to Don Juan's war of "fire and blood" against the Chichimecas. Now, more than ever, he was determined to remove the opposition to his appointment as Conquistador.

"The vermin are quiet for the moment," he told me, when he returned to Zacatecas. "But I find my position little improved at the palace. I am still a villain to Oroz and that group of Franciscans that would have us all killed by the heathen. If we had rescued de la Puebla before it was too late. Ah, but that is past."

"You must go to Mexico, now," he said, "while the Chichimeca's are inactive. I have told the viceroy that you are my emissary. Seek an audience with him. You understand the workings at court."

"Yes. When do I leave?"

"Now. I have set up an apartment for you close to the colegio. I want you to make friends with Father Oroz. In the colegio, you should find this Luis Carvajal. He is the Judaizer I told you of. You will, no doubt, find him engaged in some heretical act."

"Ah, but this is treachery. I cannot stoop so low as treachery, sire. I beg you not to ask me," I replied, sad in my heart to refuse a request from my commander.

"Nay, man, it may seem like treachery, but it is not. This man, this Franciscan, will stop my appointment based on timid council and his own weak judgement. This is treachery, I say." He paced uneasily before me. "You understand? I only intend to weaken the priest's position with the viceroy. Connect him with Carvajal and a heretical act and he will be finished, but no harm will come to him. I can give you my word . . ."

I knew what Don Juan said was true. Father Oroz had been against his appointment, favoring instead that criminal Espejo and Juan de Lomas.

"Very well. I will do what I can. But, Don Juan, I am not given to ty and I may not be successful in this spy mission. Whom do I report to?"

"I will be in Mexico from time to time. I will send a messenger to bring you. Report to me. No one else."

I took up residence in Calle San Francisco, not far, as Don Juan promised, from the colegio of Santa Cruz de Tlatelolco in one direction and the viceregal palace in the other. Father Oroz was in residence at the colegio where he had been rector, dedicating the school to educating and Christianizing the Indians of Mexico. He was revered by most of the other friars and adulated by the Indians.

When I first called on him, he was busy translating the Pentecostal mass into Nuhuatle. His knowledge of the indigenous languages was excellent. He also knew Castillian (his own tongue was Basque), Provençal, and, of course, Latin. While he was formal at our meeting, when I expressed an interest in his work he relaxed and ushered me into his scriptorium. There I saw pages decorated by his excellent hand lettering in Nuhuatle and Otomi words. There were grammars and translations of scriptures for use by friars of the province. He showed me a biography he was writing describing the lives of all the Franciscan missionaries sent to the Province of Mexico and, in particular, the first 12 Franciscans sent in the year 1524, who are now revered almost as much as Christ, our most Holy Lord. It was the work of which he was most proud. When I questioned him further, he told me that the writing included descriptions for the first entradas in New Mexico, made by the Franciscans with all their bloody ordeals revealed for all to know, and described how all had traded their cloistered lives of meditation for the blood and sacrifice of the New World, confronting the unimaginable paganisms of the Indians.

The scriptorium was a bare cell but still pleasant. There was a scriptboard from which, through a small window, the friar could see the perfumed gardens below and overhear the song of rare and lovely birds. The shelves exuded the pleasant odor of green and seasoned cypress mingled with that of ink and sealing wax. I saw that this simplicity was in itself a beauty not found in the more cluttered apartments of the wealthy citizens, a privileged beauty, known only to those keen to the sensorium of God.

Father Oroz insisted I see the buildings and works that comprised the complex of the colegio. The main structures of the school were built of small stone as was the large church. The interior of the friary was vast and housed many friars and Indian workers. The walkways were covered porticos surrounding large courtyards filled by well-tended gardens.

He showed me the large library he had spent many years assembling; it was as fine a library as I have seen anywhere. There were works by Augustine, Cyprian, Jerome, and Aquinas as well as that old Greek, Aristotle; the Romans, Virgil, Pliny and Cicero; biblical works of every type (and mostly forbidden); dictionaries, encyclopedias and a large collection of medical histories and practices. The friar was much interested in native medicines and other cures, and manuscripts on these subjects abounded.

The library became one of my daily pleasures. It was here that Father Oroz engaged me in great philosophical debates over the works of Aristotle and St. Thomas' interpretations. I felt myself bound by Nicomachean Ethics and yet Oroz pointed out how my life as a soldier was a virtual contradiction to those ethics.

"Aristotle says all human activities aim at some good. But I ask, what good is there in conquest, if the aim be to enslave those conquered? We are dealing with the irrational soul, here."

"Why yes," I agreed. "Perhaps we two represent Aristotle's divided soul. You are the rational and I the irrational." It seemed to make sense. "But happiness is the ultimate good," I continued, "and happiness is achev-ed through virtuous activity which achieves a balance between pleasure and pain. Now, is not courage a necessary fundamental for a soldier's temperament?"

He smiled, "why yes, I believe so . . . but it must be proper courage . . . the overly courageous are foolhardy."

"But I must possess the minimum courage needed to face the enemy. Thus, I am virtuous. I meet Aristotle's requirement for a rational soul."

"Ah, good argument, my friend. But let us turn this philosophy to some good and examine the position of the Jews."

And so we spent many days engaged with each other's thoughts until I found myself gaining a deep admiration for this friar. I also began to come more to an understanding of his wide-ranging views.

One day, while searching for the early pastoral works of Virgil, I was in-terrupted by a young, handsome fellow dressed in a coarse, grey garb. He said boldly that Father Oroz had sent him to be of whatever assistance possible. He introduced himself as Luis de Carvajal, serving sentence under the spiritual guidance of Father Oroz. I was stunned. This was the first con-victed Judaizer I had met, and I quickly recalled the dark mission Don Juan had given me.

"I am Captain Gaspar de Villagra," I said in a severe tone for which I was quickly sorry.

"Your servant," he replied. "are you a friend of the good Father?"

"Yes," I replied, surprising myself. "I am here in Mexico City on tem-porary duty with the viceregal court representing the interests of Don Juan de Oñate."

The mention of the name Oñate caused a brief change in his expression.

"I would be pleased to help you, Captain. I am, in a humble way, the keeper of this beautiful library. Father Oroz has brought together some of the most illuminating manuscripts in the entire world."

"Yes, yes," I myself had been struck by the fine collection. "I am for the moment looking for a copy of Virgil's pastoral works."

"Ah, yes, the Ecologues." He went straight to a shelf and returned with a book.

He opened it and with much skill read the opening lines of vulgar Latin verse. He gave the book to me with a slight tremble in his hand and excused himself.

The meeting had been brief but tense. I could feel the tenseness evaporate as he left the room. Yet, except for those almost imperceptible signs of discomfort, he was bold in my presence, almost to the point of defiance. My request for the Ecologues told me that he knew the library as well as he had said.

Father Oroz later explained that Carvajal was a genius with the classics in the library, that he could read Latin, Greek and Hebrew.

"Hebrew?" I asked.

"Yes, Hebrew. A venerable tongue which has and shall continue to reveal many mysteries to us, I mean to all of us. Perhaps someday we shall all be elightened and it will no longer be prohibited to possess such texts." He then explained about Carvajal's conviction by the Inquisition.

"In case you are curious, I allow him to go about this colegio without the sanbenito. Damned, infernal robes. He has a great hand at lettering and is now assisting me with revising my biography of the 12 fathers. He is of great service in this respect."

I felt uncomfortable and he sensed this.

"We must not condemn those who believe the old laws," he said.

"But," I said, "they are against the Holy Faith!"

"Ah, my son, it is sad that we think this is so," he replied.

"But how can you say this?" I protested. "It is well known that they attempt to convert the faithful . . ."

He shook his head. "So it seems. But they are only converting those forced to turn from the law of Moses. Our faith will benefit greatly if we allow others to live in peace. We must not let the Holy Office become an instrument of oppression. Only through faith should we convert souls, not through violence and intimidation."

Then, for some time, a wall of silence grew between us. "I will arrange for you to meet Luis more often," he sighed. "These things are always difficult at first. You will find that he is a great scholar."

That evening I went to the cathedral and prayed. I was under compulsion to report the activities of Father Oroz to the Holy Office and to provide Don Juan with the information he wanted. It was not fit to allow a convicted heretic to use the library, particularly one with the forbidden words of the Bible. Yet, I returned to my apartment that evening knowing that my growing friendship for the priest prevented my taking any action.

It was not long after that I was approached by a friar in the library. I was alone, reading an essay on medicine written by Oroz himself. A deep, penetrating darkness had settled over the monastary and my lamp burned low. Immersed in the medicinal philosphies of the brilliant friar, I was startled by a hooded figure that suddenly appeared before me. I had heard no sound.

"I fear I have frightened you," the robed figure said in a voice cracked with age. "Please . . . I am sorry. But I was sent to speak with you on matters relating to your inquiries here at the colegio . . ."

I tried to discern the face in the shadows of the hood, but with no success. It was as if therein lay nothing but darkness. I shuddered.

"Who are you?" I demanded as the figure moved in my direction.

"My name is of no importance. But what I have to tell you is, and it can be verified by the Provincial Mendieta himself, should you doubt the veracity of my words."

"I prefer to know who you are" I said, disturbed by the anonymity of the figure.

"Very well, I am Brother Leo. I have been the custodian of this friary for the past twenty years. Many are the things which have transpired within these walls that have become known to me. For example, I know of your recent meeting with Luis Carvajal, the Jew. I know that you read the heretical works of Virgil. You see, there is very little I don't know."

"I see . . . you must know all. Why do you keep heretical works in your library? Why do you allow Jews to read the forbidden texts from the Bible? Why do . . ."

"Please, Captain, one question at a time. I am old and cannot abide more than one question at a time!"

"Who sent you? Answer that first!"

"A council of friars concerned about the friary. They would, as I, that the truth be out. As for your other questions, Father Oroz has seen fit to litter this library with works of the heathen, including that clever Greek exhalted by Aquinas. There is enough heresy contained herein to send us all to hell!" His voice raised to a squeaky pitch.

"It wasn't always like this," he rasped. "But this Oroz. He believes that enlightenment from words will help us understand faith. He believes that knowledge is good! But our Father, Francis, said only God can be good."

The lamp flame flickered, nearing its end. I moved to retrieve a candle from the basket beside the table where I sat. The figure flinched as I moved.

"The lamp. I must light a candle," I explained. I lit several from the smoking torch in the adjacent hallway and as I returned I passed the candles close to the monk's face. Yet I still could not identify any features.

"I believe you have something to tell me about Father Oroz?" I said as I sat back down. The monk remained standing.

"There are others, too. Some have already been punished for their outrageous behavior. It is a story of great shame for us Franciscans, but one that must be told if only to clear our names. I know why you are here, and you are the first outsider to visit us these many years since the incident."

I was much intrigued by the figure before me, as all fear vanished. "Please sit down Brother Leo. Tell me this story."

"I will stand" came the stern reply. "Your presence here has caused us much concern. Things have happened here which are better left unsaid but my brothers cannot contain their gossip. Before you hear this gossip, which may damage us forever, I will tell of the terrible three years filled with many troubles which the demon himself contrived.

"It all started some years ago when Father Oroz was made temporary commissary-general for the Holy Gospel Province of Mexico. While he pretended not to seek this honor, he used the appointment to fill the friaries with novitiates from all over New Spain and to influence the Minister-General of Rome. It was his purpose to keep out those of us from the mother country, we who have taken the habit in Spain. He also fancied himself a writer, an author of books. For years he has labored with the documents he showed you the other day."

"How did you know that?" I asked, piqued by the old monk's remarks.

"I told you, gossip. I have a hundred eyes and ears. That of which he is so proud is really a copy of works created by other, more humble souls. Author indeed! He steals the work of others and then gloats over his success! And what's more, he reads and he reads. This Library is filled with the heretical works of Galen, Avicenna, Virgil and other too numerous to mention — to fill his hours with heretical thoughts. Did not Saint Francis say that ignorance and proverty opened the door to understanding true faith? Is this reading not a demonstration of a lack of faith?" Brother Leo was becoming exicted and spittle dripped from his cowl.

"I know nothing of what you claim," I said. "I too love our Holy Faith and Saint Francis, but cannot agree with this assertion — based on ignorance!"

"Oh yes, excuse my stupidity," he said sharply. "We are schooled in the life and wisdom of our founder, but I forget that little is known of him in the outside world beyond the miracles. You see, the desire to become worldly was considered by Saint Francis as a barrier to a true understanding of the gospels. Desire, he said, is based on satisfying the self in the world. There is a desire to know, a desire to become, and a desire to possess. Fulfilling these desires leads to recognition, a worldly status, a satisfied self. But understanding faith and the gospels is not possible while desire controls the mind and heart. The key to true faith and understanding is humility. And true humility is found only when the desire to know, desire to become, and desire to possess are eliminated from the mind and heart. This can be achieved only in a state of absolute poverty and total ignorance of worldly knowledge."

"I see. So to desire to become an author, say, would be a barrier to understanding faith and our Lord?"

"Yes. Furthermore, desire has long since been raised by the devil himself amongst my brethren. We have become a worldly order! No longer a simple brotherhood. We have lost our ability to accept true humility as our natural condition. Nowhere is this manifested with more intensity than with this Oroz! He clearly has become worldly, an author of books. To further this worldly desire, he wrote to the Minister-General in Rome, none other than Gonzaga himself. Oroz knew of the great work being prepared by the Minister-General: *De Origine seraphical religionis eiusqul progressibus, etcetera.* He offered his work to fill the needed datum for the Franciscan history of New Spain.

"Minister Gonzaga was interested. But at the same time, he had asked Father Mendieta, a well-known Spanish friar resident here in Meixco for a tract to be entered in the great book. It turned out that Oroz's work was really only an annotated copy of Mendieta's histories. Minister Gonzaga waited to decide on which work would be accepted.

"Later, when a new Commissary-General was sent to Mexico, Gonzaga asked him to interview the two priests and decide which work would be used. The unfortunate Father Alonzo Ponce was chosen for this mission."

"Surely to be selected for the post of Commissary-General is a great honor and harbors little that could cause misfortune," I said.

"Ah, were that true. I told you that desire is evil. And all this vanity over authorship divided us into warring factions. It's curious you know." He paused. "Yes, curious," he continued. "Father Oroz is a Basque. But so is Ponce and Mendieta. You would think that they would get on with each other. These Basques have so much in common, even that course tongue, but it made no difference.

"At that time Oroz had some influence with the court and he complained when he learned of Ponce's appointment. He wanted, rather, that a criollo be appointed to the post. Thus Oroz resigned his temporary appointment and caused Father San Sebastian to be in charge of the Holy Gospel Province of Mexico. But nothing these two scoundrels could do would stop Commissary Ponce from arriving in Mexico." He paused, licked his dry lips, and remained silent for some time, apparently thinking of what to say next: "After Ponce arrived, they did all they could to undermine his position," he continued. "Ponce, at first, was not fully aware of the move against his authority. He immediately set about reviewing the documents and interviewing Oroz and Mendieta to determine which version would be entered in the *De Origine.* After much work, he determined to accept a collective version, giving credit to all authors involved, including Oroz.

"But Ponce went much further than just reading. He decided to edit the documents and his hand was heavy on the works of Oroz. He felt there was too much detail in what Oroz had written. Why Oroz even included extensive descriptions of the grave sites of each of our Brothers who died here! *Sic itur ad astra?* absurd.

"Much *verba absurdum* was stricken from the works of Oroz, to his chagrin. His vanity overwhelmed him. This writer! Such vanity should never befall a Franciscan. Leave authoring to the Dominicans, the Augustinians! Why should we go against the rule of the Founder? Humility is our faith. Poverty is our lady. But this author's vanity, this evil of the written word, caused those two to turn this friary, that you see here, into a bordello! Under your very feet wicked females sported with soiled and heretical Monks!" He gestured wildly, stabbing a bony finger in the air. I was taken aback by his words. To hear such accusations from a Franciscan was shocking.

"How did this come about?" I asked, puzzled by the words of this wild monk. "What did the written documents have to do with turning this monastery into a bordello?"

As he opened his mouth to answer and still jabing the air, several monks entered the library. Only silence fell from his lips. Brother Leo pulled his hood close about his still mysterious face, and disappeared.

4

"This author's vanity! This evil of the written word!" The dark, cold words circulated through my mind, demanding recognition. Brother Leo's statements were outrageous. How could the desire to write be a barrier to faith and understanding of the gospels? How could this be? Wasn't I a true believer? Didn't I obey and respect the Holy Faith? Yet, I too, longed to be a writer and I sought knowledge with all my being. Was I guilty of courting evil?

The old monk must be crazed and had singled me out to vent his spleen. But what about the sporting females and the bordello? Was this also the raving of a lunatic Monk? I had much yet to learn about this Brother Leo and the working of the friary.

The following day I visited the library again and examined the shelves carefully. All the works were there as before yet now I saw them differently. I began dividing the works into categories: Those acceptable to the Faith (Brother Leo?) and those of heretical abstraction. Works in Hebrew were eaily classified as were those of the Arabs and Orientals. But what of Virgil? and Aristotle? Hadn't these two, while admittedly pagan, been brought into the Church? I brooded on this topic for a while and finally conceded that these two must be pagans, but not heretical. I picked up a volume of *Summa Theologiae*. I read through the fine vellum pages until I came to a section I felt was meaningful to the issue at hand:

Does a Man's Happiness Consist in any Created Good? I remember St. Thomas' answer was that happiness is the perfect good which cannot be created. Happiness completely satisfies desire, otherwise it would not be the perfect good. Happiness cannot be achieved through any desire, but rather only the fulfillment of the desire for the perfect good. Thus happiness cannot be found through any created good. But wasn't a written work a prime example of a created good?

I replaced the *Summa Theologiae*, dissatisfied, and continued my classification process. Only a few volumes could be classified as non-heretical. Was this then, a library for heresy as Brother Leo had said?

I fled into the garden fearing I had become as crazed as the monk. The light and fresh air helped clear my mind and I sat quietly for a while, thinking nothing. My eyes fixed on a burbling fountain a few yards away and I concentrated on the crystal droplets of water as they shimmered in the air like vaporous jewels only to drop and disappear into the mass of water, into nothingness. My observations, now bordering on some conclusion, were abruptly interrupted by a figure standing before me.

"Don Gaspar, I am Father Martinez" the figure said, in a firm but not unfriendly voice. "I am a colleague of Father Pedro Oroz and have come to see if there is any way I can help you. I know you have been recently visited by Brother Leo and I fear there is much to expalin."

I looked up, "That is kind of you, Father," I said. "I would be happy with *any* explanation. Brother Leo is . . . I must say, strange. I am afraid I understand little of his commentary. He seemed distraught and threatened."

"Ah yes, Brother Leo has been with us many years and still has not learned how to deal with secular visitors. But if you would be kind enough to join me, I will try to explain."

I followed him back into the hall leading to the library and into a small room adjoining it. There was a crude desk and chair and he motioned for me to take the chair. The room was poorly illuminated as there was only a small opening high up on the wall.

"Brother Leo, is, I must say, a very dedicated servant of the Lord," he began. "While he has never been ordained, it has been his wish to remain a Friar Minor. His dedication and love of our Lord is unbounded and because of his great faith, he has been custodian here for more years than we care to remember. He is an original Franciscan: dedicated to humility, proverty and prayer."

"Yes, that was clear from his words. Yet he also seemed to fear learning and knowledge. He branded them as vain and self-fulfilling evil notions in league with the devil. I find this very disturbing."

"It is so with friars such as Brother Leo," he replied. "They adhere to the fundamental rules of our founder. St. Francis had a dream, a beautiful dream of all mankind marching together toward salvation. For him, salvation came about through purity of the heart and mind. And purity can be realized only when lust and pride are eliminated. But, you see, pride is nourished by learning and knowledge. Thus, St. Francis felt that knowledge external to the scriptures was the source of vanity and puffed men with pride and self-satisfaction. He felt that knowledge was an object of worship in the universities and that these institutions plant the seed of pride in men. And pride makes men susceptible to the will of the devil. Thus salvation was possible only through ignorance and poverty."

"And . . . do you believe this?" I asked.

"Oh yes," he replied. "I believe, as all Franciscans must, that our founder was correct on these points. And we all try to practice his preachings. But long ago it was recognized that it was beyond the pale of ordinary humans to try to emulate St. Francis. You see, we are weak sinners and cannot achieve the purity he demanded. Thus we have turned to the world around us and admit learning and knowledge into our midst. We join orders, become priests and bishops and even inquisitors! And learning has become an essential element of our existence. Now we study languages, science, literature, medicine — all the things St. Francis abhorred. Knowledge is our sin, our vanity. But amongst us are those who remain pure — those who still follow the just rule — as Brother Leo does."

"I understand, but it does not explain his behaviour. Brother Leo spoke of sinister events — he alluded to a terrible three years with events contrived by the devil; to the friary being turned into a bordello!"

The Priest shuddered and after a long silence, sighed. "He told you that, did he? It is more serious than I thought." He was silent for a moment. "Please wait for me here, I shall return shortly." He disappeared into the refectory but never returned. After awhile, I left more disturbed than before.

4

At some time later, I visited the library again, staying late into the cold evening reading Bonaventure, Boethius and Augustine. Although I longed dearly to read the Aenied, I felt the presence of guilt gnawing on the sin of my pride. I was still puzzled by these friars and their strange beliefs although reading the life of Francis by Bonaventure had clarified some of what Father Martinez had explained. But the sudden disappearance of these two informers left me puzzled and a growing curiosity kept me returning to the friary and the library.

I wondered how they knew so much about my movements, but simple logic made it plain. Admission to the convent at Tlatelolco was through a large beautifully carved wooden door that fronted on the street and faced the Indian park. When I first arrived, a tug at the bell-rope produced a novice whose duty it was to admit no one without invitation. My stated purpose was to visit the rector, Father Oroz, and this produced a waiting period at the entrance while the request was verified. Following this, Father Oroz gave the novice orders to admit me to the library or the garden and thus it was that he always knew where I was. How could I leave, without his knowing, since the door remained locked at all times? It had to be the novice who informed others of my coming and goings. Easy enough, but the rest would depend on prying eyes, hidden perhaps by dark recesses or hidden openings of which I was unaware.

I was happy at my ability to arrive at this conclusion but now I felt watched. The more I thought of this the more my skin crawled until I felt I was under the scrutiny of the demon himself! I got up and pretending to examine this or that volume, I looked carefully for any signs of a prying eye. My search was not fruitless. A niche in the wall holding a crucifix and other religious artifacts was backed by a small iron grill. The wall behind the grill was almost impossible to see and could easily contain a sliding element through which prying eyes could see all.

I wanted to confront Father Oroz with all this, but even more, I wanted Brother Leo and Father Martinez to finish what they had started. Perhaps there was enough scandal here to indict Oroz without resorting to the extreme measures demanded by Don Juan. Surely involvement in what seemed to be the makings of sordid scandal would reduce the rector's influence with the viceroy.

I continued my visits to the library and one evening as darkness filled the windows and I lit the reading lamp, I became aware of Brother Leo's presence once again. I could see him now, a thin, pinched face wrinkled by age with eyes that seemed vacant. I noticed as he moved from the entrance to where I stood that he did so with the cautions steps of the blind.

"I am sorry I left you here the other night" he stammered, "but what I have to tell you is for you alone. There are those here who would not let me speak to you,"

I noticed a changeless countenance, as if his face were frozen. "I am glad you returned. I want to hear the rest of what you have to say"

"You are a Spaniard," he said "You will understand. I told you of Ponce's decision to severely edit Oroz's manuscripts. This infuriated Oroz and he and San Sebastain decided to use their influence with the new viceroy, Don Alvaro Manrique de Zuniga, Marques de Villa Manrique. This viceroy had close ties with Franciscans because many family members had taken the Habit and moved here to Mexico. The Provincial San Sebastian was also a great favorite of the virreina, Doña Blanca."

He paused for a moment and looked furtively around the library and then moved toward the niche I had noticed earlier. Reaching inside the small opening, he pulled a panel across the opening which sealed it off.

"We have many ways of observing the happenings in this library," he said. "The Inquisition is particularly fond of secret . . . ." Again, he paused and looked around. Then he continued:

"If ever there were a true manifestation of the evil of women, it would be this Doña Blanca," he said, his voice trembling. "She was, nay is, a great whore and has brought the black evil of lust into this house."

"How could this come about?" I asked, not believing.

"You don't believe me? I told you, ask Mendieta, yes, and ask Martinez, and above all ask Oroz. They will not deny what happened here. They will confirm my words. But there is more, much more.

"This virreina liked to tempt our simple monks, to disrobe them, to fornicate with them. She loved the novices and would lay with them wherever she could. She was invited to live here — here! I say, with an entourage of lusting whores! San Sebastian let them move in amongst us! Day and night we would be tempted by these lusting bitches. They were forever taking baths in the lavatory without the least regard for who saw their nakedness." He sat, holding his face. "It was a time of trail for us and we lost, lost to the great whore." He was sobbing.

"But how could this happen? Didn't the Commissary General know?

"Oh yes," he continued. "He begged the viceroy to remove the virreina and her companions from the friary. You want to know the result? His voice was now pitched almost to a crackled scream, "he ordered Commissary Ponce into exile! Exile for the Commissary General!" again he began sobbing. I waited quietly for him to continue.

"Poor Commissary Ponce! He took a few Spanish monks with him and started the long journey to Guatemala. He asked me to go, but I could not abandon this friary to the demon.

"But that was not enough. Oroz wanted Ponce to sign documents stating that he, Oroz, was the sole author of the history and further, for Ponce to resign his position as Commissary General. Oroz pursued Ponce into Oaxaca and finally confronted him with these demands, all certified by the viceroy!

"Poor Ponce. Even in exile he was pursued by his enemies. Oroz's demands were the final blow. Ponce became enraged and excommunicated Oroz, San Sebastian, the viceroy and the virreina. Then, the Spanish monks said, Ponce became violently ill and took to his bed. Oroz stayed at their retreat, offering to care for Ponce. In realty, we know he was attempting to get Ponce to sign the document before he died. Every time Oroz approached the sick bed, Commissary Ponce would fall into a rage of vomiting, a black vile substance flowing from his mouth. It was the demon! The black vomit of the demon!" He sat down, exhausted. When he looked towards me the lamp fell full on his face and I gasped, startled by his countenance. His keen ears detected my reaction:

"Yes, I am without eyes. The Chichimeca plucked them out long ago. But it is a blessing the Lord has given me. You understand? When the whores danced naked before us, I could not see them!" He pulled his cowl tightly about his face. He continued:

"The virreina openly sported here in the convent until finally I went to the legal secretary of the Provincial, Dr. Juan de Salcedo. He too, was horrified by the happenings here at the convent and now it was said that she wanted to sport at other convents as she had tired of our monks, Salcedo challenged the viceroy, against the will of San Sebastian, and ordered him to remove Doña Blanca from the midst of our brethen. But the viceroy produced a papal indult, which he said made it legal. Besides, he said, his wife would soon tire of these minor indiscretions and would leave the convent.

"In the meanwhile, Oroz viciously pursued Ponce. The Commissary General continued the spells of black vomiting and developed a tumor on his chest and severe gout, swelling his feet like melons. I am sure Ponce would have died, but at that point San Sebastian ordered Oroz to return as Doña Blanca had asked for him!

"Now Doña Blanca decided she would sport with this old and foolish monk. She stayed with him for several days and when they emerged from his cell he looked haggard and ruined but with the promise of her support to have his writings accepted at Rome.

"This sad state continued until even I became sick with grief. But Ponce would not give up and though deathly ill, he returned secretly to Mexico taking up residence with a heretical group of monks at San Cosme who were determined to eliminate San Sebastian. Through this group, he finally got word back to Spain, but only by avoiding the spies of the viceroy. Our salvation came when minister Gonzaga appointed a new Commissary General who quickly brought the scoundrel San Sebastian into line and exiled him and forced the virreina to leave our convents. Oroz himself was hauled before the Inquisition to explain his evil deeds, his lust, his vanity. They kept him in irons for weeks and he surely would have been whipped as a fornicator had not his relatives intervened. Punishment still awaits him! The Lord will see to that."

He stood before me, a sightless ghost, trembling. I noticed again that the library had become cold and I pulled my cloak around me. But it was the chilling words that had caused my actions. I could not believe what I had heard.

"Now you know, you will have him punished. Don Juan will do much with this . . . information . . ."

5

Brother Leo's story was sordid and damning, indeed. But before I would use the information in any way, I had to confront Oroz with the allegations. Before I could reach Oroz, I was visited at my apartment by Father Martinez. It was the day after my encounter with Brother Leo.

"My dear Captain," he began, as he settled into a great highback chair, "I do apologize for leaving you so suddenly the other night. But I went to consult with Father Oroz and found him very ill. I could not leave him for some time and when I returned to the oficium, you had already left."

"I have seen Brother Leo again," I said. "His story is very disturbing, if it is true."

"Yes, I know. Brother Leo's story is, in essence, correct. But there are circumstances which I believe make the presence of the virreina here in the convent less scandalous than Brother Leo would have you believe. As I told you, he is a conservative and the presence of such distractions herein caused him great alarm. But I believe you have been reading Bonaventure?"

"Yes." I said, surprised again that he knew so much. *Itinerarium Mentis in Deum.* The Cardinal weaves a fine synthesis between the Augustinian Theory of illumination and Artistotle's sensory stimulation of the intellect. Here was a great academic mind. He made great reason against those friars who would deny the pursuit of studies and insisted instead on evangelical poverty, friars such as Brother Leo."

"As you have seen, our order is greatly divided on these points. Bonaventure tried to make the case for academic pursuits although I fear we will always be so divided. But for our purposes, Pedro Oroz is following in the footsteps of Bonaventure. Brother Leo, on the other hand, strives for the pure mystical experience of our founder. Normally we have room to accommodate both of these interpretations of the sacramental element bound into our rule but here you see also the great schism between Spanish and criollo monks."

"It is true about Father Ponce? Was he so persecuted as to become violently ill?"

"Well yes, it is said he became ill. But the illness was caused by his own stubborness. He came from Spain and sought to replace many of the brothers here with novices from Spain. He would not listen to Oroz who argued that the order needed the criollo monks for their great experience with the natives. But Ponce felt that the brothers of New Spain were too weak in resisting the colonist's abominable practice of slavery. This was of great concern to the king and court and has been a scandal world-wide.

"But the Brothers here have always resisted slavery with every drop of blood in their veins and the charge was foundless. This is what caused Ponce's downfall, and his own gall made him sick."

"I see. What about the virreina? and San Sabastian?"

"San Sabastian is a friend of the Viceroy's family. He invited the virreina to use the upper levels of the cloister with her entourage and escorts. The virreina was working for Minister Gonzaga on the *"De Origine."* Her stay was perhaps, overextended, and when some of the women with her overstepped the bounds of decency, they were asked to leave. The rest is a product of Brother Leo's fervent dislike of females. There was some scandal but not what he claims. Doña Blanca was perhaps indiscreet with her request for help in researching certain Latin and Hebrew texts. That is why she requested the help of Father Oroz. Poor Father Oroz. He is a frustrated intellectual with a great desire for writing. His relationship with the virreina was without defect, except for his zeal to get his writing recognized. Towards that end, he dedicated his manuscripts on the history to Doña Blanca. There has been much unfounded speculation on his motive.

"And the Inquisition?" I asked. "Was he, indeed, arrested?"

"No. Never arrested. He was ordered to appear before the Inquisitor, but not for behavior related to the virreina. What was required was an answer to certain charges concerning his writings. They were considered speculative theology and some sixteen theological interpretations were suspected. Oroz remained at the House of Inquisition until he could bring himself to reword the passages. No, he was never arrested, but the Archbishop did condemn these writings which in some cases challenged his authority to exercise control over our order."

"Father Oroz challenged the authority of the Archbishop?" I asked, amazed at the audacity of the old friar.

"In a way, yes. But it was never his aim to challenge papal authority. Only to point out what he considered certain excesses in exercising that authority. For example, he argued against the condemnation by the Archbishop of certain writings of St. Thomas based on Aristotelian concepts of an eternal universe."

The wild stories of Brother Leo and this subsequent illumination by Father Martinez made me eager to speak once again with Father Oroz, who was still recovering. Now I felt I knew him much better and greatly respected his audacity. When I finally did get to see him, he was pleased with my understanding of his spiritual dilemma.

"I fear I am a great sinner," he said. "I cannot put my vanity aside. It is in the nature of man to know. Man must suppress his nature to be pure in heart, yet I find I am too weak to do so."

From the Franciscan viewpoint I could understand his dilemma. I was glad to be free from such guilt.

"But tell me," he said, "have you managed in your inquiries to learn more about Luis Carvajal? He is currently diligently researching the latest entrada into New Mexico. I would be greatly in your debt if you would assist us in this enterprise."

6

I met Luis Carvajal several times after that first encounter. Father Oroz was apparently not satisfied with my initial reaction to Luis. I found what Oroz said was true; Luis was a brilliant scholar, devoted to studies of the ancient texts. I discovered views and philosophies that had been ignored in my earlier education at Salamanca.

I was please that Father Oroz had asked me to assist him with his research for the biography, particularly of entradas made into New Mexico and the sacrifice of friars who tired to convert the barbarous natives. Luis was engaged in this research and was writing a history for Father Oroz based on the recent entrada of one Castaño de Sosa who was now under arrest and awaiting deportation to the Phillipines. Castaño had been appointed by Luis' uncle, who had recently died a prisoner of the Inquisition. This uncle, I was told, had been the governor of Nuevo Leon and also an acquaintance of Don Juan. He said Don Juan and Carvajal had combined forces earlier, in 1585, when the Chichimecas were the scourge of the entire frontier.

"I was a captain in my uncle's militia," Luis said one day as we read the latest communication from Castaño de Sosa. "I used to be very active in Nuevo Leon against the Chichimecas. I considered them vermin and would not hesitate to kill all if I could."

I asked him why he had left Nueva Leon since his uncle was governor.

"My uncle was a fool. He did not throw his tainted relatives out of his home. You see, he was a New Christian, a converso." He said the last words with hate dripping from his tongue. "A Christianized Jew. The Inquisition makes short work of Christian Jews who dare to get rich."

He paused for a moment, testing my reaction. I said nothing.

"He was arrested by the viceroy," he continued, "for capturing and enslaving the Chichimecas. That was only a pretext to turn him over to the Holy Office. There has never been a real Christian arrested for enslaving Chichimecas! Can you tell me of any?"

"When did you come to the City of Mexico?" I asked, ignoring his question.

"When the Inquisition arrested my mother. You see, she is a hopeless Jew. She tried to convert my uncle back to the old faith. In his own house. Still, he refused to move her out and his own lieutenant reported him to the Holy Office. He was arrested and thrown into prison. The fool."

At that point, disliking the tone of the conversation, I insisted that we review the recent report from Castaño about his travels in New Mexico. I wanted to learn what I could about that mysterious land and every report I read only increased my curiosity. Luis seemed disappointed, but he took the yellow parchment and began to read:

"*January 13, in the year of our Lord, 1591. On that day we journeyed to another settlement, five leagues from the two mentioned before, arriving there an hour before sunset. This pueblo was situated in a valley between sierras, and I cannot say what it contained, because it was buried under snow a yard in depth by actual measure, such as we had never seen before; it was so deep that the horses could not travel. Consequently, when we arrived no one came out to meet us, not even the Indian guide we had sent ahead from one of the pueblos previously visited. The very sight of us frightened the inhabitants, especially the women, who wept a great deal. In view of this situation, we circled the pueblo once, but no one appeared, other than a man who was going from one section of the town to another, and he was fearful when he approached us. In order to reassure them all, I dismounted, embraced this Indian, and led him by the hand around that quarter of the town.*

"Near the limits of another section of that pueblo, some men were coming out of an estufa. I walked toward them, ordering my men to stay mounted and prepared; then I saw another group of Indians on my flank, and I turned to meet them. They waited, and when they showed no sight of hostility, I embraced them, which to them was a very curious way of greeting. They in turn performed the ceremony of blowing on their hands and placing them on my face and clothes, after which I kissed their hands and spoke soothingly to them; asking their people to come down from their houses; but no one heeded. I gave them gifts and returned to my main force, waiting outside the pueblo.

"We all agreed to camp that night in some huts but a harquebus shot from the pueblo. As we approached, some nomadic Indians who were there to trade with the pueblo fled to the south. A few Indian men from the pueblo who had been trading with the nomads before our arrival, huddled in fear at our approach. I reassured them and asked them for corn, tortillas and firewood as it was bitterly cold. A few men returned later with negligible amounts of the provisions we had asked for. We foraged for firewood and spent a miserable night in the huts which were made of willow branches. In the morning, no one came to us except an old Indian who pretended he wanted to trade something; we knew he was spying on us. We then saw that the natives were out on the terraces, piling up stones and supplies of water and, in general, preparing for an assault.

"The pueblo was very strong in people and supplies and the houses were seven or eight stories high."

We were astonished at this revelation of such a superior culture so far to the north, and indeed I was disappointed when I found there was no more to this report. We would have to wait for the continuation. Sometimes there would be long delays between pages received from Castaño's confidante.

As time went on, I found that Father Oroz was also spiritual guardian for Luis' mother and sister. When he suggested that I join him for dinner at their house, as he and Luis had told them about me and they wanted very much to meet me, I reminded him of the mother's great heresies. He told me that I would never learn anything if I insisted on treating life as a closed book.

I agreed reluctantly, hoping not to find any scandalous happenings. I found traveling to the Carvajal house interesting. The residence was well-placed close by Calle Tacuba, a generous, tree-lined thoroughfare with passage for six carriages and a large canal down the center, bordered by trees and plants of every description. Dark boatmen poled canoes up and down the canal, filled with goods from Chapultepec or the main plaza of the city. The street surface was well packed and we were not bothered by dust so common in those parts.

We stopped in front of a well-built house of two levels, made of white stone. A carved stone lintel arched over a massive doorway. Above the lintel was the armorial sign of the Carvajal family.

That first evening went well and was far from scandalous. Francesca, the mother, and Isabel, the sister, were interesting women and their conversation was well informed, not the usual parlor talk. There was no hint of discredited politics or religion. I was relieved when I learned that Luis' brother, Gaspar, was a Dominican priest and that his sister, Isabel, showed great enthusiasm for the Holy Faith. It seemed that my suspicions concerning these new Christians may have been ill-founded for this family, in spite of their trial and conviction by the Inquisition, seemed devoted to the Faith. It was possible that Luis' bitterness was against the Holy Office rather than the Faith.

The house was well furnished and had an excellent collection of oriental rugs and Arras cloth. I spent several evenings there and my relationship with the Carvajals became relaxed. I didn't suspect then that I was involved in a prelude to disaster.

My duties at the viceregal court became more meaningful as the months passed and I began to understand something of the corridor power structure. A new emissary usually found himself walking the long corridors with other advocates trying to open the same doors. It was much the same as it had been in Madrid. Until one understood which minor corridor officials were important to the scheme of things and found a way through their steely indifference, a thousand petitions for an audience with the viceroy would fall on deaf ears.

I found in these corridors a preponderance of apes, the likes of which I had hoped had stayed in the old country. They wore the courtly black prescribed by the king himself and strutted with the grotesque, stiff-knee'd pomposities of the court. I longed for the simple fare of the frontiersmen at Zacatecas as these minor aristocrats were unlearned and lazy as well.

But the court itself fascinated me. The palace was the same building construced by Herman Cortez some seventy years earlier. It was built of handsome stone and fronted entirely on one side by a plaza of such size as to compare with St. Mark's in Venice. Tall, elegant windows overlooked the square from the second level. At one corner stood a tower from which large weights were suspended. I discovered these were part of the marvelous clock mounted on the tower which could be seen and heard from a great distance.

The palace continued with wings down each side of the square and completely enclosed the square. The porticos housed diverse shops and reminded me of Rome. The number of merchants and tradesmen was reminiscent of the Bourse in Antwerp. Completeing the architectural tone of the plaza were large, ornamental fountains.

As I waited for my audience, I attended the public courts-in-session to better understand the proceedings. The courtroom itself was large and decorated in the classical style, a room that commanded a reverence. At one end, four judges sat around the enormous chair of the viceroy, all on an elevated platform to demand respect from the audience. Since the viceroy sat at court only on special occasions, it was usually a chief justice who issued decrees and rendered justice. I noticed that the viceroy's chair had an ample and elegant green velvet cushion.

In the spring, Father Oroz told me that Don Juan had taken residence at his home in Mexico City and that Doña Inez was to visit the colegio. She came, accompanied by two Indian servants, on a particularly warm spring day. We walked in the cool gardens of the friary. The servants were sent to a nearby market. But the beauty of this charming day and lady was marred by her purpose.

"You are watched," she said. "Father Marquez has many friends here. You and Father Oroz are watched. You must be careful. There is much talk."

I asked her to explain. "Father Marquez spends much time with Don Juan. He always has with him a terrible . . . I mean angry . . . looking man who is from the Holy Office . . . a head Inquisitor." she paused, seeming to think about what she had said.

"Who is this man?" I asked.

"I don't remember exactly. Señor Peralta, perhaps that is it. You will know him if you see him. He dresses all in black, much like you."

"But who is watching us?" I asked.

She looked at me with fear in her eyes. "They talk of Luis Carvajal and what is happening here at the colegio. Your name is mentioned often as is Father Oroz. I believe someone within these walls is a spy for the Inquisitor."

I thought that her words made much sense. A spy! But there was nothing really happening except what I now perceived to be insignificant infractions of the rules. Something greater than what I had seen would be required before any trouble could be made.

"I will be careful. But, Doña Inez, there is nothing for them to spy on . . . yet"

We strolled in the beautiful gardens for some time and I listened to the soothing sound of the crystal fountains and a chorus of wild songbirds. I felt a sudden urge to take this beautiful woman in my arms.

But, I am a coward when it comes to such things and I did nothing. She left as soon as the servants returned, their baskets filled with fruits and herbs. I held her hand briefly as she parted and felt a gladness in having her as a friend, and when she was gone, I felt a sense of vacancy that I had not known before.

7

It was immediately after this that I suspected that the Holy Office was not fully informed in its assessment concerning the Carvajals and at peril to myself, I decided to do what I could to help correct this. I began frequenting the Carvajal's home with Father Oroz who, more than anyone, influenced my thinking on this affair. That is, until one evening in mid-summer.

We had gathered to celebrate the birthday of Isabel Carvajal's daughter, Marianna. I had not yet met this girl and I was told that she suffered from certain afflictions. She was the last member of the family I had to meet, before I could report to Don Juan the normal behavior of this entire group and perhaps ease the doubts of the Holy Office. I also knew that it was time for me to withdraw from these gatherings or I too would be under investigation.

That day there was a large gathering. They were there, I was told, because of Marianna's birthday. Several priests accompanied Gaspar to the celebration and I felt a sense of relief at seeing so many from the Dominican order present. Little did I know that he had been reckless with these many invitations and that amongst his friends was a spy.

As I recall, it was late in the afternoon. The girl had not been seen yet and Gaspar was telling an extraordinary tale about Jorge de Almieda, a friend and relative, who had been saved from arrest by the Inquisiton in Mazapil by a bull. It seems this bull had escaped from the Plaza de Toros and killed the bailiff of the Inquisition who had been sent to arrest him. Gaspar felt that the hand of God had played a role in Almieda's rescue. We were all commenting on this strange event when a young girl of considerable charm walked into the room. She was, shockingly, entirely naked. We sat fast in our chairs as if stricken dumb.

Before anyone could react, she started whirling and screaming obscenities at all in the room. Isabel stood up and backed aways towards the wall, a look of terror in her eyes. The naked girl then fell on her knees before Gaspar and the other priests and at that point, I could see that it must be Isabel's daughter, Marianna. Sobbing hysterically, she begged him to remove her from that house.

"I want to die," she screamed. He pulled her towards him and made a clumsy attempt to cover her nakedness with his cloak. The Dominicans were in a state of great alarm and started praying aloud.

"I must go to the Holy Office and confess," she continued. "I must die in the true faith. My mother, my aunts bring evil thoughts to my soul. We all shall perish!"

"It's Marianna," Farther Oroz told me. "She is subject to fits of madness. At such times, the devil possesses her soul. I must find a way to rid her of this evil."

It was a terrible sight to see. The girl's face had been twisted grotesquely as if she were in the hands of the black devil. But it was clear that heresy was taking place. I left as soon as the girl was sufficiently calmed to be removed.

I never visited there again. I felt deceived, and that the poor girl had been suffering for her faith. I did nothing for fear of endangering Father Oroz. When I could no longer contain my despair, I asked him how he could countenance such behavior.

"She is mad, you see. She was tortured cruelly by the Inquisitors. This young child, mind you, had her mind destroyed by those who confess the Faith. And you ask me how I can countenance such behavior? You saw her living a nightmare from the past."

"I don't believe you," I said, surprised at my own words.

"Believe me," he said. "They are all lucky to have escaped with their lives. Do you know what they do? When she wouldn't talk, the minisiters stripped her naked and put her on the rack. They twisted the ropes, a little at a time until finally she screamed out what they wanted to hear. Obscenities! Accusations against her own mother! Then they took her mother and did the same to her."

I knew little then of the methods used by the Holy Office and this was not easy to understand.

"So you see, when her mind wanders, she becomes terrorized once again and relives that dreadful experience," he continued. "You cannot believe the accusations she made that day. She was again on the rack."

I decided to stay away from the colegio and Luis. I knew enough to bring us all down and I carried this secret with heaviness, but then I discovered the worst: Luis was secretly meeting with others in the colegio itself. I sensed that it was becoming the central meeting place for Judaizers in New Spain. I passed several months without visiting the colegio, hoping that Don Juan's application would be approved and the entire affair put to rest. I was anxious to be off on the expedition and away from the treachery of spying. It seemed that spies were everywhere. I found man's behavior (including my own) a sorry affair, filled with vice and deception to sustain a belief or prove a point. Soldiering was a remarkable cure for the excesses of libertine thought and mouldering philosophies.

The weeks passed. My meetings with Don Juan became more acrimonious as I offered no evidence against the priest. I begged to be released from this onerous mission, but he would not hear of it.

Then, one evening, while I was making notes and recording events, I received a pair of strange visitors. It was the Dominican priest, Marquez and the Dr. Peralta Inez had mentioned. He was, indeed, an official of the

Holy Office. They both were solemn and the man named Peralta had such a dark and severe countenance that he made my flesh tremble.

The visit started well enough but quickly turned into an interrogation by the fearful Dr. Peralta. It rapidly became clear to me that they were aware of my every move.

"We have given Luis Carvajal every opportunity to redeem himself," the priest said. "Yet he openly defies the Holy Office. You must understand. He is a serious threat to the Holy Faith, there are now groups of Judaizers connected directly through this Carvajal. Every day they convert more innocents over to their devil's creed. We must put a stop to his satanic crimes."

I saw the seed of truth in the priest's position. Peralta then told me things about Luis, whom he called Joseph Lumbroso, that made my complicity seem like a hideous sin. He was, according to Peralta, an open and defiant heretic. Anyone supporting such heresies was equally guilty and an apostate.

Everything I had worked for and hoped for was now in jeopardy. I had not, for a single moment, agreed with Oroz and his libertine views. I had tried to stay disentangled from these affairs, hadn't I? Yet, while I secretly cursed the carpricious priest, I knew I was indebted to him for many a word of wisdom and most of all, for setting up what was now a liaison with Doña Inez.

While I had known this moment was bound to arrive. I was not prepared for it. The two men were fiercely determined as they questioned me. I was equally determined not to betray Father Oroz. Lies were of no use since they countered with scrupulous details of each event. Yet, I stubbornly resisted each new inroad that corroded my defense. We kept at it this way for some time, the level of threat rising with each passing word. As we seemed to reach an impasse, at which point I concluded they would drag me off to prison, the Dominican, after consulting with Peralta, offered a way out:

"Of course, we do not intend to implicate Father Oroz in any way. He is innocent of any wrong in this affair. He is old and not always of sound mind in these judgements and will not be held, shall we say, accountable?"

Thus it was that the tension broke. I had no further intention of incriminating myself. Omitting Father Oroz, I admitted all I had seen, claiming prior silence on these points on the grounds that disclosure would have jeopardized everyone.

Sensing victory, Dr. Peralta drew out a parchment from his cloak and asked me to sign it. Everything I had witnessed was written down, including the details of mad Marianna's hysterical outburst. Father Oroz's name appeared nowhere on the document. I asked him how they had come about this information, but he refused to answer.

Begging God's forgiveness, I signed the document. They told me that this testimony was one of many which they had already procured. Then they told me that all of the Carvajals had been arrested and were being held in the House of the Inquisition. I understood what terror that must have meant for them. Dr. Peralta's black eyes burned accusingly into mine. I knew I had been close to arrest and perhaps some more terrible fate.

8

Here in Triana, what I share and all that I share with those who are guilty of heresy is the fear of the unknown: the fear of being unjustly accused by some malcontent without knowing it. In this matter, I believe that the Holy Tribunal should find some better method; a person has a right to know what he is accused of and a right to face accusers. But back to my account of the Conquest:

I was not further detained by the Holy Office. I cautioned Inez that we should not meet for a while and some time passed before I again visited the colegio. I found Father Oroz in his sick bed, a frial wisp of his former self. I was stunned by his rapid physical decline. He was kind to me and told me not to despair over him or Luis. Whatever happened, he said, would be God's will. Then he became greatly agitated and sat up.

"If there is anyone at fault for Luis' fate it is me! I should not have been so blind as to think that the Holy Office would not take action. I thought Luis was safe here at the colegio. The poor women. They are holding mad Marianna again."

He sank back on his bed and then said something which greatly surprised me. "Don Juan will now have his way. I am old and sick and dying. I have withdrawn my petitions with the Viceroy. I feel that you are a man of reason and I have tried to show you why I feel as I do. If you have understood, as you must, your presence on the expedition will make a difference for the heathen you will encounter. Pray to God for guidance."

"Ah, my good friend, I can't tell you how happy that makes me," I said delighted with such good news. "There is nothing I want more than to be off on this great expedition. I shall always be in your debt and will do as you wish, as much as I am able."

Shortly after that I was given the audience I had sought for so long. The new viceroy seemed amiable enough and even excited when he told me that Don Juan's expedition was finally approved.

"I have not see my old friend for some time," he said. I noticed that his posture was impeccable. "I am too busy with these minor affairs." He pointed towards a stack of papers on an enormous carved desk. "But, His Majesty is a great taskmaster. Everything must be documented, witnessed, signed, sealed. Everything! But here," he walked to his desk, "is the document that will make Don Juan Adelantado of New Mexico." He retrieved a long, beautifully scrolled parchment with many signatures affixed thereon, carrying the royal seal. "The Council of the Indies and His Majesty have approved your venture. Now tell Don Juan this good news and that I must see him soon."

His elegant manner was natural and I could see that the viceroy was a true aristocrat and leader.

A celebration followed, hosted by the viceroy. It seemed that my trial was over. The new adventure was to begin.

But that was not yet to be. Although I longed to be off, Don Juan kept me in Mexico City as procurator-general for the expedition.

It was just before Christmas, as I recall, in the year 1596, when I set out to find an office in the central plaza for my work as procurator-general. It was then that I first heard of the auto-da-fe to be conducted shortly. It was announced as the largest ever to be held in New Spain; the announcements were made with horn and drum and held forth the promise of a great entertainment.

The plaza was converted for this affair with stands and scaffolds constructed into suitable receptacles for such a spectacle. There was to be a burning two days hence; a *quemadero* was built some distance from the place in front of the great park of Mexico. By the number of stakes and fagot piles, I guessed that there would be many burned alive. I had seen these live burnings before and found them vile and grotesque, a kind of living hell. I did not, at that time, believe that the Carvajals were the intended victims. It was too soon, too close to the arrest. I knew one thing about the Holy Office, it was maddeningly methodical, scrupulously complete and forever patient. Then, I found to my great shock that I was wrong.

I returned to my apartment after seeing the *quemadero*, distraught with my own vanity and weakness of character. While I looked out of my window over the city now bathed in the rays of the setting sun, I knew that I must somehow do something to save the lives of these people. I could not be responsible for this. I decided to write down the entire vile affair and turn it over to the Holy Office. I stayed locked in my room until late that night. When I finished writing, I had produced a document which clearly could have condemned me to death. Shaken, but with my spirits revived, I tried to sleep but yet heard the crier call two o'clock. Sleep did not come. Ah, Carvajal! Why did I get mixed up with you? It had been the devil's work and I had allowed myself to be used.

I left my apartment at three in the morning and proceeded to the colegio. The streets were dark and filled with threats from all quarters. Night people seemed to be everywhere shadowing me as I walked from one crossing to the next. The dim pool of light from the oil lamps offered small security.

I found Father Oroz awake and at prayer. It seemed that he expected me and I immediately showed him the document I had written.

He could not read any longer so I read it to him. The document clearly explained the conspiracy I had formulated with Don Juan to entrap him and the Carvajals in an attempt to win the right of conquest. He asked to hold the document, which I gave him.

"This is a fantasy," he said.

"But I must take it to the Holy Office. I am not afraid to die."

"You will not die. But Luis will. Not only Luis, but his entire family," the priest said weakly.

"Why?" I asked. "Why?"

"There is nothing you can do. This document will save no one. The Inquisitors have already decided what will happen and God himself cannot change that. It had much to do with Luis Diaz, a Dominican spy. He was at the Carvajal's the day of mad Marianna's outburst. He has been everywhere and reported everything you and I have done." He paused and looked at me, "What you did had nothing to do with the Carvajal's fate. Believe me. I am more at fault than you. I gave them encouragement . . . I should not have done that . . . don't you see? It was me . . . I should not have allowed them." He fell silent.

After some time, as if awaking from a deep sleep, he continued, "The Jews have much of their own zealotry to blame." He looked at me quickly, expecting my curious gasp. "Their conversion has been too sudden to be sincere and they have become less circumspect in their defiance of the Holy Office. The Dominicans have raised the alarm and the people are aroused against what is perceived to be a great threat of heresy, as you so well pointed out to me." He again lapsed for a moment closing his eyes before continuing. "How well they have detected the seeds sprouting here under our feet."

I remained silent for some time and then asked why he hadn't said this before.

"I believed Luis," he said. "I felt it was my duty to protect him from the black hand of the Inquisition. He may have used my trust."

I could see the great sadness he felt in his face.

"I wanted only that the truth be out," I said. "But now I feel much better knowing that I have not deceived you."

"The truth is out," he replied, "and you are forgiven. Now leave here before I die of grief." Although I protested, he burned my document in the apartment chimney.

I returned to my apartment not knowing what to do. The next day, having shaken my terrible guilt, I went to the House of the Inquisition to see if anything could be done, but it was unassailable. The building stood large and cold and isolated on the street as if a reflection of its very purpose were embedded in each stone. I could not get past the guards at the entrance without written permission from the head magistrate. I tried to see the head magistrate, but at that time the entire government was off to greet some new official of the new viceroy in Vera Cruz. I tried to see the viceroy but to no avail. Don Juan was now back in Zacatecas making preparations for the Conquest.

On the day set for the executions I could not bear to go near the plaza. I went once more to visit Father Oroz. With a force unknown to me, he took my hand and we sat silent throughout that fateful day, he in a deathlike trance, praying, and me under some frightful spell. I felt close to the death around me. It penetrated my skin and made me tremble.

After being mounted on donkeys and clothed in shameful robes the Carvajals, with many others, were paraded before the jeering crowds and taken to San Francisco Street and the merchant's gate where they were condemned as unredeemable heretical Judaizers. The others were sentenced as witches, or fornicators, or bigamists but nothing was ever considered to be as evil as heretical Jews. And only the Jews were sentenced to burn alive. Luis' mother Francesa, his sister Isabel and two other sisters I had not met, all fair and beautiful maidens, were afraid to die and cried out their repentance before the fire was set at their feet. The Inquisitor relented and they were garroted to death before being burned. But, Luis was defiant to the end and was burned alive, hurling savage curses at his tormentors as his body blackened in the flames.

I was not present in body or soul on that day when their souls were put to the flame. I prayed at Santa Cruz with Pedro Oroz for their salvation and forgiveness. I prayed for myself and dared wonder at the fate of mad Marianna and how it was that a whole family could be put to death in the name of God.

BOOK IV

*". . . of the lands of the Rio del Norte
and the Kingdom of New Mexico . . .
I take all jurisdiction from the edge
of the mountains to the stones and
sand in the rivers and the leaves on
the trees . . ."*

Don Juan de Oñate

1

The sad days passed, one misty winter sunset blending into the next.
Soon the *quemadero* and the stands were disassembled and removed from
the square and I dare venture out from my apartment. On that fateful day
of Luis' death a part of me burned away and now I felt hollow inside, an
empy armored uit. I needed something to fill myself again, some valiant
soul to crawl back into this shell.

I visited the Indian market next to the colegio and vacantly studied the
blue macaws and emerald parrots. They were tethered to perches and
squawked constantly, driving me away. There were few Spaniards visiting
these markets which was what I needed, to get away from them. The
market Indians stared at me insolently, their big eyes accusing in a blank
way. I left the market knowing that I had to get back to soldiering. Finally I
was intercepted by a messenger and told to report to the plaza. I was needed to help with provisioning the expedition. With some relief I threw
myself into the unrewarding task. And so it was that my final days in Mexico were spent helping to enlist those foolhardy souls who were willing to
risk their lives and fortunes for adventure.

News of the expedition was spread throughout the city with much
enthusiasm and beating of drums. While many of low circumstance came
forward, there were also many of noble birth who pledged their service to

Don Juan. They seemed even more foolish and it took some effort to find those who were sincere and with fortitude and wealth enough to confront this enterprise.

It fell to me to inspect the goods contributed by each candidate and to cull out criminals, Jews and other undesirables. It was a tedious task, but thusly - I was able to acquaint myself with those who joined the expedition.

I contributed all I possessed. Of course, I was to receive the salary of captain, but the main reward was in the granting of the title of Hidalgo and estates of land, Indians and minerals taken in the conquest. But for me, the great reward was in soldiering. I had little use for an estate.

The wealthy enlistments were necessary as it was they who pledged much of the equipment and cattle required by the royal contract. I became acquainted with several captains of class already in the viceroy's service in New Spain. Among those enlisting, I remember the names of Pablo de Aguilar and Luis de Velasco. They contributed much of the necessary supplies. I could not know then how much grief these two would bring down upon us.

When, after some weeks the lists were closed, we had recruited more than two hundred Christian souls with their families, Indian servants and slaves. The men were, for the most part, fit for the duties of warriors and only a few had not seen combat. Their battle skills had been sharpened in the Chichimeca wars and their inventory of weapons was fine-tuned to the savage foe. Great strength and stamina were required to march the more than six hundred leagues and, perhaps, do battle without rest or food or water. These men were prepared to take on any hardship for the sake of adventure and the promise of cities to conquer and silver to mine. Those few who had not seen combat were tradesmen or ranchers and hoped to find wealth in a new colony. Yet, they too were stout fellows and ready to do battle if needed. For my own company I selected six stout Castillians as I wanted my commands understood.

The women who had volunteered to accompany their men seemed hesitant and eyed me suspiciously, skulking behind their husbands and servants, often lashing out in frustration at their unruly children. They were extremely difficult to deal with as I assayed their goods. I had rented a little-used warehouse in the main plaza across from the hall of justice and the viceroy's office. Within the space of a few days, this musty old building was filled to the rafters with goods of every sort and I found it difficult to maintain control over the growing inventory and watch over the throngs which seemed to fill very nook in the dark building. I feared thievery would reduce our stocks to nothing, especially by the black slaves who delivered the goods and seemed to be everywhere. I was impress with these people as they found in every event an opportunity to make some benefit for themselves.

I was also concerned since that servant of Zaldivar, Luis Bautista, seemed to be ever present amongst the blacks, cajoling them and threatening them to the point where they would do his bidding. Although I forbade him to enter the warehouse, he used every ruse and excuse imaginable to do so. I was kept from assualting this miscreant by Aguilar, who insisted that Luis was of value to us all.

"He was a slave boy on one of Hawkins' priate ships when she was captured," he told me one day. "A mere tot, yet able to survive amongst those bloody pirates. According to legend, he was born in a volcano, mothered by a she-bear." He laughed at this.

"He has the eye of a thief." I said, "and the tongue of a serpent. If he continues to stir up trouble with the other blacks, I'll have him flogged."

"You are right again, my good captain. Luis has been in prison and mostly for thievery. He was brought out of prison last by Juan Zaldivar." He paused for a moment. "Before that, he was my slave and servant." Aguilar looked restless and of serious countenance.

"Did he serve you satisfactorily?" I asked.

"Ah, yes, but you will no doubt find out that the scoundrel was selling children born to my slaves, both Chichimeca and black. I had him flogged to the edge of his life when we caught him. He swore that he would someday revenge himself."

"Yet you want us to tolerate his insolence?" I said.

"Yes. I owe him a great debt. Before the incident I just mentioned, he held off a Chichimeca attack at the estancia during my absence and saved my family. You see, he is fierce in combat and that is why he is so highly prized by Zaldivar. But the scoundrel took advantage of my indebtedness and well, you know the rest."

I found Bautista and the other blacks eager to set out on the expedition, perhaps hoping to find their way to freedom. On the other hand, the Mexican Indians were reluctant to leave their homeland and many were torn from their familes and fell to grieving.

On the eve of departure, I visited the colegio to bid farewell to my Religious friend. I found him depressed and burdened with age and yet ever eager to hear of plans for the expedition.

"I have spoken with all the Religious who are to join you." he said, his voice barely audible. "They have promised to see that the natives will not be abused. They are eager to meet you."

My work had kept me preoccupied and I had not had time to visit the colegio prior to this time. "I will meet them on the journey," I said, "but, let me tell you of the people who have signed up."

He seemed to gather strength as he listened to my glowing report and he admonished me to preserve the faith and to be diligent in seeking justice for the savages. I agreed, feeling strongly compelled now by some higher mission than soldiering. I left the ailing priest with sadness and turn-ed toward the task at hand.

Don Juan ordered the expedition to assemble at Aviño some thirty leagues north of Zacatecas. Here we would finally be formed under the new governor of New Mexico.

With six horses, armor, servants, and a carreta containing my personal belongings, arms and ammunition, I bid farewell to that fair dame, Mexico City, and set out for Zacatecas where I was to rendezvous with the gover-nor. Captain Aguilar joined me so we might afford a measure of security for each other. He was accompanied by his fair wife, two children, many negro and mulatto slaves and a number of Indian servants. Four covered wagons pulled by oxen transported his goods, followed by twenty horses of breeding. He had already sent herds of cattle, sheep and goats to Aviño.

"I have contributed much," he told me as we rode up the well-traveled highway to Zacatecas. "But, Don Juan has promised me a good return for my investment, as you well know."

I did know of these promises, having drawn up the contracts binding us to our fate. Aguilar had been promised a half-tenth of all gold and silver found in New Mexico. Privately, I lacked enthusiasm for such promises since I thought too much had been made of the reports of silver and gold from earlier expeditions. Common soldiers are notorious liars and brag-garts and inflate the importance of everything they do. Still, this pompous young captain had been convinced and had thrown all caution to the wind.

I asked him how he came to join the expedition.

"My father was a friend of Don Juan's father, Don Cristobal de Oñate. Do you know of him?" Without giving me time to answer, he continued, "Together, they battled the Indians in the Mixton war. When I heard that Don Juan was to be selected as Adalantado, it was only natural that I should join."

"Did you know Don Juan well?" I asked.

"No. After leaving Spain I was raised at Guadalajara and of course I am much younger than Don Juan. But his fame as an Indian fighter is well-known, even in Guadalajara."

"They say his father was one of the founders of Zacatecas," I said.

"Yes, He and Ibarra and some others . . . Tolosa, I think. All great men and caballeros, but if you will forgive me, they all have one serious fault in common," he laughed.

I knew he was referring to them all being Basques. As Aguilar was of Castillian ancestry, we laughed over the Basques and their disagreeable language.

"They were most fortunate," he continued, "and some would say brave and diligent. Can you imagine when they first arrived at Zacatecas? It is wild and detestable enough now, but then it must have been a serious temptation for them to give up and turn back."

"Was Don Juan born in Zacatecas?" I asked, curious to know more about the new governor.

"I believe that is true. Yet, I know his family still holds a great residence in Mexico where I suppose he was schooled. Poorly, I must add. You know, of course, of the vast estates in Zacatecas which he inherited from his father. He is enormously wealthy, but still I find him a bore. And you?"

"Bore?" I replied. "Hardly! Most men of his age and wealth seek the comforts and pleasures available to them in Guadalajara or Mexico or Sevilla. But Don Juan? He turns his eye on a vacant unknown wilderness and is willing to suffer extremes of fatigue and great danger to carry out this mission for the Crown. I greatly admire his courage and stamina for that!"

The captain laughed, "Yes. Yes. You are right, of course," he said. "But do not confuse greed and a great desire for recognition and power with some simple sense of duty."

I could see that this man was quick with words. He was also impetuous and difficult to deal with. When I suggested that we stop at a certain well-known location to rest, he insisted on continuing and would have done so without me.

At supper on the first day out, I chanced to speak with the captain's wife, Doña Isabella. She was not at all enthusiastic about the enterprise and thought us all to be mad.

"We had a good estate and much to be thankful for. To risk everything for the promise of more seems reckless and greedy. What will my children do?"

It was indeed the case, I observed, of many gentlemen of means to sign up for this expedition because they were stifled by the soft culture in Mexico City. This was in sharp contrast to the women who, busy with families or love affairs, had little time to be bored. It was also different for those women and men living on the frontier in towns such as Zacatecas where there existed only isolated pockets of Spanish culture and life was hard and dangerous. We had all these types on the expedition.

"Perhaps you will find the adventure stimulating for your children," I offered as consolation. "There will be several learned friars in our group. I'm sure they will not suffer for learning."

"All you men feel the same," she replied sharply. "How will the children learn the arts of civilization? Not ever, I say, in the company of savages, which is all that awaits us." She was depressed and inconsolable.

I was thankful that I had no wife or children to take on this expedition, yet I had hoped for sturdier stuff. Such pining before the expedition started was not a good sign.

Before we reached Zacatecas, a messenger arrived with disquieting news. A new viceroy had replaced Don Luis and ordered us to cease preparations until he could investigate our contract with the royal office. The messenger stated that certain "irregularities" had been brought to the viceroy's attention by citizens of reputation and good standing with the viceregal office. Such ill-timing! This new viceroy would have to be dealt with or the enemies of Don Juan would certainly prevail. To have the thing in hand and then watch it fly away wrenched us with despair.

Later, in Zacatecas, Don Juan brightened our spirits, telling us that if it was God's will, the expedition would be carried out. He told us to assemble in Aviño as planned, for he was sure that the viceroy would not delay the enterprise. Much bitter language was used by those who had already reached Zacatecas and they questioned aloud whether they should continue on such a perilous journey. When certain weaker souls decided to quit at that point (I was surprised when Aguilar held his wife at bay), Don Juan pledged all of his own wealth to back up any misfortunes that might occur. This reassurance kept the remaining adventurers in line.

Eventually, they all left for Aviño. I stayed behind in Zacatecas to help form the general's personal train. I was fortunate to be able to help Doña Inez with her coach. In Don Juan's train there were two fine coaches with iron-braced wheels. Doña Inez had been assigned the smaller coach in company with Doña Maria, the general's daughter. In the other coach, twelve-year old Don Cristobal took command. Don Juan had commissioned his son as a lieutenant on the expedition.

To my dismay, I was suddenly ordered by the general to return to Mexico. I protested since I now longed to be off. To turn back was an odious prospect. But Don Juan was forceful and I returned to Mexico alone, except for a servant.

My mission was twofold — to escort a contingent of Religious who were to join us back to Aviño and, secondly, to seek audience with the new viceroy and remove his concerns about the contract. The first was much easier to accomplish than the second.

But I was surprised at how swiftly I was granted an audience. I met the viceroy, the Count of Monterrey, and found myself facing a cold, skeletal man crowned with a tall, ribbed velvet hat. His voice swept over me like the winter winds of Castile:

"I have many reports that claim Don Juan is incapable of leading this enterprise. He is accused of barbaric cruelty with the Indians. He is also, from what I can determine, bankrupt and incapable of keeping his word. Here." He turned and pointed a bony finger at a pile of documents on his desk. "I have no need to show you these documents — but at least you will know what is behind my words."

I looked through the documents and found that Don Juan's enemies were doing him much harm. He was accused of being unable to manage his affairs and of lacking judgement in affairs of government. Juan de

Lomas was the chief instigator.

"I respect your position, your grace," I said, "but I can assure you that these charges are worthless, based on the rumors of fishwives. Don Juan is quite able to refute these statements and shall do so to satisfy your grace of his honorable intentions."

Something close to a smile flickered over the count's pale face. He sat down with a rustle of clothes and bones.

"Very well, I have nothing against Don Juan and wish him Godspeed. But I must have some testament . . . on his behalf."

I went immediately to the home of the Tolosa clan and explained the expediton's plight.

They welcomed me like a lost son and were much concerned about the new viceroy. I dined at their insistent invitation and learned much about the governor in after-dinner gossip.

"He is a great man and a leader," Juanes de Tolosa said as he drank heavily from a silver goblet. "He married my sister you know. My mother was the daughter of El Conde Cortez and the great Montezuma's daughter. Royal blood filled her veins and so fills ours." He was drunk and knocked the goblet over, spilling the blood-red liquid on his pantaloons. He was older than Don Juan, short and stocky and gray in his beard. I had heard much good about him from Don Juan. He was known as a fierce fighter and a capable miner and manager.

"My sister, Leonora, was a magnificent woman and a perfect wife for Don Juan." He continued with difficulty. "She was charming and probably most important . . .," he broke into silly laughter that seemed interminable until finally he choked and had to stand to regain his breath and composure. Then he continued, "And probably most important, she was acceptable to his mother."

I remembered how imperious and demanding Don Juan's mother had seemed during my stay at his home and how sharp she had been with Doña Inez. I shuddered at the thought of living under her dominion.

"And what happened to your sister?" I asked, eager to hear this unedited news.

"She died at the birth of Cristóbal."

"I have just met him."

"He has been in Mexico at his studies. Now he leaves with Don Juan for New Mexico."

"When did this happen?"

"Ten years ago. Can you believe it? Ten years! And Don Juan loved her so . . . his grief has been sad to watch. It never wanes. He prays for her constantly and never forgets this woman who gave him so much love. She died so young." He stopped and rested his head on his arm on the large dining table. "She made him what he is today." With that he fell asleep.

When I left they assured me that within a few days documents would be presented to the viceroy attesting to the qualities of the governor.

I then met again with Father Marquez. Although I dreaded this reminder of Luis Carvajal, I found the priest in good spirits, much different from that black day with Dr. Peralta. Although the Franciscans had violently objected, in particular Father Martinez, Father Marquez had been appointed commissary-general for the expedition. No one but Don Juan wanted the dreaded inquisitor as commissary-general.

We left for Aviño, accompanied by three Franciscans one of whom was a dedicated enemy of Marquez/ It was Father Duran, who, despite the protest of both Don Juan and Marquez, had been ordered to join the expedition by the previous viceroy. Duran was a strong defender of the savages and had little faith in those of more worldly pursuits. I wondered how the previous viceroy had set this up. If he were truly a friend of Don Juan's and trusted him, why had he selected this priest to accompany the expedition? I suspected Father Oroz's hand in this.

Other than customary greetings, few words were exchanged on the way back to Aviño. The three Franciscans walked together behind us and I rode in silence next to Father Marquez. We traveled slowly, but arrived without incident.

We waited at Aviño for what seemed an interminable period and I began to wonder if the Tolosas had been successful. Every day there would be news about yet another soul that had given up hope and abandoned the expedition. But just as things seemed at their blackest, an agent of the viceroy arrive in camp. He requested permission to inspect the camp's readiness for the expedition and if all was in order, the viceroy had given him authority to order the expedition foward.

Five days later we set out for the Rio del Norte and the mysterious Pueblos of New Mexico.

2

We headed north and after a few days, passed into wild and unexplored regions where mountains thrust violently up from the plain and deep arroyos scarred the barren plateau. As we drew further away from civilization, our feelings changed from apprehensiveness born of leaving to anticipation of the unknown. I could feel this anticipation building into an eagerness filling our hearts with a silent joy. But this joy was short-lived. A dusty rider arrived in our camp like one driven by the devil. Leaping from his horse, he demanded to see the governor at once.

"And by whose authority? I am the procurator-general and whatever business you have with the general is my business."

He dismissed me with a wave of his hand. "I have a message from His Majesty. I am to deliver it directly to Don Juan de Oñate! Now, take me to him!"

There was much in his bearing and uniform that spoke the truth. I led him to the general's tent where I found Don Juan working on legal documents with Juan de Resa.

With a flourish, the messenger address Don Juan coolly and unrolled a royal proclamation:

"To Don Juan de Oñate, Citizen of Zacatecas: You are hereby ordered to cease all preparations, movements and any and all other activites related to the Conquest of New Mexico until such time His Majesty is satisfied with all contractual conditions. By order of the king."

"The details are here." He handed a second document to Don Juan. It was a letter form the viceroy.

So the vile and evil rumors had reached the royal ear. This was a serious turn of events. We dared not disobey.

The viceroy's letter stated that there was no choice. The king was wavering on the matter of appointing Don Juan as governor based on the rumors, but mostly on the fact that one Ponce de Leon and old friend of the king, had petitioned for the honor.

The governor called us to council when the messenger departed.

"We must not lose heart over this," he said in a voice expressing bitter disappointment. "The king will soon realize that no one is better placed than we to carry out this expedition. It is important to keep up the spirit of the camp or all will be lost. I will make the announcement. In the meantime, no one is to repeat one word of the royal order."

The following day, the governor reported the fateful news as though it were a joyful message:

"My friends and comrades, we have been ordered forward to the conquest by the king himself!" The people cheered and loudly applauded. "We have been asked to halt here on the Rio Nazas until certain legal problems can be solved. But this will be resolved quickly and we shall soon be underway again. Now, in honor of this great occasion, I proclaim a celebration."

I marveled at how the governor's deception turned diaster into success. He ordered precious barrels of Castillian wine opened and had several steers roasted in preparation for the festivities. Bullfights, horse races and mock battles filled the afternoon with excitement. As darkness crept over the camp, the revelers reached a wild crescendo; loud horns and drums competed with savage yells and people wheeled and danced in crazed drunkenness around a blazing fire. Later, as the fire died to huge glowing embers, I saw Don Juan and a priest stumble into the surrounding bush with two female savages followed by several others. They were all drunk.

Returning to my tent, I found Inez waiting. She was playing a sweet Castillian melody on a lute, an instrument she had completely mastered at the colegio. I listened, enraptured, to the soothing music. A candle burned dimly in a small silver holder and Inez sat cross-legged on my fine oriental rug. I thought at that moment that no palace, no large estate, could match this elegant simplicity and beauty.

We were free, for the moment, to be lovers and later we consummated our passions with joyous intensity. I was in love with Inez and told her so.

We settled into camp by the river and when several weeks passed and no further word was received, the situation became perilous. The people had given up all their worldly possessions and now grew restless as they watched their supplies dwindle. The threat of mass desertions became increasingly real and it was with great difficulty that Don Juan kept the camp under control.

At first, the men took to making cattle raids in the countryside. This supply of meat provided some income as the stolen cattle and horses were driven south and sold. But as time passed, with no word from the king, the men became more desperate and raids were made against estancias and small villages. Don Juan viewed the raids with guarded indifference; he felt he had authority to levy support for the expedition from those regions.

The surrounding ranchers and villagers began defending themselves against this "levy" and soon killings occurred on both sides. At one large estancia, the resistance was so fierce, most of the defenders were killed and all the Indians not killed were captured and sold as slaves. Several women, both Castillian and Indian, were raped and taken as slaves into the expedition. When Father Duran heard of this, he was furious and immediately protested to Don Juan:

"You must release these captives immediately," he shouted. Duran was a portly priest even though he seemed to exist on meager fare. His jowls shook in anger. "The royal contract forbids you to molest the inhabitants of these regions or to take human souls in bondage. And some of them are Spaniards. This is outrageous!"

"May I remind you, Father Duran, that the royal contract is now in suspense. As governor of New Mexico I have the right to levy against the population to maintain this expedition. These Spaniards were forcefully resisting my levy."

"You are not yet the governor of New Mexico. And if this outrageous behavior continues, I doubt if you ever will be. Now, I demand that you honor my request and free those unfortunate souls."

"You are being impertinent, sir. I shall not release anyone until I can determine proper punishment and am sure of the success of this expedition. In the meantime, I suggest you care for their spiritual needs and leave the control of this expedition to me."

The priest was about to issue another threat when he decided against it. He glared at Don Juan and started to leave the tent with his attendants. As he exited, he said calmly, "The viceroy will be told of this things."

When he left, Don Juan knelt in front of a small altar and prayed, oblivious to our presence. After a while, when he did not rise, we noticed that he was deep in prayer, weeping, and did not recognize us. We left silently and returned to our tents.

The next evening, Don Juan summoned us to his tent. I was unaware until that moment, how much these political maneuvers were affecting him.

"Gentlemen. God is trying our will to carry out this mission. We must persevere. Inasmuch as any lack of resolve at this point will have disastrous consequences, I am sorely concerned about some soldiers and a captain who have not been seen for over three days. I have reports that their families are missing as well as wagons and supplies belonging to the expedition. If they have deserted, it will open the gate for disasters. They must be found!"

Captains Aguilar and Sosa, the sergeant-major, which is what Don Juan had named Vicente de Zaldivar, and myself, set off in search of the suspected deserters. We scoured the countryside around our campsite and found their tracks headed north. We had expected that they would have headed south, returning to their homes, and this new turn of events led to much speculation.

"Rather than desert, they are leading their own expedition," de Sosa told me as we followed the tracks. "there are many who can no longer stand the waiting. They are penniless, without hope and have used up all their goods."

"Yes," Aguilar joined in, "and Julian de Resa is a good man, certainly no coward. I have heard of his skill in battle."

"I know him well," de Sosa said. "It must pain Don Juan greatly because this man was in his service."

"What can their plans be?" I asked. "Surely, they know we will follow them? Why have they taken such a risk?"

"Desperate," Vincente said. "We have a camp filled with desperate men and women. If something doesn't happen soon, the entire expedition will disintegrate!"

It was true. Many of the families had already returned to their homes, including Aguilar's wife. Yet others had remained, staunchly supporting Don Juan's efforts. Over the year, the camp had taken on the look of a small village as shacks were erected rather than tents. But it was a shabby, forlorn place and after some time, the people sank into bizarre behavior to counter the gloomy prospects. Some of the women, married and unmarried, openly pursued favors from the governor and captains and were reduced to little more than whores. After a while, they were indistinguishable from the camp-followers who decended upon our group like desert wolves searching for prey.

We were able to follow the fresh tracks and within two days we over-took them, arrested the men without a struggle and returned them and their families to camp.

Don Juan ordered us to attend a hearing. The unfortunate captain and soldiers were not present and the hearing was conducted by Father Marquez in the style of the Holy Office.

"Is it clear that these soldiers fully intended to desert the expedition?" he asked us, his face expressionless in the candlelight.

"No doubt," said Vicente. "They were fully prepared to set out on their own."

"And is it true that they had stolen wagons, cattle, horses and supplies from the expedition?"

"Yes, your grace. I have a full inventory of items stolen by these people." I handed him the list. He put it aside.

"And is it true, Don Juan," he continued, "that you issued an order, both written and posted, that forbade anyone to leave camp without permission and that should desertion be the aim, it was punishable by death?"

"Yes. I also announced such at a general meeting of the entire camp."

"Then it is my opinion, Don Juan that you have a legal right as leader of this expedition to punish or pardon these soldiers as you see fit." The priest left.

Don Juan returned to the altar and knelt in prayer. He arose after some time and kissed the black crucifix at the top of the wooden structure.

"Gentlemen, as captain-general of this expedition I order that Juan Gonzales be jailed and Andres Martin Palomo and Captain Julian de Resa be put to death. Sergeant-major, see that this order is carried out."

We were shocked at the severity of this punishment, but, except for Aguilar, we made no protest. Aguilar was furious and demanded that their lives be spared as he had much admired their daring move.

Don Juan went into a rage over Aguilar's demands.

"For the love of God, Don Juan, do not kill these men. It will serve no useful purpose but will only encourage our enemies," Aguilar said.

"I have made my decision. To show mercy to deserters will only aid our enemies. I have spared one life. Have you failed to see this? Now, forget this demand of yours or I may change my mind." His eyes glowed with contempt.

Aguilar's face turned red and he had a vile fit of coughing. "You have a black heart, sir, and an empty soul," he said through his coughing.

Don Juan started to draw his sword but Vincente grabbed Aguilar and pulled him from the scene leaving Don Juan mad with rage.

The two prisoners, wild-eyed and unbelieving, had their throats cut that very day. The families were held prisoners in a nearby village. Father Duran knew nothing of the proceedings until Aguilar showed him the severed heads spiked on poles in the center of the camp. Then it was as if the devil himself had arrived in camp.

"This bestial crime shall not go unpunished," he shouted at Don Juan as he prepared to leave for Mexico City. "This camp is no longer recognized by the Holy Order. We are leaving immediately."

Don Juan tossed curses after the departing Franciscans. Farther Marquez told the governor it would be best for him to return to Mexico as defense against the Franciscan charges. He requested that I accompany him since I had already achieved some success with the new viceroy. We knew that to save the expedition, we had to be released to leave quickly and that new Religious would have to be persuaded to join us. It was a critical moment.

I escorted Father Marquez and the Franciscans back to Mexico City. I was again given quick audience with the viceroy after he had seen Father Duran. He seemed greatly agitated.

"These acts are outrageous and must be stopped. I cannot have a rebel army in the field raiding every outpost and estancia."

"Your Excellency must know the great difficulty of maintaining a field army in camp for such a long time without pay. Such raiding is commonplace in Andalucia and even Castile."

He tossed my remark aside. "I have had no word from the king," he said, "but a recent ship brought a letter from a *confidante* who states that Ponce de Leon is no longer capable of fulfilling the role of Adelantado."

He paused and puffed on a tube of tobacco. "Father Duran tells me I must replace Don Juan as head of this enterprise. Yet, clearly the crown has already invested much which cannot be recovered and to stop now means many years may pass before a new attempt can be made. In the meantime, the French and English are pushing in from the north and east."

He finishing smoking and walked over to a large window, He looked down at the plaza for a moment and then said that it was his decision to send Don Juan on the expedition. He would issue the order, have the camp reinspected by a royal inspector and explain what he had done to the king.

"Your excellency has made a wise decision," I said, smiling.

"Yes. And I cannot permit Father Marquez to accompany Don Juan. It was the one point I conceded to Father Duran. And all prisoners taken during these illegal raids must be freed. Now, if you go to the monastery, you will find a new group of Franciscans willing to accompany you. You will escort them back to the camp. The royal inspector is already on his way to make the inspection."

I returned once more to the rectory at the *colegio* with a mind set to see my friend, Oroz. The intervening months had brought little change to the convent and *colegio* and as the year was nearing end, there was much preparation for the advent of the holy season. The friars liked to decorate the gardens with pig-fat and seeds for the wild song birds and strings of flowers. A new novice led me from the gate into the refectory where the evening meal was about to end. There once again I encountered Brother Leo who greeted me with a toothless grin.

"Welcome, Captain." he said, his voice much softer than before. "I am glad to see you. As you can see, I am old and death approaches. But I am not a coward who fears death. Nay, I have even asked for a great favor from God now that I may finally leave this convent. Have you heard the news?" His grin broadened and before I could say anything, he turned and disappeared, leaving me with my escort. Puzzled by the wild monk's remarks. I asked to be taken to Father Oroz once more. Without comment, I was led out of the refectory and to the oficium where I found Father Martinez.

"Captain. It is good to see you again. I have spoken with Father Duran and have agreed to take his place on the expedition. We talked much about the, ah, incidents you have suffered on the expedition. But perhaps now the tide has turned and you will march gloriously forward. You have of course, heard that Father Oroz has most recently given up this feeble life for the greater glory of God?"

Even though one expects it, such words always bring sorrow. I would sorely miss this philosopher of God. We had arranged for mutual correspondance by which I would have kept him informed of the events of the Conquest. With the outrageous delays, this has not been possible.

I spent time in seclusion and prayer, writing panegyric verse for my friend. The prayers I uttered in the nave were those of a eulogist's oratio for the newly missing intellect.

"Brother Leo is happy, not because of the death of Father Oroz, but because he is relieved of seeking sinful vengeance." Father Martinez explained later. "He had been heavily burdened by the Ponce affair. He now asks to be relieved of his duties here and to join us on the expedition."

I was glad that Father Martinez had agreed to replace Father Duran. This was only because Father Marquez, an enemy of Martinez, was no longer on the expedition.

I congratulated him on becoming a member of the expedition. "but isn't Brother Leo too old to join us? The march is rigorous even for the young. And then, he is blind."

"Brother Leo is blind but surely he can see. God has given him inner vision which guides his way without help. I cannot believe how well he gets about. And while he is old, he has the endurance and strength of a rock. No, he will not be a burden for us but rather an inspiration." Father Martinez was inspired by Brother Leo's determination.

"When will you be prepared to leave?" I asked.

"I must find two more Brothers to join us. Those selected have been sent on other pressing matters by the Bishop. The group should be ready to leave within two days. But let us talk of the executions, raids and slavery. I shall not abide that any more than Father Duran!"

I was taken aback by his blunt approach. "I can understand your position. The executions were most unfortunate, but I will venture that such an enterprise as ours will not long endure without strong-willed leadership and discipline. The measure was, perhaps, too severe. Yet as a soldier I understand desertion cannot be tolerated."

"It seems like excessive cruelty to me. Don Juan is not a man long on reflection and his impetuosity has caused difficulty in the past. He is, as you must know, a penitente and punishes himself severely with the instruments of penitence. Such cruelty to one's own body does not bode well for those to be judged."

"But many of your own friars are penitentes," I said "Surely their charity has not been displaced by a more cruel nature."

"It is different with Religious. I do not approve of inflicting pain on the body, yet it certainly is a cure for the fear of pain. Not to fear pain is something we must learn early for our ranks are legion with potential martyrs. And we all fear that when the moment comes, we may fail in the face of cruel tortures."

"Such a philosophy would serve a soldier as well," I said. "War is cruel and painful and one must show no fear in the face of death!"

"Nay man, you mistake military valor with faith. A soldier's valor should be vested in his ability to fight and bear arms. It is the soldier's task to become skilled in using the best armaments obtainable. His lack of fear should be based on confidence in winning any encounter, not on being able to bear pain. For us, it is different, since we have no means to resist."

Here was a man of great logic. He was also much more of a diplomat than Father Duran and this we needed with Don Juan.

"I see your point, Father. But should desertions occur again, I doubt Don Juan would hesitate to have the offenders executed. I too, would carry out such measures." I now felt it necessary to defend the actions of Don Juan.

"We shall see if a more moderate approach won't serve as well to deter desertion. But surely, there are degrees of desertion. In this case the desertion was one of form only. The deserters, I am told, were actually marching forward towards your ultimate destination. An impetuous act, perhaps, and thievery to boot, but surely not desertion in the classic sense. These people did not break rank or attempt to avoid the mission."

It was true. Father Martinez had put clearly what had bothered us all.

We stayed in Mexico for several days waiting for the friars to prepare for departure. Finally, we left just after Christmas, 1598, to rejoin the camp at Casco. Father Martinez approached me: "Just before he died, Father Oroz asked us to keep this parcel to be given to you at the first opportunity. He made us swear that none be allowed to open it but you."

He handed me a package bound and sewn in leather. I stored it away for examination at a later time.

After several weeks, we reached the camp at Casco only to find it abandoned. We passed through the still-standing rambling shacks, by the well we had dug and in front of the rough altar Don Juan had erected. The wind slapped loose boards together and raised wisps of dust. We were startled when a naked figure appeared suddenly from one of the shacks. I quickly drew my sword and approached the bearded figure:

"Please, your grace, do not be alarmed. I am a poor soldier, Manuel Francisco, left behind by Don Juan to guide you to the expedition."

"Why are you undressed, man? Where is your uniform?"

"If it please your honor, I have been waiting for more than three weeks. I was sleeping, you see, when you arrived."

I could see he was drunk and freezing without clothes. When I dismounted and approached, an Indian woman appeared in the doorway of the shack. We collared the rascal, made him dress and sent the wench off with a whack.

As we started to leave the camp with the wretched soldier at our head we came across the spiked skulls. Father Martinez became greatly agitated.

"These skulls, are they the Christian soliders executed by Don Juan?" he asked.

"Yes," I replied. "They were the soldiers."

"Then we must bury the remains of these unfortunate men with their bones. Where are they buried? It is not fitting for a Christian to be so separated."

We did as the new Commisary ordered, burying the grisly heads in the graves, although it was not possible to know which head went in which grave. We then prayed for their redemption.

3

The wagon train was something never seen before on God's earth. From the head, where Don Juan rode with an escort, the wagons and animals stretched out for several leagues in a long winding column from which great clouds of dust billowed across the landscape. Such was the sight that greeted us when we finally reached the expedition.

Don Juan greeted us with enthusiasm and shortly called a halt to celebrate the arrival of the new Religious. An altar was built and named after the saint of that day. Mass was conducted by Father Martinez and after a sumptuous meal and some rest, we continued the march.

"Your efforts with the new viceroy have been very successful," Don Juan told me as we rode together at the head of the expedition. "I am grateful. But the inspector, Juan Salazar de Frias, he is an enemy. He is a friend of Juan de Lomas. He prevented us from leaving quickly and continuously insulted me and the men. I thought for a moment all was lost. I could have killed him."

The wagon train moved north until we reached a swift river. The wagons were heavily loaded and this was the first challenge of the journey. We had tons of arms and ammunition, armor for both horse and man and five pieces of heavy cannon. There were machines for silver mining operations; barrels of quicksilver for smelting and refining; huge bellows and other tools for a blacksmith; iron plowshares, hoes and rakes; axes, adzes and saws; barrels of nails; bolts of fine Holland and cotton cloth; barrels of olive oil and good wine from Galicia; bushels of wheat seed and corn; salt, flour and sugar and a host of medicinal preparations and surgical instruments to combat every scourge and ailment. We were moving a whole culture into the savage wilderness.

Several men tested the swirling waters and found them deep and treacherous. We searched until dark for a passage but to no avail.

The next morning we tried again but it became clear that all fordings would be dangerous. Don Juan became impatient when none would attempt the crossing and he plunged his own horse into the stream. He had neglected to remove his breastplate and halfway across the cauldron of water swept him from the saddle. A cry went up from the river bank and we searched the brown water frantically as both he and his horse disappeared. Just as it seemed that all was lost, the great white stallion struggled up on the far side of the river with Don Juan clinging to his mane.

The governor lay still on the bank but to our great relief, jumped up and signaled that he was unhurt. He shouted that the river was too dangerous. Nevertheless, we had to get across.

"Gaspar, we have to float the wagons." It was Bernabe de las Casas who spoke. He was a native of Tenerife, a seaman in his youth, and practical in these affairs."

"How?" I asked.

"We can use empty barrels tied to the axles and pull the wagons across with ropes. No?"

We found four volunteers who could swim and they stipped themselves. The horses were freed of their livery. Each man tied a strong rope around his waist with the free end held by another on the bank. With a prayer, they plunged into the water and both men and horses were swept downstream rapidly. The men on the banks had to run with the ropes. Two ropes were set free when the running men could no longer keep up but all four managed to gain the other side. We then had two ropes, four men, and four horses across the river.

The first wagon carried two men and floated across unloaded. A rope from the other side was tied to the front axle with a rope from our

side to the rear. The wagon was then pushed into the water where it bob-
bed like a cork. A man on a horse using Don Juan's saddle carried the rope
as the wagon moved rapidly downstream, pulling it as he went towards
the bank. We watched in amazement as the wheels struck bottom on the
far bank and the rushing water capsized the rig. The barrels soon floated
the wagon back into deeper water and the two men were able to right the
wagon. The horseman continued to pull the floating wagon and it was
God's will that brought him to succeed.

With that experience, we were able to judge the operation properly and
the next wagon went over without difficulty. Once the point of entry and
exit had been established, the horses on the far bank were harnessed with
rigs sent in the second wagon and the operation became less perilous.

We crossed some twenty wagons before sending the women and
children. Once the wagons were across, the drovers began herding the
horses and livestock into the river: they would have to swim. The first
sheep to enter disappeared in the muddy waters, their great masses of wet
wool pulling them under. We built a crude bridge from some nearby trees.
And so most of the sheep crossed although many leapt or fell into the river
and drowned.

Finally, we were across. We celebrated with a mass and camped,
exhausted, gathering our strength for the ordeal ahead.

4

The next morning, Don Juan called a council in his tent.

"I propose we seek a route directly to the north," he said as we examined a crude map of the northern frontier.

"We will have to leave the Rio Conchas. The river takes us hundreds of
leagues to the east out of our way."

The map had no entries to the north and we would be the first not to
follow the Rio Conchas. It was a bold strategy and would save months of
travel if a route could be found. We agreed with Don Juan that it was
worth the risk.

We set out the next day in a party of seven, commanded by the
sergeant-major with two guides recruited from local Indians. They claimed
to know the territory to the north but it soon became clear that these
guides were liars and hopelessly confused. In a few day we were lost. We
wondered through the difficult terrain for a week, often having to back-
track because of impassable mountains or rivers. After ten days we had
made little progress to the north even though we estimated our travel at
100 leagues. We were running low on supplies. We were on the verge of
turning back, but that evening we saw the first signs of others in this
wilderness. The glowing dots of campfires in the fading light sent chills up
my spine.

"Do you think they are Chichimecas?" I asked Vicente.

"Aye, could be, but I doubt the foul beasts would be this far north."

After observing for some time Vincente called a council.

"They haven't seen us. I believe they are savages from this region. We have counted seven campfires. I would guess there are thirty-five. I propose we attack," he said calmly, "and capture prisoners. They must have food and water and may be able to show us a route."

We waited for full darkness then crept like foxes towards camp. As I crawled past a hummock of bushes, a large bird flapped and screeched, scaring me witless. I waited for some time, my neck tingling with fear, but nothing happened.

We encircled the camp and I was waiting to fire my heavy musket at Vicente's command which was to be the cry "Santiago". I could see several savages sleeping by the fires and laid my sights on one when I felt a sharp point pierce my back followed by a loud grunt. In a daze I rose to my feet. For a moment I saw fires in the eyes of the black savage who held a spear poised to kill. We had been captured.

We were taken to the center of the camp without being disarmed although they watched our every move. After poking us with sticks, they began laughing.

"These are not Chichimecas," Vincente said.

The Indians, ever cautious, spoke in a tongue so strange that even our guides failed to understand all they said. They were mostly naked and tall and very black — their hair cropped across foreheads with large topknots and would have been frightful except they were grinning all the time. They were armed with bows similar to those of the Chichimecas and powerful-looking spears.

The leader issued a rough bark and we were quickly disarmed and bound together. The fires were dying and the moonless night made it difficult to see. This leader was more than two yards tall and missing half his face. His teeth gleamed yellow in the dying firelight. I then realized that he had no lips.

We were forced to sit and the leader and a large number of Indians sat around a fire across from us. They fed wood to the fire and attempted conversation with our guides, tracing figures in the sand. We discovered after many hours that they considered us to be troublesome devils sent by the great spirit to make them behave. The leader seem amused by this.

Vincente told us to be calm. "I don't think they will kill us if they believe the great spirit sent us. If they try I have pistol hidden under my jacket."

But suddenly, the Indians melted into the night and soon we heard nothing but our own voices.

We tried to slip our ropes but the more we struggled, the tighter the bindings became. Finally, exhausted by out efforts and frustrated by the darkness, we lay quiet on the sandy ground.

"It is better to rest," said Vicente. "At daybreak we will set ourselves free."

I lay on my side and tried to sleep. But great pain in my arms and legs kept me awake. A sliver of moon rose on the horizon. The sky was deep black and bejeweled with stars, reminding me of the sky in Andalucia. Suddenly my wandering eye caught a movement in the sand. A strange creature came into view against the rising moon waving claws as it searched the sands in agitation.

The scorpion advanced towards my face and in panic I yelled and tried to struggle to my feet. But the victim was Juan Rodriguez. The night passed in great misery for Rodriguez as he moaned over his swelling arm.

In restless sleep, I saw many men on horseback carrying a large cross with someone nailed to it, moaning in pain. The face of Luis floated across the barren sands towards me. Then the face of Inez replaced that of Luis and it floated before me as clear and brilliant as the stars and then began to fade as the terrible pain in my limbs came soaring back. Just as death seemed a sweetness to embrace, the orange and pink streaks of dawn broke the illusion.

In the morning light I and the others saw a large covered bundle. A knife was stuck firmly in the ground nearby.

We dragged ourselves to the knife and with some effort cut our bindings. Free at last, we opened the leather sack and could not believe our eyes. The Indians had left us food and water and our weapons.

With happy hearts we fell on the smoked hares and other wild meats and drank deeply from the clay pots. It was a miracle. After a while we regained our spirits and strength and administered medicaments to Juan Rodriguez.

"We will return to our campsite, send Juan back with the guides and then follow those bloody savages." Vincente was bitter about being captured.

"They spared our lives," I said. "They could easily have killed us."

Vicente grunted. "We are alive because they think we are demon spirits. Nothing more."

When we reached our old campsite, the horses were nowhere to be seen. Without horses we knew we would perish.

We returned to the Indian camp and gathered all the supplies we could, then took the trail the savages had followed. The remainder of that day we marched north without gaining sight of them. The landscape was changing as we turned up a large valley enclosed by rugged mountains and strange mesas. As we continued, the valley floor rose and sweet grasses were everywhere as well as many bushes bearing berries and wild grapes. There were many clear springs of pure water.

At nightfall we arrived at the end of the valley where it climbed steeply into a craggy mountain. At a point near the summit, we found a pass and on the other side a steep descent into a wide, arid wilderness. As far as could be seen there was red sand stretching to the north. We made camp and waited for morning. During the sleepless hours we heard strange noises from the crags overhead.

"It's only the wind," Vicente said as he stirred the blazing fire to a new fury. But we had a feeling of being watched, of being surrounded. But the dawn broke clear over the horizon and finally, with resolve born from desperation, we stirred ourselves and conducted a search of the awesome peak. We soon found a way to get the wagons down.

Consulting our charts, we felt certain that we were within striking distance of the Rio del Norte. Vicente sent a guide back to the general's camp to guide them this far.

We descended to the barren plain below but lost sign of the tracks we had been following. Soon we picked them up again when we reached the basin. There was still no sign of horses. We followed the tracks across the plain. There was no water here and only thorny bushes grew.

At evening, Vicente ordered us to camp in a large arroyo and keep our fires hidden.

"I have a feeling they are nearby," he said. "We will search tonight for their campfires."

Later this feeling proved correct. Campfires could be seen off to the north, several leagues distance.

"We must attack immediately," he said. "surprise is our advantage."

When we were within a short distance of their camp, we began firing and shouting from all directions to seem a much larger force. It was as Vicente had planned. They fled in terror except for the leader and three warriors. They were about to return our attack when Vicente shot a ball through the heart of the lipless leader. His face froze into a cry of pain as he fell back into the dust. The other warriors fell silent and dropped their bows.

"Careful," Vicente warned as we approached but they gave in without resistance. Suddenly when we were within a few arms' distance Vicente leveled his pistol at the nearest savage and firing, knocked the hapless man back with such force that all three fell to the ground.

"Now they will know that the death of their leader was no accident," he said with a savage twist of his lips. The two remaining lay quietly in the dust, expecting the same fate.

As was our custom at that time, Vicente took the scalps of the two slain Indians and we returned to camp with our captives. The bold strategy worked. We saw no sight of the remaining Indians that night or into the next day.

Our captives were fearful and refused to eat or drink. We left them with a guard who was ordered to treat them kindly and at times our Indian guide attempted to speak with them. I noticed that they reacted with more fear to the guide then to us so I tried.

One of the savages seemed to recover from his fear and began to display a surprising ability to understand Castillian. With much patience I finally understood that his name was "Mompil", a strange sounding word for my ears. As he continued to talk, I realized that I could make no sense of his efforts. But the more I said, the more he seemed to understand so I questioned him about the Rio del Norte and New Mexico. He soon drew a crude map in the sand and pointed towards the mountain peaks we had passed. Above that point he drew a crooked line and I understood that it was the Rio del Norte. Just above the crooked line he drew the outline of a Pueblo.

I was amazed at his knowledge. He continued to draw and put in many towns to the north and finally the oceans and seas surrounding this area of world. He then drew a star map and explained locations of the North Star and evening star and morning star. He then pointed me towards the correct points on the horizon and labeled those points on his remarkable diagram.

I brought Vicente over but the Indian fell silent in his presence and attempted to destroy the map. I sent Mompil away and we examined the map which was several yards in length and width. Because Mompil had been so accurate in describing where we had been and knowing where we were now, we concluded that we still had a ten day march to reach the river. It also seemed to be no more than a seven day march to the first Indian Pueblo beyond the river. I then drew the map on my writing paper.

That night I was restless and unable to sleep. My thoughts were with Inez and those marks in the sand drawn by Mompil. I knew they were her people and I feared she would return to her former life and find me an unwelcome stranger. I loved her deeply and vowed that I would marry her. But I had to make my overture before we reached her country.

I was dozing, when I heard a strange, soft cry just beyond the firelight. I roused the camp and Carbajal and I went to investigate. In the dim moonlight, we found a crying woman and brought her, without resistance, into the firelight.

She was dusky and wild but seemed like Venus in the firelight — a remarkable beauty with perfectly shaped breasts glistening with oil, naked except for a short deerskin skirt. Through her tears, we were able to understand that one of the captives was her husband. I found myself with a sudden urge which I was able to, suppress. God forgive us, but here in this cruel and barren landscape, to have such a vision float before us was overwhelming and I could see lust in the eyes of all the men. I covered her with a blanket and even though the air was cold, she tossed the blanket aside. She was not one ashamed of her nakedness nor did she recognize desire in the Castillians. I took her to one end of the camp and put her under guard. We had to make a decision.

"We cannot accept her story," Vicente said. "Not until we know it is true. Anyway, we are only guessing. We don't know the real meaning of her words."

"We should bring Mompil here and see if he recognizes her," I said.

Vicente agreed. When Mompil saw the woman it was certain that they knew each other well. She was placed with the two captives under guard.

I fell into an exhusted sleep and it wasn't until the hot rays of the sun touched my cheek that I awoke. I jumped to my feet and found that the captives and the woman had escaped. I realized then how exhausted we all were, incapable of performing even simple sentry duty. We realized the fleeing savages had taken our best hope for success with them.

"It is God's will," Vicente said, "Accept it as such and you will find that we no longer need their help."

With Mompil's map in my jacket and the rising sun on our right shoulder we left in search of the mighty river. Without horses it was a perilous undertaking. Before us stretched the strange and hostile wilderness which impeded our every step. The nights had been bitter cold and the hot days grew less tolerable with each passing sunset.

5

At that point, fortunately, we found our horses tied and grazing on the thorny scrub just a short distance from camp. We could see from the tracks that the woman had brought the horses to that point the night before. Her visit now seemed miraculous and we named that spot after the Blessed Virgin.

With renewed spirit, we marched for seven days, always due north unless forced around by impassable mountains. On the eighth day with supplies exhausted, we arrived on the edge of a great sand desert with dunes as high as the viceregal palace in Mexico. Waves of sand stretched north to the horizon as far as could be seen.

We sent scouts east and west to search for a way around the dunes. Without water direct passage seemed impossible. But the next day there was nothing to report. The dunes seemed impassable. We decided to strike eastwards hoping to encounter the river at some point. Suddenly, we were given a reprive. The heavens parted and sent down life-giving waters and soon there were pools where there had been only lizards and baking rocks. It was the second miracle of our journey and we named this spot after St. Jude.

Again refreshed in body and spirit, we set out across the forbidding dunes, sensing that the long-sought river was now within reach. We marched for five days and the dry, searing air sucked the moisture from our lungs and too soon the meager supply of rain water dwindled to nothing. On the morning of the fifth day, Zaldivar spotted the snaking line of green shadow, the unmistakable footprint of the great river. Our prayers were answered.

With a drive born of hope, the horses plunged wildly toward the river, sensing the water even from this great distance. By midday, we were through the dunes and into thickly laid hillocks covered with thorny mesquite and sharp plants that tore our clothes and bloodied the flanks of our desperate horses. We reached the banks of the mightly stream just as the sun turned toward the horizon.

The horses, so carried by their thirst, plunged into the rolling stream and two of them suddenly were swept from sight. But undaunted, we bathed in cool water and spread out to rest under sprawling trees along the banks. Our remaining mounts browsed on sweet grasses. Bees swarmed amongst the wild flowers that grew nearby. After our rest, we set out to explore the river before darkness overtook us.

The river teemed with fish, particularly a white *bagre* that grew to a yard yard in length. We caught these easily and the hunters bagged ducks and geese and that evening we feasted like monarchs of the realm. The river was a source of life and beauty and reminded me of the Rio Guadalquivir below Sevilla. Filled with awe and admiration for this place, we almost forgot the ordeals of our journey and our purpose. We basked in the simple joy of living throughout the next day.

On the second day, off to the southeast, we saw a rolling cloud of dust. We raced to greet the expedition and our leader, Don Juan. He had helped us to achieve what no Spaniard or Frenchman had done before.

As the long column of wagons and men approached I could see that the people looked haggard and thin. There was a loud cheer from the governor and from the friars who had walked all the way. We rushed to greet the governor and Juan de Zaldivar and one strange story followed the other as we related our adventurous trials. Winded by so much talk, the governor called a halt to the reunion and proceeded to the river bank. He fell to his knees and we all knelt in a prayer of thanksgiving. Our joy in the Lord was unbounded and unabashed. Don Juan immediately called for an altar to be erected and within an hour, Father Martinez blessed us with our first mass on the Rio del Norte.

My heart bursting with anxiety, I found my way through the dusty band to the wagon where I found Inez. After so much time apart, we greeted each other shyly but with joy in our hearts. We walked to a secluded spot on the river bank and exchanged our tales of adventure.

"You are thin like a willow branch," she said as I rested close by on the soft grass and she pointed to a branch overhead.

"We helped poor Juan Rodriguez heal from that horrible poison," she told me when I asked about his health. "He rides in the carriage with Don Cristóbal."

I watched a large fish-hawk swoop down on the river with a splash and lift a glistening fish out of the water, writhing helplessly in his steely talons.

"We followed to the spot where wild ones had trapped you. Here the second guide found us. Then we followed the tracks made by your boots. I was always in prayer for your salvation. We saw you had no horses."

She told me how the expedition ran low on water and how Don Juan had sent the cattle and horses to the east in fear of losing them in the sand dunes. They too had been rescued by the deluge from heaven and had named the spot Socorro.

"We saw no sign of the wild ones. The two dead ones must have been taken by their brothers."

The fish-hawk had disappeared into a tree on the other bank. Occasionally I caught a glimpse of the shiny remains as the bird tore at the fish's body.

"Will you marry me?" I blurted out, the words tripping over my tongue like wild sheep.

She was silent. She lowered her eyes and refused to look at me. I was shocked, both at my words and at her silence.

"I cannot," she said finally. "I am sorry."

Being ungifted with a tongue for love affairs, I did not know what to say. We sat quite for a while.

"I made a promise," she said finally. "When I keep that promise, I will be free to marry. Will you believe me?"

I turned aside and looked into the swollen stream. It looked muddy and dangerous. The horses had drowned quickly that day.

Suddenly I found my tongue. "Can you tell me of this promise?"

"Yes, but not now. There are many things I must do to prepare to meet my people. It will not be easy after these many years. I have forgotten our ways."

"You will not leave me? I could not bear to lose you," I said with truth in my heart.

"You are like the eagle," she said. "I am like the fishhawk in that tree, we are different but we both fly. We can fly together if we try."

I walked with her back to the wagons, deep in thought about this turn in my life. I then went to visit Juan Rodriguez and found him much recovered. He told me how Inez had created a poultice that immediately relieved his pain. He said she had learned that art, not from her people, but from Father Oroz.

"I think we were followed all the way here. I sensed the presence of those who captured us as we moved through the dunes."

I told him how we had felt the same back on the mountain. Then I told him of Mompil and the woman. And, I told him of my proposal to Inez.

"Take heart, Gaspar. Her refusal has nothing to do with love. She truly loves you. Why don't you talk with Father Martinez? Next to Father Oroz he probably knows more about her than anyone."

Suddenly I thought of the leather bundle I had almost forgotten. I must examine it before much longer.

"My dear captain," the friar said when I questioned him later that day. "Life holds strange events for us mortals from which we may learn the way of God."

We sat at a table in my tent which now seemed more elegant than ever after the rude life we had passed in the wilderness. I thought of how much I had learned from that ordeal.

"Yes, yes, but what about Doña Inez? Do you know of this promise?" I asked.

He sipped the wine I had given him and sat silent for a long period of time. Finally my anxiety burst.

"Well? Do you know anything?"

"My dear captain," he said slowly, "I will admit to knowing about this promise, but I can tell you nothing. It is something she will have to work out and tell you herself. You must be patient."

"But you must tell me," I begged.

He lifted his hand to halt my question. "Thank you for your hospitality, captain. But I think it is time to join the governor.

Don Juan had asked the entire expedition to gather at his tent. When I arrived, he was standing on a carreta, dressed in his finest slashed black armor looking like a conquering monarch. Next to the governor stood the maese de campo, Juan de Zaldivar. He too was dressed in his finest armor and wore a crested morrion.

It was a while before the crowd silenced and they could speak and during that time I noticed that both the maese de campo and Don Juan looked different in some way. When they spoke, I realized they had been drinking.

First the sergeant, then the general outlined the exploits of the expedition, recounting each trial in great detail. Don Juan was eloquent in his praise and the camp cheered as he spoke. He told of their great courage and hardships. He pointed out how Glorious Heaven and the Blessed Virgin had seen to it that there were no casualties, that all had survived with minds and bodies intact and spirits renewed.

"We have marked the trail of the future," he said. "Many others will follow. This great wagon train is the first of its kind to be successful. We have driven a sea of cattle all the way from Mexico. Horses in numbers that cannot be counted and the cattle and sheep in herds that rival the stars. Never before has this been done. Thanks be given to the Almighty Savior!"

The soldiers and colonists drank in every word. They were inebriated by his praises. The maese de campo started to speak, but then only cheered the ringing words of Don Juan.

Suddenly, I saw Captain Aguilar and his clan at the edge of the crowd. They were talking insolently and loudly as if to drown out the general's words.

That devil servant, Luis Bautista, was in their midst. There was talk that this man was evil incarnate, an evil I sensed that day in Fresnillo and in Mexico. It was said that he would murder for a few gold maravedis. I know now that his presence with Aguilar's group bode evil for us all. As Don Juan continued speaking, I moved closer to this band of malcontents to see if I could discover their motive. They were so preoccupied with their insolent talk that they failed to notice me. I stood hidden behind a large carreta.

Aguilar's mistress was voicing bitter resentment and she said that the past few weeks had been beyond endurance. She would not go one step further into that infernal wilderness and insisted on turning back.

"Don Juan will not allow it," Aguilar said to her. "Listen to him now as he boasts about these accomplishments. Remember what he did to the others who tried to leave. But, I am tired of this constant complaining. I will make arrangement for you to return if you insist!"
But, I am tired of this constant complaining. I will make arrangement for you to return if you insist!"

"Begging your grace's pardon," Zaldivar's servant said, "but I could be of use to you in this respect. There may be ways to achieve your desires without the cruel punishments of Don Juan to contend with. Since I now serve the maese de campo, I can . . ."

At that point I was rudely grabbed by the arm and, turning to defend myself, I quickly drew my sword but it was only Father Martinez.

"Calm down, man!" he said as he jumped out of my reach. "Didn't you hear? Don Juan wants you up front by the wagon. He intends to honor your band of explorers."

Crusing my luck, I moved to the wagon with the others. It was a monment of honor and yet I could think only about Aguilar and the servant.

After Don Juan's lengthy account of our exploits, the celebration ceased and we return to the reality of our new environment and our planning for the final march to New Mexico.

Our earlier scouting had revealed that to the west, the river passed through a gap in a string of mountains that ran like the back of a bull from the north. there were no maps of those regions and our reports could provide only what could be seen. These mountains were bare of vegetation, wild and strung with sharp peaks. We observed from earlier journals that our course should follow the southern bank of the river until we reached the gap. Then it would be necessary to cross to the other bank. Since the river at the point where we camped was almost a half-league broad and very swift, we hoped for a crossing point better than the last.

Early the next morning, we were called to council in Don Juan's tent. He seemed depressed and out of sorts.

"Gentlemen, we are not in a good position," he began, so contrary to the speech from the night before. "We have lost many of our cattle through thievery and I suspect some of the thieves are amongst us. The drovers report that at the present rate of slaughtering, the herd will be finished in two months. We have that much time left to march before we reach the land of the three friars."

He took a drink and had the servants serve us water from clay jugs.

"I have two proposals," he continued, "and would like your opinion on these. First, we must cut the meat allowance in half. I realize that some of you have donated much more cattle than others but I think it is time to ration. All of us. Secondly, we must send out scouting parties to secure support from the Indians hereabouts, a move that many cause hostilities. I defer to your judgement," he looked at Father Martinez, "but I must remind you that all supplies are dangerously low and there is talk about returning to Mexico from some of our leading gentlemen. They use the lack of foodstuff as their excuse. I will brook no desertions for any reason, but it is best to remove this as a source of discontent." He sat down heavily.

We agreed to his propositions with only Father Martinez offering a voice of caution. At that point I addressed Don Juan.

"Your excellency, may I suggest that you send Captain Aguilar out as head of the scouting party? I think this will help."

Everyone murmured agreement, for it was well known that the captain harbored mutinous plans. Don Juan thought for a moment and then agreed. Aguilar was an elite member of the Council of War and could not refuse such an assignment.

"Tomorrow," Don Juan continued, "in the name of His Majesty and the Holy Mother Church, I will take official possession of all the land north of this river as my kingdom."

It was the day before the last day of April in the year of Our Lord, 1598.

BOOK V

*"The first and not the least cause of this
expedition was the death of those saintly
preachers of the holy Gospel, those true sons of
Saint Francis, Fray Juan de Santa Mariá, Fray
Francisco López and Fray Augustiń Ruiz . . . "*
                                        Don Juan de Oñate

1

My sister's husband informs me that new charges have been brought
against us by some friars of New Spain. He tells me that there is a letter to
the king telling of convictions of Don Juan and myself and a document
claiming that I murdered two deserters. Murder. Now I am accused of
dastardly deeds by those louts, relations of those beggars who stayed
behind in Mexico while we braved the trails of the wilderness. But soon
my own account of events will reveal the truth.

I am astonished by the convictions carried out in New Spain. Don Juan
and I were accused of murder and cruelty and found guilty, although
murder has been reduced to "unnecessary killing." But what fault was
mine? I, a captain in the governor's service, was sent to capture and
execute deserters. I was bound to carry out those orders. And of what con-
sequence is it that I executed those worthless vermin?

The sentence, as set out here, is infuriating. We have been stripped of
rank and sentenced to exile from Mexico for five years and banished from
New Mexico forever. How am I to pay the court costs of five hundred
gold pesos called for in the sentence? My rewards have been spartan (I asked no more than to serve the Chruch and my king). If I cannot reverse
these convictions I will end up in debtors' prison.

It is the king himself who now detains me in this cell in Triana. My sister's husband believes that the Holy Office has no further interest in me and that I am being held until the king decides my fate! The gold pesos have something to do with it, no doubt.

The enemies of Don Juan have pursued us to the mother country. The king seems inclined to listen to these distortions of the truth and Don Juan seems to be in danger of being convicted on these charges. The case of Captain Aguilar is most precarious for him and I will relate this shortly. But back to my account of the Conquest and the truth:

This was the first contact we made with savages that did not run from us in terror. They seemed much as they must always have been from the birth of time. Because of this, the friars asked for a delay so they could introduce the learning of Christ to these heathen. Don Juan agreed as they seemed so ready to do whatever we asked.

They went about their daily works completely naked. The women in our group were embarrassed whenever the naked men walked among them as these men became lustful and aroused, seemingly by the women's clothes and jewelry.

The unattached savage females tried to entice eligible men to take them hoping to catch one as a husband. While these children of Eden were amongst us there was great consternation between our married couples.

I was ordered to take Fray Martinez to teach them shame.

"They seem to understand signs," he said as we approached their rough settlement. "Maybe we can get them to cover their shame!"

"I doubt it. These people know no shame of their bodies. I have seen their wickedness and I hope you will be spared these sights." I felt there was little hope to change such primitive behavior.

We entered an area where the huts stood like beehives. They seemed to be part of the terrain and as natural as if constructed by beavers. A band of naked children and adolescent girls followed us. We went from hut to hut and sometimes a man or woman would emerge, look at us and then disappear back inside. We tried to speak to them but there was no answer. Suddenly, several men came from nowhere.

"Zacra tu," they shouted. We had no idea what it meant.

"I have come to help you," Fray Martinez replied. The men smiled and ignored him. They came up close to me for a look. One reached out to touch my sword and I jumped like a cat. They laughed and seemed unafraid even as I menaced them with steely looks.

"Zacra tu," they said and sat down in the dust and motioned for us to sit beside them. After several hours, with our doing the talking and their grinning and saying, "zacra tu," we concluded that we were not making much progress.

Meanwhile, several dusky maidens brought us smoked meats on a mat of woven grasses and a hellish-tasting drink.

"In the beginning there was only one man," Fray Martinez expounded. "This man was called Adam and he lived naked in a beautiful garden."

He dramatized his words by pointing at himself or me or an Indian man, repeating the words over and over.

"Man." He pointed at me. "Man." He pointed at himself.

The Indians nodded as if they understood and then drank their fill. "Zacra tu malupe, malupe," they said.

"But this man was lonely and so God pulled a rib from his side and created a woman." He reached a hand to his side as if pulling out a rib and then pointed at one of the maidens nearby. "Woman," he said again and repeated this as he pointed to different maidens.

The Indians jumped up excitedly. "Malupe, malupe, banaga," they shouted and dragged one of the women over and pushed her down in front of the priest. Fray Martinez was astonished and rose quickly to his feet.

"No, no, you heathen!" He was sweating profusely "I do not want this girl. Take her away. I mean you must not go about so exposed. You must cover your shame!" After a short time he sat down and continued.

Just as he was at his most eloquent about the sins of wantoness and the body, a handsome youth with a great swelling lust quickly took one of the maidens and committed a bestial act directly in front of us. Fray Martinez let out a groan like a man run through and jumped to his feet, struck with terror. The savages laughed and yelled, "Zacra tu." As we departed, not wishing to offend them, I held out my hand in the universal sign of friend ship and smiled. After this failure, the friars decided that these savages would have to wait for a permanent missionary of exceptional fortitude.

The river was crossed at a shallow place where the stream bed passed from west to east between two mountains. We could see the tracks of heavy carretas which must have been those of Castaño de Sosa. Because of this we referred to this place as El Paso del Rio Norte.

The Indians were of much help and I think, greatly relieved when we were across. For some time we traveled up river, which now ran in an easterly direction. The Indians of those parts told us that the first great settlements were several days' journey to the north. I remembered the accounts of Castaño and my blood stirred when I thought of the strange, mysterious civilizations which lay ahead.

That night in camp, I visited Inez. We talked of her homeland and she seemed agitated by these conversations. It was, she said, like walking back in time. She warned me that I would see things that I would not like and perhaps cause me to dislike, even hate, her and her people.

"There is nothing that could cause that," I replied.

"The ways are opposite."

"But I already know you."

"Yes, but not all. I am more than one."

"Will you still love me when you return to your people?"

She shifted uneasily.

"Will you?" I asked again.

"We are like the eagle and the fish-hawk."

"Damn your cruel philosophy," I said, and drew her into my arms. "Inez, I love you. You must marry me."

She gently pulled away and stirred a roasting bird in the campfire.

"You are my life," she said. "I will always be your love. But I must keep my promise."

2

We proceeded at a slow pace. There were more curious Indians who came to look at us and trade goods. All were eager to tell us of the Pueblos to the north.

Don Juan called us into council. "Our situation grows steadily worse," he said. "Even as we cut our rations, the onset of this infernal heat has eveyone debilitated. We must make contact with the first Pueblo and evaluate our chances for getting supplies."

Before him on a small table lay the crude map we had been steadily developing. He pointed to the spot where we were.

"Just north of here lies a great expanse of wasteland." He continued, "we cannot follow the river much beyond this point because it passes through a deep canyon in an easterly direction. We will have to pass through the wasteland." He stroked his beard in thought. "Water is the problem. We will be ten leagues from the river. We must fill all barrels before striking out."

Earlier exploration parties had discovered that the river bed eventually turned north again, ten leagues from the trail we were to follow. They had recorded the problems through the wasteland and pointed out that passage to the river was possible if we did not encounter springs. The cattle could not be sustained otherwise.

At council on the third day, we decided to send Captain Aguilar and a party of four men to scout the closest Pueblos to the north observing locations, defenses and vulnerabilities.

"You are not to enter any town," the governor ordered. "And you must remain invisible so as not to spread panic amongst them."

"But your honor, we need food which I could take."

"The penalty for disobeying my orders will be severe." the governor said coldly. "We will get food soon enough."

Aguilar left the next day at dawn and we continued slowly northward. At this point, I noticed the governor had taken the servant of Juan de

Zaldivar as his own and now had more servants than I had seen at any time before. I also noticed a change in the governor's entourage and in his manner and bearing. He now consulted only with the friars and spent much time in courtly black dress and formal armor, and spent more time than ever in prayer.

We traveled one more day and then halted on the river bank waiting for Captain Aguilar's return. The land apart from the river banks was now more difficult to travel and the heat was oppressive. We were short of meat and water but the river was abundant with fish and fowl and cool shade.

The land, though severe, was beautiful. Sunsets cast a purplish light of great intensity on a high sierra with needle-like peaks of white rock several leagues east of the river.

"Those sierras remind me of the wild mountains around Valencia," Captain de Sosa remarked one evening. "We should explore them. They must be filled with game."

"I would like that very much," I replied. I liked this de Sosa although he was part of Aguilar's circle. He was, like myself, a native of Castile and longed for the homeland.

We traveled by horse to the foot of the sierra and both carried musket in the hopes of finding deer. Deep canyons penetrated the steep walls and were filled with trees and flowers and delicious water from underground springs. Many animals, including golden eagles of such size as to frighten a man, abounded. We found deer as abundant as rabbits and with little difficult secured our quarry. While our servant skinned and butchered the kill, we climbed the nearby steep walls and surveyed the sweeping countryside.

"It is pleasant here, in this spot," he said. "but I fear for what lies ahead. My wife and children have suffered much and I now think my joining the expedition was foolish, a mistake. Do you think we will find gold?" He seemed subdued and was clearly nervous about expressing these feelings.

I looked around. Everywhere dark mountains loomed on the horizon. "Somewhere out there, de Sosa, there is gold, there is silver. You can feel it. This country is mining country. All we need to do is find it. But patience is our only course and first we must build a suitable town. Your wife and children will fare well if we see this through." We left the white sierras and returned to camp with a load of fresh meat.

The next day Aguilar returned and was greatly disturbed by what he had seen. Before he could tell his story, the general bellowed like an angry bull and had Aguilar seized.

"You have deliberately disobeyed me. I warned you the penalty would be severe!" Don Juan's eyes burned with rage and he drew his sword as he rushed toward the captain.

At that moment Aguilar's mistress entered the scene wailing for his life. "Don Juan, your honor, I implore you, do not do this thing." She fell on her knees in front of the raging governor, between him and Aguilar who now stood in a daze. As he pushed her aside, the governor cut her severly across the forearm.

"Get out of my way or it will be worse with you," he yelled at her.

A protest went up from several in the company and Father Escalona attempted to intercede but was knocked to the ground. Quickly several friars rushed between the captain and the general and for a few moments there was an uneasy silence. He seemed ready to cut them all down. At this point, the staunch Robledo stepped in, and being close to the governor, he spoke to him quietly. This calmed the situation and the governor's anger subsided. He lowered his sword and was led to his tent by servants who seemed fearful of his every move. It was only a miracle and Robledo's bravery that spared Aguilar's life that day.

I learned later that the ensign assigned to accompany Aguilar had returned moments before the captain's arrival to report that Aguilar had gone into the first Pueblo visited.

3

The general decided to set forth immediately with a band of men to approach the first Pueblos, secure the needed supplies, and subdue any attempt at resisting our progress. We were accompanied by Father Cristobal, a devoted Religious and I was delighted to be one of the chosen. At last. We were on the verge of conquest. Our blood raced with anticipation and we talked around the fires about the strange civilization we would encounter. Although we all had a common goal and were in good spirits, my enthusiasm was damaged when I heard that wretch of a servant, Luis Bautista, was to join us. Later that evening, I caught him looking over my prize warhorse.

I prepared my horse armor for the upcoming expedition. I selected full regalia, including breast, head and flank leather coverlets, expecting much disturbance from the Indians. "El Zaqal", my Mexican warhorse was of Moorish blood and there was great spirit in this animal. He was extremely difficult to control. Yet it was this indomitable spirit that projected a fierceness from both horse and rider and somehow gave me great confidence in the outcome of any encounter. This horse was not meant for one who would listen to timid council.

The devilish Bautista said nothing to me although he was preparing a pack mule close by for transportation which included a bevy of hampers for Don Juan. I could read a vicious envy in his eyes as he stared at my marvelous steed. I felt he would commit murder to possess such a horse.

Later that evening, at a distant grove, I met with Inez. The sunset was lingering, covering the desert with a blanket of dancing light. We embraced and remained so for a good while. Her face was sad and reflective and I sensed a struggle within.

"Must you go? To be first to meet my people? I fear again that many will die," she tightened her embrace.

A warm wind rushed in and thick clouds began to circle the horizon as if to dampen and destroy the dancing lights. I held her in my arms until they went numb and I knew she was right.

The adventure, the conquest, was now about to begin. The prelude of exploration was over. Yet I felt an emptiness draining my spirit and I was sorely pressed to discern the cause. Images of desert beasts crossed my mind and I felt the hot breath of fate on my neck.

As we left the grove I promised I would do all in my power to prevent bloodshed, that Our Lord was commanding us to save souls and not destroy life. She sighed and said that it was a battle of the gods and men were the unwitting victims of jealous spirits.

I was stunned by her blasphemy and looked to the horizon, hoping to settle my fears which now grew with each of her words.

"You have searched your soul," she said, "and found that you must do these things. It is in the nature of man to kill. You have already killed many. You will kill again. What can I say?"

Her hand was in mine and I could feel it turning cold.

"I wish you would marry me," I cried, "and cease this melancholia! I do not kill except to protect and defend. I am not a ravenous beast."

We stopped and I looked deep into her stormy eyes as our lips met in a passionate kiss. We lingered but the darkness was fast approaching and the black clouds now seemed more threatening. I quickly returned to camp.

I realized that my mind was completely given over to this talk of conquest and love. I no longer invoked the Romans or Greeks nor sought philosophic council. The physicalness of life had enveloped me and it was then that I discovered what the emptiness of spirit had been caused by: I no longer had Fray Oroz to help me search for the meaning of truth and reality.

The camp was full of excitement and anticipation. We bristled with arms like fighting cocks and I knew then what Inez meant the night before. It was beyond my control and death was surely my companion. Not that I thought much of it at that time. A soldier in action has no time for reflection.

I was dismayed to find that Don Juan had invited Inez to participate in the journey. I should have suspected. When I questioned her she replied that it was Don Juan's wish. She was the only available interpreter.

I sought an audience with Don Juan but found my way barred by his servant. "He has given orders not to be disturbed." It was Luis Bautista who spoke. His lips curled with surly pleasure as he spoke.

"I will brook no lip from you!" I shouted.

"I meant no disrespect, your honor," he retorted, "but the governor is not in good spirits since yesterday."

"Out of my way, you cur," I said as I started to draw my sword The servant fell back and Juan de Zaldivar suddenly appeared from the governor's tent.

"Let him be, Gaspar. What he says is true. The governor will see no one." He seemed drawn and pale.

Disturbed, I retreated to preparing the troop for the march as ordered by Juan de Zaldivar. I was about this task when Fray Martinez came rushing up to me.

"Ah, my dear captain," he said, blowing the words out of his lungs. "I almost forgot! I . . . well, it is now that Father Oroz wanted you to open the parcel he gave you. His words were 'to open the package no sooner than a day before the first entrada.'"

I had forgotten the parcel in the excitement. I thanked Fray Martinez and raced to my tent.

Out of the package spilled a tightly packed cloth and a folded document printed in Father Oroz's excellent hand. I opened the cloth and found it to be an old robe of sorts, patched and dirty. It was neither brown or black nor Franciscan nor Dominican, but just a dirty robe. I examined the curious cloth for some time before reading the document. Father Oroz's words leapt up as if he were reading:

April 1597

"My Dear Captain Villagra,

"I am about to die. When you read this I will already be dead and in the hand of the Holy Spirit. But for now, I am only about to die. Each day brings a further weakening of my eye and hand and I only hope I can finish this letter before it is too late.

"You may wonder why I am doing this after the death of Luis Carvajal. I do not blame you for that any more than I blame the Holy Office. We are caught in unfortunate times. It is the fact that you can recognize this evil that makes us friends. Or at least, makes me understand that I need you as a friend. You see, while many people worship me, I have none who understand me as you do. I am a priest and have only religious relationships with my peers. The Indians adore me but can never be close to me because of this adoration.

"I as a priest and you, as a soldier, have very often been on opposite sides. Yet, our common ground is a bond that overcame this opposition. As my friend, which I wish I could have acknowledged before now, I must ask you to do two favors. These favors are of the utmost importance for my career as a writer and as a dedicated priest. To complete them for me would be the

ultimate confession of faith and I will reach out and thank you from the grave in a special way. We have such powers, you know.

"The first favor is to help me complete my Book of Histories. I must have the truth set down about Frair Rodiguez and Fathers Lopez and Santa Maria. Until such truth about their demise at the hand of the heathen is known, my book will forever be incomplete. I had hopes to be able to outlive your expedition but now I know I will not. I beg you to follow my instructions as I have great experience on a firsthand basis with the savages.

"Except for Fray Martinez, do not entrust any of this information to the good brothers on your conquest. They are excellent Religious but so filled with zeal to Christianize the savages that little truth will be brought to light. A sad truth I will admit to no one but you: our mission has largely failed. The savages accept Our Lord only by force. If you remove the threat of force from missionary work, the Indians would never convert. Dear God. I fear I have blasphemed, but I can see through the blind veil of zealotry and understand that Christianizing by force will not work. We must bring Christ to the savages through love and dedication. Can you see this? The other brothers cannot see and fail to see that our missionary zeal is what brings the sword down on the savage. That is why I feel you must get the true and final stories of the three Religious without aid from my brothers-in-Christ.

"In order to accomplish this I provide you with the robe. Doña Inez has seen this robe in use and can tell you how to use it. Explain what I want, she will know the rest. Do not let the strangeness of the robe stop you. It will open up your understanding of life.

"My second request is related to an Indian servant on your expedition. He now serves a Captain Alonzo and was assigned by my charge. Upon payment to this captain of twenty gold pesos, he will be released to you. Ask Fray Martinez and he will give you the twenty gold pesos which I have given him for this purpose.

"This Indian is Pedro Oroz. Surprised? He is a Tiquex Indian whom I have Christianized through love and service. If he is released back to his people, he will have the greatest effect in Christianizing the savages for his love for Our Lord is great. Do not tell anyone except Doña Inez. If Don Juan should discover the origin of Pedro Oroz, he would be pressed into the vile service of a Malinche, something he could not stand. He desires, more than anything, to return to his people from whom he was taken by Chamuscado. I ask you this great favor so I may spend my final days in peace.

"God bless you, my good captain. I will always remain yours in Jesus,

FF. P. Oroz"

"P.S.
"Since (as I must know) you have agreed to these requests, please tell Doña Inez that she has my permission to carry out her wish . . . P.O. SS"

I folded the parchment and placed it carefully inside one of my hampers. I felt strange and even angry at the priest for having reached out from the grave, charging me with these tasks. Why should I try to deceive Don Juan to satisfy this Religious? Why? Why did he dare ask me to deceive his brothers? Wasn't this heresy?

But, it wasn't long before I again felt the warm rush of friendship for this dead prelate and deep gratitude for what he had done for me. I knew I could not refuse these final wishes. I also understood his great confession and how much faith and trust he finally had placed in me. Our minds were linked through a transfusion of literature and philosophy. We were both Aristotelians but we dueled mightily over the fate of the savage. My position was that of a soldier, but Fray Oroz had clearly demonstrated earlier in Mexico the contradictions under which I labored.

Yet, this newfound position of trust depressed me as I returned to the advance party. I decided to wait before telling Inez and Fray Martinez.

4

The country now changed into a hostile, violent landscape, crevassed by great arroyos walled with devilish dagger-like plants of extraordinary strength capable of sorely wounding man or beast. It was this very instrument of evil that caused Robledo's horse to stumble, pitching him to the ground. I pierced the calf of my leg and this left a great wound which resisted healing. The heat was intolerable and we found it impossible to march beyond the hour of noon. The oxen, so strong before, now succumbed to the heat and became footsore and lame. A two-yoke team pulled our logistics and we were not able to replace the beasts with horses when, as if at a signal, they gave up the ghost. We transferred the supplies to pack animals and continued, sending a contingent back to the wagon train with the much needed meat.

We traveled north up a valley that seemed carved out of hell. To the east black mountains thrust jagged peaks through the blue cover overhead, locking us in their grip. At times, great thorny trees and giant thornsticks formed impenetrable thickets that even Toledo steel failed to dent. Our detours forced us through deep canyons filled with boulders and here we lost several horses. Carbajal and Pinero, normally staunch fellows, were exhausted from this effort and asked for rest. The very ground boiled under our feet and we felt light-headedness as our water rations diminished.

As the hours and days passed, the terrain changed from a black pebbled flatness split by arroyos to a country of rolling sand hills covered by poisonous plants and snakes. Otero tried nibbling a leaf from a plant that exuded a pleasant smell and became violently ill. A terrible wind blew for a

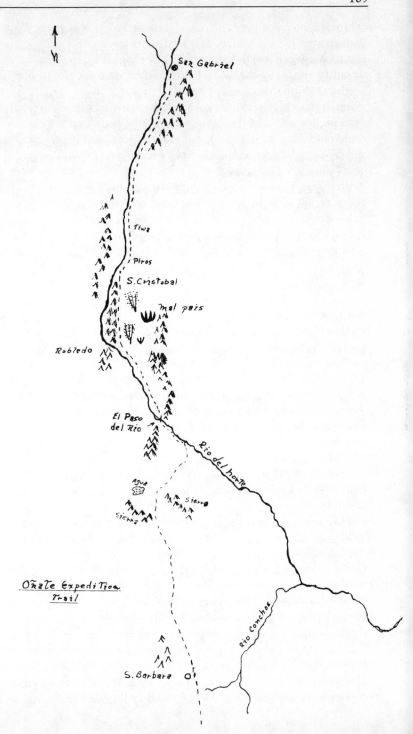

Oñate Expedition Trail

day and we were almost suffocated by thick clouds of red dust. Sand filled our nostrils and our lips cracked in the dry wind.

On the third day out, Robledo took a turn for the worse and we gathered around the carreta where he lay. The entire forced stopped.

"Ay, this wind is like a vision of hell," he said weakly as we gathered in the lee of the wagon. The wind howled so that his voice was barely audible above it.

"You must be strong, Robledo," I shouted, hoping to encourage the old man out of his melancholy state. "We have much yet to do and learn. Your experience is much needed."

"Ay, Don Gaspar," he rasped. "I fear fate has other things in store for me. I do not want to die. I do not want to leave you."

Robledo was one of the oldest men on the expedition. Yet he undertook challenges that would have daunted younger men. He never hesistated when called upon to serve and always encouraged those who were ready to give up.

His body was racked with an illness that none could discern. The wounds he had suffered in the fall were grievous but did not account for the pain he exhibited. Inez administered the best of medicaments yet Robledo sank quickly, his pallor turning yellow, then a deathly gray. Finally, his frail body rattled and trembled.

During a particularly violent part of the windstorm which blotted out the sun. Robledo succumbed and, poor soul, we carried his dried, frail body through that ghastly wilderness without friend or relative to pray over his remains. Fray Cristobal said mass but we decided to postpone burial until his family could be contacted. Later, we returned his remains and he was laid to rest at the foot of a great mountain by the river. We named the mountain in his honor.

The loss of Robledo was serious. He was a stabilizing influence over the dissenters and had he lived, perhaps things would have turned out differently.

I became concerned about our survival. I visited Inez in the lead wagon and found that she was still vigorous and but little diminished by thirst. She was gladdened by my visit. I then read the Oroz document to her.

"Why did you wait to tell me?"

"I was unsure."

"It means very much. Didn't you know?"

"What exactly? I am confused by the robe, the wish . . ."

She smiled and I could see that there was much more to these pages than I realized.

"I know now how much Father Oroz thought of you to trust you with this robe." She held it, rolled, in front of her as if it were a sacred object. "You see, he believed this robe is blessed with a miracle. Anyone wearing it will know the truth and be protected. But not everyone can wear it. Only special people. People who are in grace and understand." She seemed overcome.

"Where did it come from?" What am I to do with it?" I did not much believe in miracles.

"Father Oroz was given the robe by a man named Gregorio Lopez. This man was as close to Our Lord as anyone could be. He was almost a saint. Father Oroz said that many believed he was the dead son of King Philip, Don Carlos. This man had the powers to cure the sick and heal the wounded. He wandered among the Chichimecas wearing this robe and never came to any harm." She stopped for a moment.

"Later, whenever there was trouble among converted tribes, Father Oroz would wear this robe and walk among the angry warriors. This was the way he learned the source of their troubles and brought peace without ever being harmed."

I looked at the robe and touched it. "Why would Father Oroz want me to risk my life to complete his book? I don't understand that."

"I will tell you. Don Juan has many times stated his intention to punish the heathen responsible for the Holy Fathers' death. It is a sacred mission in his eyes. Father Oroz feared this would soon amount to a general massacre of my people. Now you know why I am so concerned. A cough interrupted her speech. I offered water but she waved me aside.

"We must go to the first village before Don Juan. It is my duty to Father Oroz. He would want us to enter each village first and protect the innocent."

I thought this request amounted to treason. Don Juan would have us executed if he found us disobeying his orders. Before I made my decision I told Inez that I would talk with Father Martinez. His opinion was important.

That night I told him that it was Father's Oroz's belief that I would be of great importance in protecting the heathen from injustice. He believed I should help prevent bloodshed in the name of God.

I finally agreed to Father Oroz's strange request because I really believed that I could spare the innocent. But, alas it was mostly my desire for adventure. To be first into those strange places, I put my faith in the protection of a rotting robe while resting under the blade of Don Juan's wrathful sword. With the help of Inez and Father Martinez, a plan was laid to secretly enter the first village.

BOOK VI

"*Let not mercy and truth forsake thee:*
bound them about thy neck; write them
upon the table of thine heart."

(*Proverbs 3:3*)

1

For reasons I cannot explain, I agreed to Inez's request to accompany me. While great danger stalked us, both from the heathen and Don Juan, I felt Father Oroz had the powers he claimed.

Making hasty preparations in the dead of night, we stole up to a hill overlooking the first pueblo, spiriting our horses out of the Spanish camp undetected.

We approached the village entrance unaware of any sentinel. Walls loomed up into the moonlit sky. I wore only the robe and my hair had been made into a wild style using tallow. Inez blackened my face and hands with charcoal until I was almost afraid of my own reflection. I began quite unexpectedly, to fancy myself a madman bent on some mysterious mission.

As we entered the pueblo yapping dogs clamored at our intrusion. Pale firelight flickered through openings in the walls on upper levels and the air was thick with pleasant but unfamiliar odors. Inez strode boldly towards an opening in the wall and called out in a strange tongue.

We were soon surrounded by a crowd of torch-bearing Indians. They were unpainted but looked fierce enough in the firelight. After some talk, they led us to a building in one corner of a rounded plaza at the end of a crooked street. There in the dark, I felt as if I had entered a village in

Altamira. The crowd had grown and we were ushered off the street into a small room. Water and bread were laid before us while several of the savages pointed at me from a distance through a constant flow of babble. They were greatly agitated.

I glanced around the strange room for an escape route if needed. This was a clean structure with many drying condiments suspended from ceiling beams. There were numbers of hideous beings painted on the white walls which seemed alive in the vibrating torch light. The skin at the back of my neck trembled at this sight as I recalled the savage visage of the Chichimecas. I asked Inez what they were.

"Gods,' she replied. "Gods of our people. But, I am afraid we are in a bad way. I cannot speak well with these people. They are from a different place than my own. They are suspicious. I think they called a cacique."

The murmuring ceased and a small old man entered the room in ceremonious fashion. Over his shoulders he wore a great fur robe the likes of which I had not seen before. Underneath he wore a shirt which appeared to be made of an excellent cloth and pantaloons which reached his knees. On his feet were soft leather boots reaching to his knees. Behind him, women carried earthen jars which they shook constantly. He stood before us and said nothing but look straight at the wall behind us. Suddenly the women tossed the contents of the jars into the air and the room filled with yellow powder which covered all of us.

"He is purifying us," she said. "Do not move."

The men shuffled and sang in a strange fashion, almost a lamentation and at times, such sweet melody as may be heard in a choral jubilate. Then, as abruptly as he had entered, he left the room with the others following. For the moment we were left alone.

Soon a man appeared and spoke with Inez. She smiled and I learned he was familiar with her tongue. Later she told me that the conversation had gone well.

"We are messengers," she had told him, "sent to help and protect you. To the south is a great force of Castillos. This man of the robe seeks the bones of three Religious who were here many ages ago. If he finds them he will be able to keep the Castillos from being angry."

The man had replied that he knew nothing of the three Religious. He asked about the Castillos and if they were the same as those who had come before, seeking the three Religious.

"No," she said. "these are different. They have come for another purpose but are ready to punish those who may have harmed the three Religious."

The man left the room, stealing a fearful glance at me. We were free to move about but we did not move from where we sat. Inez said the man had been lying about the three Religious. She could tell by his voice.

He returned shortly and said that his people had done nothing and would receive the Castillos in peace. However, the Castillos should not be angry because it would be very bad for everyone. He asked that the demon man (me) use his powers to keep the Castillos from harming them.

Inez told me to act angry

I was surprise at her request and found I could not stoop to this indignity. The best I could do was yell at the savage in full voice.

The man's eyes widened and the strange robe and my odd appearance made me seem possessed. Presently, the cacique reappeared in the room and when he saw my seething anger, he quickly withdrew with the others. Later the cacique and several men lead us to another, larger room. When the light flickered on the walls I could see, much to my astonishment, a large painting depicting the vicious death of the Religious. Several savages were portrayed stoning and clubbing the priests to death.

We were asked to sit and a small fire was lit. The old man who had entered first told the story to the man who translated to Inez. The story was told like a song and I was intrigued by the gestures and music. Inez translated.

"As I told you, the three Religious were at my village and were accused of witchcraft. You see, amongst these people anyone who claims to communicate with spirits is either a holy man or a witch. There are only certain ways in which holy men communicate with spirits. But, Father Ruiz, like a witch, would talk with spirits in heaven at night. The other two priests were assistants. Many people died at my village of unknown illness during this time. It was such that cacique decided they must be witches and would be driven out. They refused to leave. He had them killed. This painting celebrates their passing."

I felt this was the truth.

We told the men to cover the paintings and that we would talk to the Castillos about what had happened. Then, with much caution, we eased back to the encampment undetected. I had been transformed by this adventured and the marvelous civilization around me and much relieved that on this first attempt I could help fulfill Father Oroz's wish without losing my head.

2

Morning broke over the seared plain with a welcome coolness and we noticed a large mountain to the northwest covered with snow. It was the first time we had seen snow since leaving Mexico and as the rising sun spilled over the peak, it shimmered like a jewel. Soon the cool blue color changed to pinkish hues and finally the snow-capped peak glistened white against the sky. Our spirits lifted to new heights and expectations.

We followed the same trail as the night before, the brutal terrain now giving way to a more temperate region with occasional sweet grasses and small lakes providing succor for exhausted animals and men. After some time we were again within sight of the river bed and the first pueblo. It was next to a large black mesa. Adobe buildings were silhouetted against the mountain wilderness. Never have I witnessed such a scene. The houses were terraced to three stories and were sturdy and straight-walled. The buildings rose one on top of the other until an irregular pyramid emerged, reflecting the massive strength of the mountain framework behind. We had come five hundred or more leagues since leaving Mexico and this sign of civilization thrilled us. The savage cultures of the wild lands we had passed were primitive compared to these civilizations before us.

We stopped a league west of the pueblo on a small hill. From here most of it could be seen above the river bank and we stared in wonderment at this apparition in the desert. Several men standing on the elevated terrace of the houses looked back at us. Don Juan appointed Juan de Zaldivar, Francisco Vasquez, Cristóbal Lopez, Juan de Olague, Munuera and myself to approach the village.

"I want no bloodshed but be prepared. At the first sign of trouble we will follow. Otherwise we wait for your signal."

"I demand to be the head of this party." The voice came from Fray Cristóbal.

"Ah yes, my dear Father, I should have known. My only interest was in the welfare of you and your brethren. But please, join them if you wish." The governor's tone reflected displeasure at this interference.

But suddenly before we could proceed, an unexpected thunderstorm rolled over the black mesa and enveloped us in a wild cloud filled with lightning. The animals bolted and we crouched on the windswept hill in fear for our lives. Father Cristóbal called out to the Lord for forgiveness and as quickly as the storm had appeared, it dissipated. We all gave thanks and rounded up the frightened animals except for Zapata's horse which had fallen off a cliff and had to be killed. In honor of this great miracle we named the nearby mountain range Fray Cristóbal.

We descended following a well-used track which led through a shallow arroyo and approached the first house in the pueblo. We were dressed in full armor and long swords and I think we frightened the savages mightily, for when we reached the town we saw no one. In silence, we walked the horses carefully down a crude street which I could now see contained large boulders and even small trees. This disorder in the street did not match the orderly architecture of the buildings. Later, I realized clear and straight streets were not needed since these people had neither horse nor any other conveyance. The road served only as a footpath and workplace.

Suddenly, several savages appeared and ran up to Father Cristóbal who was leading us on foot. We prepared for the worst and started to draw swords, but the Indians fell on their knees and kissed the cross carried by the priest. I could see one of them was the old cacique we had seen the night before.

Juan de Zaldivar approached the old men, staying on his horse. They were frightened by the animal. He pointed to the remainder of our group now visible on the horizon and then, dismounting, attempted to embrace the old man who shrank back from the armored figure. Zaldivar held out his hand in a sign of friendship and the old man blew on his hands and cautiously touched Zaldivar's arm. This peculiar greeting went on for some time, each gesture significant of goodwill. Finally Zaldivar could no longer contain himself and asked Fray Cristóbal to speak to the Indians in whatever tongue possible. He had been instructed to ask permission for the remainder of the group to enter.

The friar rattled out a great number of sounds of which I understood nothing although I'd swear they were not Indian but really that cursed tongue of the Basque.

The old Indian replied, and for some time this strange dialogue with much hand waving went on. Finally, the priest turned to Zaldivar and said, "I'm sorry, but I can't tell you much."

"What can you tell me?" Zaldivar demanded.

"Well, it seems this old Indian doesn't understand a word I'm saying."

"Well, did you understand him?"

"Not a word."

Zaldivar cursed but I couldn't help but laugh at the priest's pretention.

The cacique finally tugged at Zaldivar's arm and led us to a small cache of maize, dried vegetables, smoked hares, and several tethered turkeys. He indicated that they were for us. He then led us to a room containing earthen jars painted in a most excellent manner and filled with water. The jars were held with a woven grass mat with a handle.

We were delighted and called out for Don Juan to move up to the city.

"Where are the people?" Don Juan thundered when he arrived.

"We don't know," replied the priest. "We can't seem to understand this fellow," he pointed towards the cacique.

"Doña Inez, speak to this man," Don Juan said. "Ask him where his people are."

From behind the front riders, Inez appeared unmounted. She walked up to the old cacique and questioning him in that strange tongue which sounds so dull to my ears. He couldn't understand her, but somehow there was a telepathic system of understanding.

Inez told Don Juan that she understood little, but she believed the people had left the village because they were afraid.

"Of course," he replied. "But how did they know we would be here today? Do you think they have spies?" he asked, looking in my direction.

"In this country, our approach is well announced by the clouds of dust that follow us everywhere," I said. This was always a problem but very often forgotten.

Don Juan grunted approval of my observation and looked at the provisions offered by the old man. He told the priest to set up a cross in the main plaza and to instruct the Indians not to remove it. Then Don Juan ordered the cacique to open the houses so they might be inspected. He ordered the troop to seize whatever was of value in each home since the people had chosen to abandon their goods. He asked Inez to explain this to the cacique.

We searched the houses but found little other than works of art, some painted demons, and other heathen items. I investigated the room where we had been the night before and found the incriminating painting covered by a new layer of stucco. The sergeant with me failed to notice the ruse and I, for some reason, felt relieved. Here I was, plotting with the savages.

During this search I noticed how orderly the village was laid out. The terraced houses seemed to work towards a pyramidal structure overlooking the river and centered at the main plaza. Works of art and excellent pottery were everywhere.

When I stepped back out into the main plaza, I reflected on this curious state of affairs. Here before me stood an old savage who, except for his excellent clothes and jewelry, could be easily mistaken for one of the uncivilized people we had encountered since leaving Zacatecas. He was dark, of low stature and had a rugged and crevassed face.

Yet this man was the leader of a race that could erect graceful buildings of the most crude materials; harvest excellent crops in an inhospitable climate; raise and domesticate wild animals; create fine art, jewelry and excellent cloth; and place all this within the confines of a pleasant town.

I knew that Father Oroz would have been delighted with these people. They seemed hardy and vigorous and at the same time had an eye for design and art and they carried out this enterprise without the aid of wheel or iron. No horse was to be seen in their midst. Yes, I was greatly taken by all they had wrought.

After some further attempt at conversation with the cacique, Don Juan ordered us to retreat from the village. He thanked the old Indian and had Father Cristóbal bless him. He made it known that we would be back.

3

We proceeded up the river valley, sending as much of the supplies as we could spare back to the wagon train. Having entered and "conquered" the first village, we headed to the next as seen on the crude map we had fashioned.

The country now became more temperate and the cruel valley we had passed seemed to be at an end. The river banks were covered with large trees; a veritable forest for leagues on either side. It was less than a day's march to the next village.

"Don Juan has posted double sentries," I told Inez. "It will not be possible to visit this village during the night as before without being seen."

"I think the cacique has sent a messenger to the surrounding towns," she told me. "They may well be warned. But now I must tell you about my promise and what Father Oroz meant about my wish. You see, I had made a promise not to marry any man until I should be free to return to my people and the man I married had the approval of Father Oroz. My wish was that you would be that man."

I was stunned and embraced her with great joy.

"We should make arrangements with Father Martinez for a wedding as soon as we get back," I said.

"We can be married by Father Cristóbal. Why wait until we return? Something could happen to . . ," she didn't finish.

I paced the ground around our campfire. I was worried about Don Juan.

"You are wrong. He would be delighted. You see, he wants you to marry me. That is why he had me in the room that first night you came to Zacatecas."

I told her what he had told me about her being his mistress.

"Ah, he would have liked that to be so and yes, he wanted me very much. But . . . remember his mother? She refused any relationship with me because I came from New Mexico. Don Juan was always under the influence of his mother. Because of her, he was trying to encourage our meeting and yet couldn't give in that easily. Anyway, he has lost interest in me except as an interpreter. He will not be angry."

The next morning I asked for an audience with Don Juan.

"We would like to be married as soon as Father Cristóbal can perform the ceremony."

"Splendid. Why did it take so long? You had a difficult time I would say," Don Juan smiled, a rare occasion.

I was happy. To have captured this savage beauty was more than I could imagine and my blood coursed through my veins like fire. Me. The black dwarf.

Don Juan set the ceremony for three days hence, and we set out on the march again.

This village contained many people. Apparently word had spread and now the people were hesitant to leave their towns. This pueblo was not so splendid as the first but Don Juan demanded tribute of food and quarters.

The reluctant inhabitants provided us with rooms and a small cache of maize and turkeys. They showed great reverence for the crucifix, which they again kissed.

We were given quarters off the main plaza and the walls were also painted with fierce demon gods. These gods represented many forms of heathen life.

We spent the day in the village and observed again the custom of these people to parade their damsels naked in public view. They are allowed to lay with any man, but become chaste and of one man after they have married.

The savages brought us many gifts but Inez told me that it was not out of friendship but out of fear. They had fine blankets made of turkey feathers which they seemed especially pleased to show.

While examining one of the rooms we were shocked to see the same painting of the murder of the friars. The Indians had hastily whitewashed the wall over the painting but as the whitewash dried, it became transparent to the colors.

Don Juan also saw this painting and I feared for the pueblo. Yet, after a short period of silent anger he showed rare judgement and asked us to act as if the paintings had not been seen. He had decided, however to quit this village as the Indians could easily overpower us as we slept. We kept vigil through the night and before the light of dawn we stole into the blackness of the surrounding wilderness.

In this same way we visited several of the pueblos of the southern regions while continuing our march to the north. We discovered several Mexican Indians who had remained when Castaño de Sosa returned to New Spain. These fellows reluctantly became our interpreters since Inez was not inclined to perform this task.

As we progressed, a fresh countryside sprang forth from the desert blooming in a bounteous, well-tree'd, elevated plain, surrounded by mighty snow-covered peaks. Sweet grass and water were abundant and even our weakest horses improved greatly.

Finally we arrived at a large, handsome village overlooking the great river. Don Juan calculated that the river would supply quantities of fish and game as well as life giving water and that the village would house all the colonists on the wagon train following us from the south. He decided to establish our first colony even though many protested, especially Captain Aguilar, who considered the site too primitive. He would have continued the search to the north. We named the place "San Juan de Los Caballeros" in honor of those who had first raised the cross in these heathen regions.

Most of the inhabitants of this pueblo had fled into the hinterlands so Don Juan felt no reluctance to occupy their homes. We cleared the walls of demon figures and added a few touches of Iberian culture such as doors and windows but most of the house were useable as the natives had left them. Father Cristóbal immediately set to the task of finding a suitable place for the church.

4

For many reasons my marriage was delayed and then, just as we had settled on a date, an attempted desertion took place. The settlement was set in an uproar. It was again the troublesome Captain Aguilar and Alonzo de Sosa Peñalosa who, seeing that these regions offered little in the way of civilized amenities and were bare of any sign of silver, decided that their families would return to Mexico. When Don Juan discovered this plot, he was furious and called for the execution of the would-be deserters. But because of Aguilar's high rank and standing, Don Juan finally relented and accepted the pleas for mercy. The captain appeared stunned by this turn of events and a somewhat shaky pledge of allegiance was given.

The soldiers and priests then decided to hold a thanksgiving ceremony to celebrate the reconciliation and several cattle were slaughtered and roasted. The savages from all the pueblos nearby were invited to join the festivities and were astonished by the arms and instruments of iron we had brought and fascinated by the cattle, horses, mules and burros. Don Juan would not let them handle our armaments except for the large cannon but they were free to examine everything else.

By God's good will, I was secretly united in marriage with Inez on the first day of the celebration in mid-summer of 1598. The ceremony was performed by Father Cristóbal and attended by Juan Rodriguez with whom I had become fast friends and Captain Geronimo Marquez another gentleman in whom I had great faith. We completed the ceremony trusting in God from whom all things must come. It was Inez's wish to keep the marriage secret.

That evening, around a great fire which served the celebrants, I felt calm and happy indeed.

"Are we near your home?" I asked my new wife.

"Yes, it is, as I recall, about a day's ride." She looked especially beautiful on this most magic of days.

"When do you think to return to see your family?"

She lowered her eyes and remained silent for some time. "I will not return," she finally said. "When I decided to marry you, I had to break with my people."

At that moment several savages approached us, wanting to speak. They asked if they could sit with us and we agreed. Apparently, Inez understood their language. One of the savages spoke for the others.

"I am Gicombo," he said. "This is Qualco and Buzcico." he pointed to the others,

"We are from Ako," he pointed his arm to the west. "There, in the setting sun. We are happy to meet you. We are very strong, not like these fleas amongst whom you have settled. When your leader is ready, we will be pleased to have him visit us."

I sensed an arrogance which I had not seen in these people before. Before he left he made it known that his pueblo would never submit to such occupation as we had brought upon this place. But, after some conversation with Inez, he left friendly enough and seemed to be fascinated by us.

I asked her what they intended.

"They asked how it came that I was with the Castillos. I told them about my capture and removal to Mexico. They remembered that time. As you heard, my name is Luzcoija."

I had heard them say that name excitedly many times and wondered about it.

"Are you related to this tribe?"

"We are of the same people. I have many relatives who live in Ako. I spent some time there. It is a city favored by the gods."

"Luzcoija. Luzcoija," I said several times.

"Please do not call me that name. To you I shall always be Inez. I am not Luzcoija." She seemed tired from talking with the savages. The night darkened and the fires grew in intensity. Rodriguez asked me about the savages.

"Don Juan said that they are spying on us. What do you think?"

"If the situation were reversed, wouldn't you like to know what invaders in your land are like? I feign to call it spying to know what's going on about you. But I think we must be careful. Those savages seem very proud and assured that they can defend themselves."

He grunted and said if that were the case we best find out what their defenses were like. I agreed. I looked into the glowing embers and thought of the haughty Gicombo. But there was something about him that I admired. Even in his fierce defiance there was a sadness that made my blood cold.

We were all living on edge, sleeping little and greatly awed by our position. While we said little, I think we were sorely disappointed by our circumstances which now seemed to depend on the forced hospitality of the surrounding savages. We had not expected this when we set out on the adventure but now it was real. We were cut off from any source of supply from our fellow countrymen and were but a handful surrounded by a sea of savages. Our only hope for survival was a determined face in confronting these heathen, and in that we were most fortunate in having a fearless leader such as Don Juan. His love for God and the king was unshakeable and he faced all odds certain of the outcome. Without such men these missions would be impossible. The simple strength of the penitent is called for here.

I don't know what we expected, but it was more than what we had found. Don Juan was following the tactics of earlier explorers who had occupied the Indian towns they conquered and then built on them. What we lacked was a principle, a true battle. It is in the cleansing blood of battle that the thing becomes a test of strength and courage. This conquest was robbed of glory when the heathen ran into the hills and left pieces of their lives behind to remind us of our occupation, our theft. Such people cannot be converted nor defeated and this causes us to live in constant fear of the unknown. Better the bloody battle right off to decide the issue than this. I think this was why we felt as we did and an uneasiness developed in the camp even as the festivities progressed.

Then, like the sting of the dreaded scorpion, the poison spread and we now found that four soldiers had deserted. It was another shock and Don Juan, in a public announcement, ordered me to lead a squad to capture and execute the deserters on the spot. I was to bring back their heads to put on display.

Don Juan said that if this act went unpunished, the venom of desertion would spread further through the expedition and that all would be lost before the start.

Yes, but what agony greets such a venture. After six months of unending hardship without the trappings of civilization with which we were all accustomed, we looked for an end to the savagery around us. We yearned for the music and decorated parlors, the plays and literature, news of the world, the trappings of full life. It would take time to replace this desolate waste with a new civilization. But the men could not wait. Disappointment with our plight was more than they could bear and lacking confidence in the future, they deigned to put much time and space between themselves and New Mexico. It was weakness we could not tolerate.

Marquez and Ribera joined me in the pursuit. I left Inez in the hands of Rodriguez as we picked up the trail. The deserters were headed south by east, avoiding the approaching wagon train command by Ensign Peñalosa.

We tracked them for several days and when we reached the first stretches of the vast desert waste we could see the great dust storm far to the south raised by the wagon train.

Of the four deserters, two of them, Juan Moreno and Matios Rodriguez, had family on the expedition. I felt certain that although their tracks indicated they had passed far to the east, they would have contacted the wagon train somehow. With this in mind I sent Ribera and Marquez westward to intercept the train and gather whatever news they could. I would follow the deserters. We would join at the point where the river bed became accessible.

Again the real enemy was the endless heat. I followed the trail slowly; haste would lead to certain death. As the days passed, the great clouds of dust passed to the north and I felt comfort knowing that the train was nearing its final destination. I made my way through that infernal region again without a sign of the deserters. Their trail became muddled and confused at certain places.

When I reached the rendezvous, Marquez and Ribera were camped and waiting for my arrival.

"We spoke with Ensign Peñalosa," Marques said, "and it was as you thought. Two wagons and the families of Moreno and Rodriguez are missing from their train. They are fleeing towards Santa Barbara."

We immediately headed down the green river valley, across the river and back into the northern reaches of Nueva Vizcaya. Within days their dust trail was in sight and soon, with little effort, they were our captives.

I read the sentence of doom proclaimed by Don Juan. They begged for mercy and I knew if I listened I would not be able to carry out my orders. Begging God's forgiveness, I hastily cut the throats of Manual Rodriguez and Juan Gonzalez begging them to die like men. But they were cowards until the end and their pleas continued to hiss and bubble from the slits in their throats.

Before Marquez could execute the others, the wives put up such a wail of woe that we were forced to relent. I let them go and offer no apolgy for so doing.

When Rodriguez and Gonsales were dead I cut off their left hands and packed them in a bag of salt. Since we were close to Santa Barbara, we decided to file a report of this incident before the surviving deserters would tell their lies.

What I did seems cruel but it was necessary to preserve life and limb on the expedition. If these deserters had gone unpunished there would be no province of New Mexico for His Majesty to administer. I was under direct orders from the governor and would have been derelict in my duty to have done otherwise. The deserters did not beg to confess their sins before dying. They begged only for their miserable lives which I had no power to give.

When we returned to San Juan, Ensign Peñalosa had arrived with the colonists. The first white settlement in those regions was about to begin. We did not then know of the great ordeal that still lay before us.

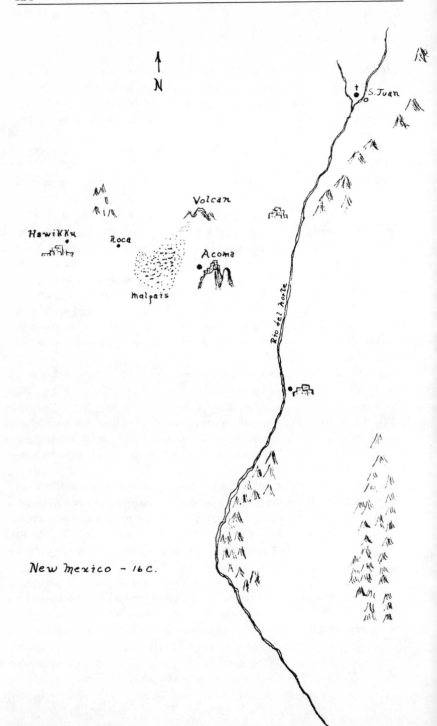

New Mexico - 16 C.

BOOK VII

*"And Moses sent them to spy out the land of
Canaan, and said unto them, get you up this
way . . . and go up into the mountain and see
the land, what it is; and the people that
dwelleth therein . . ."*

(Numbers 13:17)

1

San Juan was not so well-sited as we had thought and the governor
decided to settle some of the company in another pueblo across the river.
This one was larger and except for a few sturdy savages had remained
empty since our arrival. We named the pueblo San Gabriel in honor of the
day we moved and it was here that we began to build the colony.

The Lord willing, we placed much faith in finding silver in the ground as
Don Juan's father had found in Zacatecas and his father before him in
Asturias. Mining was the very life of these Basques and that is why we
hauled all the equipage those many leagues. The governor sent out those
who were expert in these affairs to determine location from the Indians.
This was dangerous, as splitting the company placed us in peril of attack.
But the governor knew our venture was doomed unless we found some
compelling reason for colonization. Few of us were fit for farming or other
coarse endeavors.

But these few set immediately to exploring the grassy plains for forage
and places for tillage and had their markings down before the trees turned
orange and gold in the waning year. It was too late to sow a crop in spite of
the promise of Juan de Pedraza to have us filled with chick-peas by
Yuletide.

Also Martín and Juan Ximenez started sheep and cattle rancherias on the
great plains that abounded in grass and the few remaining cattle prospered.
If the Lord provided and we could survive the perils of the coming winter,
the venture could succeed. We remained dependent on the savages for
foodstuffs since it would have been folly to slaughter the

decimated herd as was being demanded by certain captains.

As providor-general, it was my duty to inspect the colony, control the store of provisions and see that all effort was made to maintain the enterprise. Alonzo Martiń, dressed in buckskins and a huge sombrero, guided me over the regions he hoped to have granted to him. We rode many leagues to the north, across a sunny open flatland, completely denuded of tree or bush, rimmed with majestic mountains. We halted on a ridge and before us spread a view of eternity. At one point the path led to the edge of a narrow, precipitous gorge. Directly below, at a frightening depth, the current of the great river plunged and roared around the canyon walls. Martiń led me down a path which raised the hackles on my neck. I was grateful for my sure-footed mount. We crossed the river at a wide. shallow place and climbed out of the canyon on the opposite side. Again, vast, open land spread before us. It was here that Martiń had his cattle grazing, still more than a hundred strong, but weak and bone-thin from the long journey. The vaqueros were camped on the plain, watchful for wolves and bears. These wild beasts had already done much harm to the heard and Martiń said that as the herd prospered, he would graze them further out away from the mountain forests and the fierce beasts. He had not had trouble with Indians.

I spoke with the vaqueros and found that they were pleased with the country. It was as fine a place for cattle as they had seen. The grass was endless, stretching as far as the eye could see, and there were cold springs of the best water. Juan Torres de Saavedra, a gaunt-faced Tabasco Indian was supposed to be one of the best vaqueros in the colony. He smiled a loose-lipped, big-toothed grin when I told him he looked as poorly as the rangey cattle he herded.

"Yes," he said, "I have lived with the cattle so long that I must be careful around Senor Martiń. He might slaughter me some day by mistake." He howled gleefully but then, in a more serious tone said that he was concerned.

"I have seen morning mists burn off with the rising sun. Lately the sun is losing this battle with the mist. Last week, the mist was frozen and it was noon before the grass dried. Everyday it takes longer. People say that winter will be bad for the cattle. What think you?"

I looked at the high sierras and thought that I too had seen the snow Line rapidly descending.

"The Lord will provide, Juan Torres," I said. "And if not, we can always eat you." We left the swarthy vaqueros in high spirits.

After that, I met with Juan Ximenez, a husky Basque. He too had placed his marks on a vast region where his sheep would prosper.

"But the savage beasts kill many of my animals," he told me. "I wish I had the great wolf-dogs from my homeland. Such perils would then be short-lived. But such dogs are not obtainable and I have only my hunting dogs. They fare poorly here."

"I have heard that the Indian rely on their dogs," I said. "they are large and even pull a cart. Maybe they could be trained."

He promised to pursue this possiblility. "I have many local Indian herders but they do little to discourage the wolves," he said.

I asked if the Indians were afraid of the wolves. "Not at all" he replied. "But they will not kill them for fear of angering the wolf-spirit. They say only certain people can kill a wolf. It has great significance for them."

As I left he promised we would have good meat and plenty of wool soon. "With God's help, I will solve this wolf problem," he said. "It is the only thing between us and prosperity."

Juan Perez established a busy blacksmith shop at San Gabriel. He soon became our doctor as well as blacksmith as many of his remedies seemed to work as well on humans as on animals. We lacked a real doctor, but Juan Perez was skilled in bleeding and extractions and soon had a thriving business. Once, I noticed a line of Indians outside his shop. I found him busy at pulling a tooth from an old white-haired Indian.

"Come here," he said, while he struggled to get a grip on the tooth. "Look at this old fellow's mouth." I peered into the cavern. The old Indian didn't move but followed me with glazed eyes. He was resting against a tree and held his head back. Perez had his giant hand jammed into the open jaws, working a tool that was intended for removing nails from horseshoes. Soon Perez removed his hand. "There it is," he said. "Almost rotted off. This tool keeps slipping off that stump. I could use some proper tools I tell you." The old man did not move.

"These people have the same infernal miseries as we," he continued. "They have wonderful herbal cures but know little of the art of extraction." He drew some dried plants from a shelf. "These plants are new to us. They make a powerful remedy for pain. I covered that old man's jaw with it. Otherwise, he would have left long ago howling with pain." He showed me a paste made from the dried plants.

I noticed that Perez had a large store of grain and dried meats. He said the Indians had given it to him for services even though he had never asked for anything.

"They come back the next day or maybe weeks later and leave this grain and meat. They are good people and very healthy. They do have these problems, though," and he pointed to the old man's mouth.

Perez asked me to help and I held the grizzled jaws apart. He succeeded in loosening the tooth with an awl and got a grip on the stump with the nail puller and with much force pulled the rotted tooth from its socket. A gush of pus and blood flowed from the wound and I marveled at how adept Perez was. Soon the old man's glassy stare disappeared and his ashen face flushed with life. Throughout the ordeal he had not uttered a sound.

I checked our stores, knowing that dental tools had been included in the inventory. I found that many items had disappeared. Our delay in Casco had cost us more than time. Probing deeper I found that *fanegas* of grain and cattle counts had also been tampered with. Many barrels of oil and wine were missing. The official inventory maintained by my clerks agreed with the amounts on hand so I knew something foul was afoot. As providor-general I was responsible for this thievery. After completing my inspection of the settlement, I would investigate this matter further.

I visited Juan Perez and found him busy making a table from logs he had cut when we first arrived. The wood was seasoned and he said the nearby forest were filled with fine wood of every variety. It would be no time at all before he could start hauling in construction timber. He said that he would prefer a well-built house constructed as was done in his father's homeland in Galicia.

"Wood and stone," he said, "build the finest house. You Castillians can have all this adobe." He laughed as he pointed towards the settlement buildings.

I saw several Indians working in his shop.

"They want to learn," he said replying to my question about their presence. "When they first observed my great saw in action they were struck dumb as I cut through a log. Now they want to learn about tools and help me whenever they can."

"Do you pay them?" I asked.

"No. I give them boards. They will not work on a steady basis. I never know when they will be here. They are as free as the wind."

Perez was a big man with sad eyes. His sadness was said to spring from the soul of his wild daughter, a comely wench who made it her business to solicit all the men in the colony. His wife had died years before in Guadalajara and his second wife had taken a strong dislike to this girl. He hoped that the rigors and perils of this expedition would settle her down and bring marriage, but as time progressed, this became more unlikely. She spent most of her time with the few camp-followers and bawdies that had taken up residence down by the river. When all they found was hard work and little pay, these women wanted to return to New Spain. Helena Perez led this group and she would soon cause us all a great deal of trouble.

The weaver, Alonzo Martinez, had set up looms to make rugs and blankets and, as a novelty, began adding designs found on the Indian jugs. He too had local Indians in his employment.

"They are natural weavers," he told me as I inspected the fine blankets. "They make a fair cloth and look at this blanket of turkey feathers!" He displayed an example of feather-weaving, a gift.

"They have crude looms but their work is good. Now they want to learn to use this Spanish loom. They can do much more with this. The men have an excellent eye for this work and seem to admire weaving."

"How many blankets can you weave?" I asked him as I was concerned about the coming winter.

"Until we harvest wool, I can make only a few," he replied. "I have looms and willing hands but we are short of materials, all materials. I sold my wool to survive in Casco.

Juan Griego, the Greek, became butcher and greengrocer for whatever goods he could obtain. Although we provisioned mostly from central stores, the Greek carried on a thriving trade with the Indians through shrewd and, I suspected, sometimes crooked bargaining. I noticed he had a large store of smoked hares, badger and venison.

"What did you trade for that meat?" I inquired.

"Ah, some fine Holland cloth. The men are exceedingly fond of Holland cloth and make sashes of it."

We had an abundance of Holland cloth and little use of it in this wilderness. But the Indians maintained small provisions and I was surprised at their improvident behavior.

Griego sold the meat to the colonists, sometimes for gold or silver, but mostly for traded goods. Gold or silver was of little use in the colony at that time and for some time to come. It was the will of Providence that so many were seeking the very thing that had little or no use in our enterprise.

Other small businesses and shops were established in San Gabriel and San Juan, including a bakery that produced an excellent wheat flour bread from what little flour remained. We would soon have a thriving community.

2

When I completed the inspection, I started my investigation into the shortage of goods. Night after night I poured over the documents. Where were the lists with my signature, Don Juan's and that of the inspector? Everything was in order and all with exact tally counts. These documents must have been tampered with since they were completed when we resumed the expedition after our long delay. It would not have been possible to steal goods after we resumed the march.

I told Don Juan and Father Martinez of the missing inventory and promised to discover the cause. The goods must have been stolen during our delay in Casco, they agreed. I would have to determine how.

I interviewed the priests and captains since they had access to our storerooms and only had to list items they removed. I had clerks controlling the lists but often they had been intimidated by these captains who claimed the goods were theirs to start with. I employed Father Lugo, who was schooled in the ways of the Holy Office to help.

Interviews were conducted with little trouble. However, Captain Aguilar was, as usual, furious.

"What matter is it of yours?" he retorted when questioned. "You may be the providor-general but most of those goods in the warehouse were contributed by me and I owe it to no one to take my own goods."

"If you removed goods without recording it, we invite you to inform Don Juan. He would be most interested." Father Lugo was direct.

"Damn it, I took no goods, Why should I? I had wagons full of provisions. I'm only saying that I had every right to take them if I wished."

"Not without recording such on the tally sheets," I said. "Don Juan's orders, punishable by death."

The captain cringed and I saw a momentary wild expression in his eye.

"I took nothing," he insisted. "Further, you have no proof. Your lists show a full inventory when we left."

We finished interviewing every captain and I recorded the results. In addition to Aguilar, there were two others who had been insulted by the interrogation.

We interviewed the priests. Father Lugo was stunned when we found evidence of pilfering in almost ever case. The priests were unable to lie and we easily detected their activities. They protested that it was their right to some of these goods as Don Juan was obliged to support them. Seeing no connection between the pilfering (mostly wine and oil) and the shortage of goods, we stopped investigating at this point. Father Lugo said he would talk with the commissary-general about this behavior.

Lastly, we interviewed the clerks in charge of the lists and the servants sent to fetch the goods.

"Do you know anything about the missing goods?" I asked Manuel de Salas, a clerk.

"No sir," he gargled, as the priest looked deep into his eyes. He was very nervous and almost unable to speak. We found the same reaction in another clerk. They both must know something. Father Lugo agreed so we decided to force the truth from them.

We questioned them a second time in the manner of the Holy Office. Fray Lugo conducted the interrogation in a darkened room of the pueblo.

"The goods were stolen. We know you had something to do with it. You were in charge of the stores. God sees all." He looked as firece as any Inquisitor.

"No . . I . . . did nothing," the clerk replied. "I recorded all actions."

"Why is so much missing then?" Would you like to pay for this crime yourself? Are you willing to accept full responsibility for the missing goods?"

The clerk squirmed in the candlelight. "I had nothing to do with this,

God's word. It was the servants doing. Ask them."

"Servants? Which servants? Quick, man, and your life will be spared."

The clerk was frightened and blurted out a sordid story.

"We kept watch as you know, sir. However, during that long wait in Casco, there were times when no one seemed to care. Even you, sir, spent most of your time traveling." He was talking to me. "The captains kept at us constantly and the priests insisted on taking goods without charging the tally."

He lowered his voice in great fear. "Then Madam Perez entered our lives. We were restless and lonely and she granted us favors in exchange for goods. She said she would get the captains to sign for the goods so as not to put us in danger. And so it began. At first small amounts were taken by servants sent by the captains. Then larger and larger amounts. But, I swear it had all been signed for."

"How could this be?" I asked, irritated that my own responsibilities had been so seriously shirked. "The tally was checked every week against stores. Such reductions would not have gone unnoticed!"

"I . . . don't know, sir."

"Who signed the lists?" I demanded.

"Well, sir, we gave the list to Madam Perez who had the entries made by the captains."

"Which captains?"

"I know not, sir."

"Yet the lists we have now agree with the final tally held on the days of inspection. How can this be?"

"I don't know, sir. We meant no harm."

"Who collected the goods?"

"It was a mulatto servant, sir."

With trepidation we visited the house on the river to further this investigation and found Madam Perez haughty and defiant, ready to feed us any lie that would serve her purpose. She was a young woman but already her beauty had faded, replaced by a hardened, sardonic grin.

"I have nothing to tell you gentlemen."

"Do you deny the story told by Manuel de Salas?"

"Who cares? I did nothing wrong. Is it a crime to lay with a man?" Her boldness infuriated the priest.

"Who were you taking the lists to?" I demanded.

At first she refused to answer but under repeated questioning, she relented.

"Luis Bautista," she said. I suspected as much.

I again studied the lists of inventories and could find nothing wrong. Since I had other business to attend to with Don Juan, we delayed further investigation.

3

As providor-general I was responsible for collecting tribute from the pueblos. Don Juan ordered me to determine a fair tribute and I decided the tribute would have to be heavy. Because of our long delay at Casco, we were in dire need of foodstuffs to support the more than four hundred people in the colony. The onset of winter boded ill for the venture and we had few heavy blankets. It would be possible to make blankets and robes from the wild shaggy beasts that roamed the plains nearby. The Indians use these skins for blankets and they are warm indeed. Unfortunately, we had not been able to bring off a successful hunt up to that time.

It was not in the king's interest or our own to levy such tribute from the Indians as would cause them harm, so, working out our needs, I came to the following conclusions:

For a large pueblo of four hundred savages or more, a tribute of one blanket and one *arroba* of corn, beans or squash would be required for every eight inhabitants. This would mean fifty *arrobas* and blankets per village. For small pueblos, the amount would be halved.

I expected to collect five hundred *arrobas* of foodstuffs and at least two hundred blankets.

When I presented this to Don Juan, he thought it fair and said I should notify each pueblo of their requirement and explain how it was derived. I thought this a large task and suggested that we might offer some trade of goods. We agreed to give each contributing pueblo seeds of lettuce, cabbage, chick-peas, carrots, turnips, garlic, onion, artichokes and cucumbers, all of which were unknown to them. If a village voluntarily doubled its tribute, we would consider giving them a mated pair of sheep. Don Juan said we should never give them a horse.

I departed early in September on this difficult mission and immediately encountered strong resistance. After receiving no support at all at the first pueblo, I traveled many leagues and found that the Indians no longer feared our presence and were unwilling to part with their goods. While I demanded as forcefully as possible, we were only six strong counting two muleteers and an interpreter. It would have been foolhardy to persist. By early November I had collected only thirty five *arrobas* and twelve blankets. The prospects for more seemed bleak.

The governor was sorely displeased by these reports. He was preparing an expedition to explore the western regions and before he left he convened an assembly of the Maese de Campo, myself, Father Martinez and several other friars, along with the royal ensign. He wished to determine a correct course of action to settle our predicament.

"Good brother-in-Christ," Don Juan addressed the priests, "I will state our position here and then ask, by your leave, which course of action we should take." He studied some documents lying on his desk before he continued. For the first time I noticed an air of concern in his demeanor, a careful attention to detail not characteristic. He seemed much older now than when we had started, as if the burden of government had been more than he expected. He coughed and continued.

"As you know, we have been granted a royal license for this settlement. In keeping our agreement with the king's order, I am to collect tribute from the Indians who have rendered obedience and vassalage to His Majesty, in an amount not to be harmful to their welfare. As usual, one-fifth goes to the royal treasure." He nodded at Peñalosa.

"The providor-general has determined that we must procure at least five hundred *arrobas* of corn if we are to meet these demands and maintain this colony. This calculates to a levy of not more than one *arroba* for every eight inhabitants of a large village. This is only a few hands full for every person. This surely would do little to diminish the provisions in each village. The question I put to you now is this: Do I have the legal right to levy this tribute and does the amount seem fair?"

The priests retired to an adjoining room. After much discussion they called in the royal ensign. When they emerged Father Martinez spoke, "As to the legality of your levy, there is no question. It is your duty to levy tribute. This is required in the kingdom of Castile as well as New Spain, although in these regions it is called a tax."

He stopped for a moment and surveyed his audience. "The pueblos of which you speak have all become vassals of the king and as such, must pay their share to maintain the kingdom."

I thought of how little the savages knew of such things. We had been amongst them several months now and I was slowly learning their ways. They had little government and few recognized leaders even with their civilized ways. Wherever I had demanded tribute, I found that no single person could make this decision although one may find an old sage or cacique who could speak for the pueblo. They were free from all laws, rules, taxes, but abided by the rule of common consent. They all shared freely in a common good, no man holding himself above others.

"As to the fairness," he continued, "it seems that the amounts you have demanded are in accordance with what the subjects can yield without undue harm to their welfare."

Don Juan looked pleased. "Now," he said, "here is the difficulty. The savages, for manifold reasons, many times refuse to yield up their tribute. In New Spain such action would be condemned and punished. Because the existence of this colony is in grave peril I intend to collect this tribute by force if necessary. What say you?"

Again the priests retired with the royal ensign. When they returned Father Martinez spoke again, "We do not agree that force is necessary. We know the savages come reluctantly to the fold, but we must be patient. Using force, there would be little chance of their agreeing to fulfill their obligations peacefully."

Don Juan became angry. "Is that all? Do you believe patience will work?"

"Force will invite bloodshed."

"What would you have me do? Abandon the colony and let the savages return to the ways of Satan?"

"Is there no other way? Can't we obtain provisions from Santa Barbara?"

"I have requested aid from my supporters and the viceroy but it will be months before see a thing. No, there is no other way."

Once more the priests retired for consultation, this time without the royal ensign. When they returned to the table Father Martinez said, "Very well. But if force is used, it must be used only as a last resort and only against those who would bar collection of tribute. There will be no killing over this." He sat down and wiped his brow.

"I cannot promise that," Don Juan responded dryly. "I too want no killings and we will give all ground to avoid this. To draw blood over the collection of tribute would be a great stain on our community. But killings may happen."

The assembly adjourned on this note and the priests left. Don Juan slumped in a chair, exhausted by the meeting. Out of his desk he took a tube of tobacco. He too had taken up this vile habit.

"Use whatever force is necessary," he instructed me, "but don't kill anyone, unless you have no choice. I know this is difficult for you" He smoked and smiled at me. "But I know of no other way."

That evening I talked with Inez about the meeting and she was very disturbed.

"It is the bloodshed I told you of," she said. "The Tewa, Tano and Ako people will yield no tribute, unless the robe will work. We must do what we can."

I had forgotten the robe. Its very mention made me feel like a conspirator.

If we are to survive we must do something before the snows fill the roads." I said. "I will take a small troop to Galisteo and should they resist . . ."

"No. We must try with the robe first. Gaspar, I have relatives there."

I had forgotten. Galisteo was a large and powerful pueblo well able to pay tribute.

"I still must do my duty, Inez. Our existence depends on this."

She fell into silence. Then she said. "I will come with you."

We were at odds for the first time.

"You only know what the Castillos say. You must, as Father Oroz has asked, understand the will of my people. Perhaps the robe will let you do that. Can't we try?"

I became defenseless in the face of such arguments. The old priest had me firmly in his grip as he had said in the letter. I agreed to go to Galisteo with Inez to convince the savages to yield up the tribute peacefully. But unknown to Inez, I sent my servants to scout the trail and make emergency plans.

Before we departed, the first messenger from Santa Barbara arrived at our colony. His message brought a great gloom over us all and did little but bode evil for our venture. His Majesty, King of Castile, Aragon and Granada, Prince of the Indies, was dead. Philip the Second, the greatest monarch of the realm, was no longer with us. How well I remembered his court. His long rule had put his stamp on every corner of the kingdom and he personally had directed the organization of this enterprise.

Don Juan was inconsolable. We knew nothing of this new prince or how it would affect us.

"Don Gaspar, it seems we have been cursed," he said "First the viceroy changes, now the king is dead. Are we not to achieve our destiny?"

It was a time of great sorrow for all of us. Don Juan ordered a special mass and a wooden altar to be built. The service was held in the half-completed church being built in San Gabriel. We prayed for the king's deliverance and for Holy guidance for Philip the Third and ourselves.

4

At dawn we left San Juan on swift horses, heading south. The air was now bitter cold and since we had many leagues to travel to Galisteo I feared being trapped by snow. Inez looked radiant in the cold air and fox-skin robe she wore. She rode well and we made good time to a point I had selected based on the earlier surveys. We left the horse with my men and as nightfall approached, we entered the pueblo on foot.

Our earlier experience was repeated although this pueblo was more beautiful than any I had seen before and the people seemed larger and fiercer than any others. A large crowd gathered in the shadows before we had gone any distance and seemed to menace our progress. But when Inez spoke they understood and led us to her uncle's house.

"Gaspar, sit over there, by the fire," she said. In the middle of the room, a fire burned openly, the smoke exiting through a hole in the roof. The fire kept the cold away and I was grateful for such comforts.

"I will speak with Mataca. He does not remember me. Please keep silent while we speak."

They sat on the floor, cross-legged and faced each other. The man's face was expressionless. His wife hovered like a nervous moth. They sat like this for some time until finally Mataca emitted a frightening sound and started to rock back and forth. Inez spoke and this broke the silence. They talked for some time and finally Mataca seemed to reach a conclusion. They touched each other's hands and shoulder, blowing on their hands at the same time. Finally they got to their feet and Inez brought Mataca to where I sat. I rose.

"This is El Santo," she told him. "He is possessed because a holy one has made him so." She was referring to the robe I was wearing.

Mataca made a gagging sound, something I had not experienced with these people before. Inez said it was because I looked so curious, like one of their clowns. She said it was a good sign. He was laughing.

We were given a small room with a woven mat and a blanket and there we spent the night. Inez had told Mataca what we wanted to do. Mataca replied that the Castillos were not welcome since they had killed many Tano people before.

"I told you this in Zacatecas. It was here that my father was killed. Even I have difficulty forgetting. But that is past and it was by the will of the gods. My people do not dwell on good or bad from the past. What is done is done forever, and should not occupy the mind's eye. But this thing is still fresh, like an autumn-killed deer kept frozen through the long winter. When the last piece is eaten by men and the last bone fills the belly of the wolf, then the deer no longer exists in any mind's eye. The Tano believed they were punished by the gods for attacking the Tewa and scalping many young men. They believe the Castillos were sent at that moment. It was the predictions of the priests."

I marveled at what I heard. This had not been clear to me before. Now Inez was opening my mind to the truth, much as Father Oroz had. And suddenly, a new fundamental truth dawned on me: These savages had no distant past, no ancient history. There was no written document to be found. All things long past must, of necessity, be legend, twisted to fit the needs of the morrow. What sweetness when the bitter dregs of moldy yesterdays have been buried and forgotten forever. Suddenly, I felt a deep kinship with these people, something I couldn't explain, but something that made me want to understand them better.

I told her of my feelings. "You must be careful, Gaspar," she said. "You have much understanding, more than anyone I know. My people may not live in the past, as you say, but they do not forget so easily, and they can bloody the morrow. They are fierce in their habits and can kill quickly. You must be careful. They have not forgotten the Castillos."

In the morning, Mataca took us around the pueblo at my request. It was situated in a broad valley surround by snow-covered mountains. The air was sweet but intensely cold. The houses were terraced to as many as five stories high and a clear mountain stream passed around the south edge of the village. Smoke poured from the houses casting a glistening veil over the early sun. The sharp light reflected off the houses which seemed molded of reddish clay smoothed by the winds of time. Inez was right. The savages appeared warlike and I perceived an air of hostility.

5

But we were accepted without incident. We spent the next day amongst them and I tried to learn what I could. At first I was treated as they want to treat madmen and I encouraged this reception. I spent most of my time in silence as I could not fathom the language, but this made my observations keen. I found these Indians to be true idolaters, setting great store by augury and having many priests dressed in animal disguises of great ingenuity and variety, including hideous masks with antlered heads and wild cattle with horns. Their priests read signs in droppings, bones and feathers which the people depended on.

The houses, too, had a magical atmosphere. They were entered by sharp-poled ladders laid against the first landing, giving the look of a great leafless forest. Some of these were called estufas as we had seen in other pueblos and served, I believe, for secret ceremonies. I was not allowed to enter these places and my curiosity was only satisfied by Inez telling me of them.

In the evening of the second day, we were told that an assembly would hear my request in the morning.

"Tonight they will perform a ceremony to keep the gods happy," Inez said. "They may dance all night. The drums will bring signs and the signs will be read, all in preparation for tomorrow. If the cacique reads bad signs it could be difficult.

"I fear that . . . I should not have done this. Be careful and do not make them angry."

"I only want to convince them to surrender the tribute without trouble," I said. "I hope this robe . . . " I fell silent, afraid to voice my doubts.

We sat on the roof looking at the crystal stars. The surrounding peaks glistened in the luminous light of the moon and I sensed in this silent air a great mysteriousness. The frigid air was full of the smell of cooking fires and soon we were brought wild meats and corn cakes.

We slept in fits as the drums beat through the night, the silence of the cold dawn was most welcome. We steeled ourselves for the meeting and as we approached the square we found the savages seated in unruly bunches in a rough semi-circle. After some preliminary confusion and shouting, I was told to speak. Their hospitality seemed to have withered.

"Speak," they commanded again in their unusual tongue. Speak, indeed. The gathering encircling me adorned in every manner of devilish hue and dress and boldly plumed or horned, was enough to prevent any man from speaking. But by the grace of God and the robe of Father Oroz I became bold.

"My friends, I have here been sent by one who receives his commission from the Almighty. It was his will, as one with the Almighty, that peace and harmony prevail in this land. He has asked me to accomplish this. Thus I come before you to ask your help in making peace and harmony possible. Will you help me with this noble task?"

I employed my best classical rhetoric and hoped they would agree with only one small point at each pause. Inez translated and a great debate raged among the savages. I was praying for a quick agreement when their answer came: "Speak," a particularly wild looking savage shrieked.

Quickly, I continued, "The Castillos have come amongst you seeking this peace and harmony." This statement caused a general uproar and I was forced to the ground to avoid a stone hurled by one of the savages.

"Speak!" they screamed.

I could see this was now a deadly game. I jumped to my feet and with wild abandon shouted: "The next one to hurl a stone shall be struck dead on the spot!" I fingered the pistol under my robe. This calmed them considerably. I continued:

"Far off, in a land beyond the sea, a great king rules. He has been commissioned by the messenger of the Almighty to rule over many lands. It is the will of the Almighty that all people should know him and know his love. The Holy messenger has asked this king to do this. The king, in turn, has sent the Castillos. Soon the Castillos will show their great friendship. They will give you gifts of great magic," I paused.

The men again debated violently. Then again the wild savage: "Speak!"

"They will give you seeds that will grow wondrous plants such that you will not believe your eyes!" I paused.

"Speak!"

I needed something that would seize their attention and calm their agitation. "They will give you horses which you have seen make men as swift as deer!"

This created the impact I had hoped for. They calmed down and sat, holding muted discussions. I had lied, but this situation called for drastic measures. After all, perhaps I could talk Don Juan into giving up an old nag.

But suddenly the savages jumped to their feet. "When do we get the horses?"

"Before six moons," I replied, hoping that would give me time to make good this promise. They were silent now.

"The great king wants all people to share in his kingdom. If one Castillo has five bags of corn," I counted on my fingers, "he gives one bag to the king. The king then gives this bag to the people in his kingdom."

They looked at me vacantly again mumbling amongst themselves. "One bag not enough for all people!" the savage said.

"If a Castillo has five horses," I continuted, "he gives one horse to the king. The king shares this horse with the people in the kingdom. Now the great king," I took a breath, "asks you, his subjects, to share your corn and blankets and be part of his kingdom!"

After a short pause and while Inez was still translating, an uproar broke out. They seemed greatly aroused by my speech, so much so I thought it unwise to speak further. I told them I would hear them speak. Finally, a spokesman emerged. He stepped forward and crossed his arms.

"I am Calco. My people live here since the beginning. Before first sunrise, we live here, beneath the earth." He stomped the ground and pointed to the earth. "The god of air, all air, gave us water, fire, air to breath." He took in a great quantity of air and exhaled. "He brought us out of earth, like the birth of a buffalo. Then god of light made us see and gave us corn. Now this earth," he picked up a handful of dirt and crumbled it slowly in his hand near my face, "belongs to the gods. This air . . . , this water . . . , this corn . . . ," he swept his arm around the village, "belongs to the gods. Everything belongs to the gods. We cannot give what belongs to the gods to your king whom we do not know. The gods will punish us if we do this. It is the gods' wish that all Castillos leave this land. If not, there will be much sorrow for us all."

I was astonished by this simple but eloquent speech. Before I could reply there was an outburst and several savages threatened us. Mataca hastily led us to a nearby house.

"I will return," he said. "You must leave soon. It is not good that you stay." I knew we were now in grave danger.

Inez was sad. "The robe has failed," she said. "Perhaps we have sinned to much."

"No," I said. "The robe has saved us. These people know nothing of our ways and cannot understand our needs." I paused to see if she understood. She nodded. "They were angry with my words. Without this robe, I fear I would have been in even greater peril."

"We must leave quickly," she said. "Father Oroz said sometimes Christian charity must be offered lightly. I fear for you if we try to talk with them again."

As night closed around the pueblo, great fires were lit and streets appeared blocked. Each street was well illuminated and ghostly shadows danced off the few large trees around the edge of the Pueblo. We silently climbed to the roof once again to assess our chances for flight. I stared in fascination at a strange pagan dance in the square below. I saw no exits. We waited for Mataca's return.

At middle-night, with the moon hidden behind the high peaks, the drums went silent. We jumped up from a weary doze in time to see a band of savages moving from the plaza in our direction. At that moment, Mataca appeared and quickly led us over the rooftops, down through large rooms and out into a small path behind the houses. We had traveled the length of the village over the rooftops and through the rooms and were now at the south end. When we reached the last building, Mataca whispered quickly to Inez and then dropped from sight into the darkness.

"We go south," she said pointing to a high peak, "until we reach the stream Then we follow the stream to the Rio del Norte."

We had to cross a clearing at least a cannon shot's breadth before entering a low wood. The moon's light was still shadowed by clouds so we ran quickly. We had only gone a short distance, when a cry went up from the pueblo and the savages were in hot pursuit. As we crossed a small foot bridge, I realized we would never outrun them so I decided on a desperate measure I had planned earlier.

I held Inez and turned to face the hooting savages. Suddenly arrows rained down on us and one struck Inez in the breast. I told her to be steady or all would be lost.

The savages stopped on the other side of the bridge and were silent as they waited for my move. I shouted, "If you continue to threaten us, the great God will kill you."

Inez slowly stepped up to the bridge, ripped the arrow from her breast and threw it to the ground. The savages drew back, their faces reflecting awe in the torchlights. But one desperate youth leapt onto the bridge brandishing a war club and torch. His face was evil in the flickering firelight with eyes lusting for blood.

I pulled the trigger on the pistol and heard the hammer snap home, but nothing happened. My blood drained to my feet but just as I tried to pull the pistol from my clothing it went off. The ball ripped through the robe with a flash and much smoke and smashed into the foot bridge in front of the savage knocking him to the ground. When the others saw this they fled in terror. The wounded youth staggered to his feet, eyed me with a crazed look and also fled, dragging a bloodied leg into the night.

We moved quickly into the surrounding wood and I stopped to examine Inez. She was bleeding heavily and the wound was jagged where she had ripped the barb loose. She cried out, "Gaspar, you are wounded." She pointed at my mid-section and I saw a great hole had been burned in the robe and my skin was curled like bacon.

We struggled to reach the Rio del Norte and followed it north to the point where I had left my men three days before. Praise God, they were there, waiting as I had instructed. Inez was in poor condition in spite of my ministrations of cold water and winter leaves. Snow began to fall.

"Don Gaspar, it is good to see you," they cried as we neared the small camp. "You look badly wounded." They lay Inez on a bed of branches and Gaspar de Tavora, a Portuguese, applied a medicament he carried in his saddle bag.

"You gave me this," he told Inez as he opened the herb salve. "Soon your wound will disappear." Then he turned to me and I found the salve a great blessing for the pain of my burned flesh.

Inez seemed much improved so after a short rest, we decided to continue lest the Indians fall upon us.

Battling the now bitter cold and heavy snow, we made our way slowly back to San Gabriel. We kept a sharp eye out for the savages and arrived at daybreak. The sight of our good fellows was most welcome. We quickly took Inez to be doctored.

I then reported what had transpired to the Maese de Campo.

"We shall not collect the tribute easily," I said. "This shows their determination to stand fast. We must find some way out of this peril."

I was not comfortable with the method we were using to sustain ourselves. Other expeditions had succeeded, but always at the cost of many lives. Coronado sustained a larger army for more than a year from tribute, but the costs were great. I knew the savages resented this regardless of their token submission to the Crown. It caused much hardship for all.

"We shall bring them about," he replied. "They are not worth thinking about. Force is what they understand and respect. Don Juan has been too lenient. He fancies himself an emperor, or some bloody business like that, where he feels responsible for the savages' welfare."

It was true that Don Juan seemed burdened with his office.

"I think it proper that he be so," I said. "I am concerned about the savage I wounded."

"Bah!" he shouted. "What of it?" You should have taken his head off."

"No matter. But we still need some way to sustain ourselves through the winter. I have thought upon it and have a proposal."

I could see de Zaldivar was restless. He was miserable with his work and longed for his brother's return from the wild cattle plains so he could join Don Juan on the expedition to the south seas.

"What is this proposal?" he asked with interest.

"I will collect all the fine furs and deerskins we have gathered and take them to Santa Barbara. With an order from the royal ensign I will be able to trade them for several carretas of corn and dried meats. With luck, I could be back in a month. We have enough now to hold the colony until then."

"But we need the furs and skins. Without them, we will freeze to death," he replied.

It is my guess that your brother will succeed with the hunt. He should return with many skins for robes. When do you think he will return?"

"He is overdue now and I must stew here in his place."

I knew his mind on this. He had not changed in any way since the Chichimeca wars.

"I like your plan but I cannot give you leave. Don Juan is but five days' march from here waiting for my arrival. You should go and tell him of your plan. Since he thinks so highly of you I'm sure he will approve. If my brother arrives I will send a courier to you and prepare the skins for the trek. He may bring enough meat to feed us all."

I would have to leave immediately. But I did not want to leave Inez even though I knew something had to be done. A soldier's lot cannot be easily reckoned with concern for others. In my case, good fortune never occurs when needed. Here I was, the providor-general and responsible for the material welfare of our company. That is normally a heavy office to fulfill but in this case I was plagued with a multitude of adversities. I was sadly oppressed by my duties and more so because of my wife's condition. Yea, and forlorn is he who bears his miseries alone.

"I cannot do much more for her," Andres Perez said later that evening. She was feverish and only half conscious. "I think the salves will heal, it is more her weakness from the bleeding. I had to bleed her greatly to release the black infections in her veins or she would have perished."

I decided to wait until the fever broke to tell her of my plan. Around middle-night she sat up and called my name. I held her cold hand. Her eyes reflected like a looking-glass. I summoned Perez.

"I love you, Gaspar," she whispered as I held her. "Am I to die?"

I told her that Andre Perez would soon have her well. She sank back in my arms, delirious.

We spent the rest of the night this way and by God's will at dawn the delirium passed and she improved enough to take sustenance. I was grateful to the Lord and spent some time in prayer. By midday she was awake and I told her of my plan.

"That make my heart glad," she said. "It is the best way to avoid bloodshed. Do not worry for me but go and do this thing. I shall be in good health awaiting your return."

Relieved by this turn of events and seeing her condition much improved, I bade her farewell the next day.

The people were sorely pressed by the deep snow that now covered our community. The women and children were in poor condition and troubled by the bitter cold. The optimism I had seen just a few months earlier had now disappeared. All enterprise had ceased, everyone was engaged in survival against the bitter elements. For days, a cold wind had swept down from the north bringing the snow with no letup. Fresh food was in short supply and hunting parties sallied forth every day but to no avail as the snow kept the beasts well hid and we did not have the skills to hunt them.

6

I journeyed south with a spirited mount and a hunting dog until I reached the western trail. Here the snows had disappeared making travel much
easier. I kept an eye out for Indians as I pursued the governor's track made
not more than a fortnight ago.

As I approached a region where high mesas jutted up from the plain like
giant tables for the gods, I became uneasy and found myself alert. I passed
through a devil's region where ages before the earth had vomited up its
black innards which now curled over my head like giant black sea waves
ready to devour me and my animals. Overhead, large carnivorous birds
circled my path. They seemed to float effortlessly on the vacant air as if
propelled by the devil's breath.

I became haunted by the fear that I was being followed and was grateful
for the company of my faithful dog. The dog was calm and this helped to
settle my frantic notions. As evening neared I camped on the open plain
keeping well away from the black lava and large rocks. I dined on cold fare
so as not to raise a signal with a fire. The night passed filled with terrifying
sounds within the vicinity of my imagination.

At dawn I took up the march again and before the sun had fully escaped
the bounds of earth I was startled by barking. I turned to see a war club flying in my direction. Instantly, I flattened myself and drew my pistol as I
saw an Indian spring onto the trail. Lo! Not one, but a band of warriors ran
at me with blood in their eyes. As I leveled my pistol at the nearest in-
truder my horse reared into the air, pawing the sky with his great hooves.
This frightened the group and they hurled their clubs at me, missing, and
then fled. I prodded my steed and we headed southwest at top speed, my
faithful dog following.

I rode hard until I was sure they could not follow for I was no match for
that band and then, I slacked my pace. My horse was sore pressed and
blowing hard. The dog, too, was tired, his tongue lolling from his black
mouth. After a time I stopped to rest myself and the animals and to take a
bit of water.

I continued on at that pace for the rest of that day at which point the
trail led into a great forest of conifer trees. As I approached the area, I could
see a great forest spread before me for many leagues and as the land was
quite high, the air became bitter cold and it began to snow. I traveled until
nightfall and then made camp. I rested; it was around middle-night when I
awoke stiff with cold. The snow, which earlier had been light, was as thick
as wool and increasing rapidly. Seized by an unreasonable fear of being
trapped and freezing, I broke camp and mounting, I rode out again in

search of the trail. The snow covered all trace, but I pressed on letting my noble horse pick his way. The dog, for all my urging, would not go ahead but stayed behind the horse.

It became darker and I urged my horse on at a faster pace, hoping to find a region of more comfort and less snow. Suddenly my noble mount stepped into what seemed a small depression but I realized we were falling headlong into space. Like in a dream, we fell through the night until a sudden jolt brought a scream from the terrified horse. I landed in a twisted mass of saddle, armor and horse. I could hear my dog barking on the rim of land above. The horse didn't move but grunted weakly. I was stunned and bruised but after some time I managed to free myself from the entangled equipment. I seemed not to have any serious wounds or broken bones. But my horse was dying as great shudders racked the noble body. I could not find my pistol to dispatch the animal and I tried several times to find a path to the top but I fell more than I stood so I decided to stay in this snowy hell til daydreak.

I slept in fits, listening to the weakening tremors of my horse and my dog above and wondered if this was a trap set by the Indians. The gathering grey light revealed my prison. The rim above was ten yards over my head. We had fallen on a platform of jagged rock. Behind me the abyss continued down into a dark cavern filled with ice. My horse was now dead from a broken neck. I discovered a nasty wound on my head. I was covered with blood which I though had come from the horse.

To climb out of the devil's depression was formidable. The sides sloped up steeply and were covered by black jagged rock looking like huge burned coals. Snow and ice mixed with fumerols of smoke on the slope.

I stripped myself of unnecessary weight and left my food and water, coat of mail, helmet, shield, sword and pistol and powder pouch, taking only my dagger. Finally, I fell, torn and bleeding, at the feet of my happy dog who had urged me relentlessly on during that exhausting trial. The area around the hole was honeycombed with vicious openings which seemed to lead down into the fiery bowels of the earth.

After resting, I struggled on through the forest and found that it was inhabited by many wild animals. I headed in a westerly direction but after several days' I found I had only traveled in a great circle. I was still dazed by the fall and found it difficult to keep my wits and my heading. Finally, on the third day, I came out of the forest and upon a dry plain studded with giant rock formations that looked like the castles of Castile. My thirst by this time was unbounded and I was pressed by hunger. I began to wander with little or no direction, imagining pools of water everywhere. I passed several days in this fashion, finding neither food nor water. I found myself rapidly succumbing to weakness and a wandering mind. In this condition, I imagined that my starving dog would eat my corpse if I died.

In a fit of madness and hunger brought on by the devil, I wildly struck out at my faithful friend and gave it two deep wounds with the dagger. The terrified beast fled from this mad apparition of his former master. I called to it, hoping I might eat the beast and thereby survive. The pitiful creature, ignoring my senseless cruelty, came back to me, crawling in weakness and pain. He licked his wounds, and as if to please me, licked my hands, staining them with his own blood. I fainted and when I awoke and saw the dead animal, I wept at my senseless and shameful cruelty.

In fits of madness I fell asleep, dreaming that Inez was dying and that I too would soon be dead. My dreams swarmed with black and red devils and hideous visions of my dead dog. I saw images of Father Oroz and felt great remorse that I had not been able to do his bidding.

I awoke in the morning covered with snow and the cold, stiff body of the dog locked in my arms, its mouth choked shut with clotted blood. I threw it down with a cry. Wandering away from that terrible place, I prepared for death.

Suddenly, I came upon a miraculous rock standing on the plain like a mighty fortress. It was a remarkable structure and even in my failing condition, I was attracted by its extreme beauty. As I came closer, I noticed how the smooth white walls soared to marvelous heights and were as straight and tall as the Giralda of Cordova. Near the base I found a well-worn path and following it, I came upon a crystalline pool of clear water. The pool basin seemed to be carved out of the base of the rock which soared in rich hues overhead. I drank deeply, pouring the miraculous liquid into my fevered body. I recovered somewhat and exploring the area, I found wild dried fruits, still edible. Just then as I recall, three horsemen rode up demanding that I identify myself. My miserable life was saved.

7

For several days I slept, waking only to take food and drink. I was comfortably housed in the governor's camp near the Pueblo of Hawiku and as I recovered I was grateful to be alive.

"You are lucky." Rodgriquez said when he brought me rabbit stew. "We thought you were a wild beast dressed as a man. You would not have lasted another day."

I asked him about the rock where they had found me.

"It is a well-known resting place for travelers. The Indians have marked it well with trails. They believe the water has magical qualities."

Rodriguez had been part of a hunting party sent out to find provisions for the army. I was fortunate that they had traveled so far from their camp.

Don Juan visited me frequently as I recovered and I reported all that had happened since our last meeting.

"What makes the savages behave so? They have shown none of this behavior before," he asked.

"It is the devil's own reason," I replied. "It is the heathen priests that cause the people to resent us. They are concerned about their gods and would do us harm to appease them."

"Harm? But they have all pledged obedience to the Crown."

"We must be realistic, Don Juan. They do the act of obedience only to please us because they fear what we may do."

"But what of the friars? Are they incapable of meeting this challenge?"

"The friars can do little. The pueblos are remote from out settlement and they spend little time there. Besides, they have been unable to master the devils' own tongue, so they fail to communicate."

I knew Father Martinez was unhappy with the situation. It had been different in Mexico where a great city had been occupied and the friars were busy in those regions close to their brethern. But here. Father Lugo had disappeared for months, being one of the few brave souls to set out alone. We were a small group and unable to send men to occupy each pueblo. Thus, the friars were forced to travel and take up residence along amongst these people, who wanted naught to do with them.

"You seem to know the Indians better than any of us," he said, "yet even you were subject to bad treatment." He sighed. "Once your strength has returned, it is best if you carry out your plan. I'm afraid that collecting tribute from the savages cannot be supported until we are better established. You should be able to get what we need with my letter to Reza."

We sat in silence for some time. Then he continued. "We have managed thus far without any serious harm or bloodshed. I am determined to see that no blood shall be spilled. But we must perservere, Don Gaspar. As always, much depends on the success of your venture."

I thought of the long journey I would again have to make. Every step was fraught with danger, both from man and beast. But, I could not know then of the great calamity that was about to happen. It would change all our plans and present dangers far surpassing anything we had yet seen.

BOOK VIII

*". . . where there is no governor,
the people shall be scattered . . ."*
(Prov. 11:14)

1

Today I faced my accusers at court in Seville. Their wild claims astonish me. It seem everyone is making claims on everyone else. The vile relatives of Portuguez were determined to have me hanged and lay claim to my estate. Yea, verily, such a pittance could sustain them, they are so wretched. But I must contend with this infamy in order to obtain my exoneration. Today, more innocent souls are in jail while the criminals flaunt their freedom in the face of justice. The relatives of Gonzalez have yet to complete their new accusations but the council will not wait, for I have petitioned to free myself of those odious convictions carried out in New Spain. The commission has agreed to hear me but they asked that I have at least two witnesses of substance and not under conviction, swear to its accuracy.

Don Juan is returning to Spain to plead his case before the Council. The accusations against him are more serious and I am determined to complete this document of our services during the conquest so that he, too, may use it to right his good name. But without two witnesses, my petition will mean nothing. I wait expectantly to see Don Juan once more. It has been fourteen years since the events occurred as described in this document.

Don Juan will arrive in Spain in three weeks. I have not seen him in ten long years although I have heard of him and the colony. I pray that he is in good mind and health and that I once more may be of service to him.

I am now seeking the whereabouts of my old friend Rodriguez and Marquez. They will do witness for me and can write a good hand as well, as I will show.

2

But it was a long time ago, that I set about clearing up the murder charges lodged against Don Juan. It was after the incidents at Acoma, which I shall shortly relate, that Captain Aguilar again confronted the governor with demands to be retired from the expedition. The captain had recently distinguished himself in battle and was much taken with his popularity with the people because of this.

These events were related to me by Juan Rodriguez through letters from San Gabriel. I shall, rather than reword his observation, repeat a letter here without comment. It is a remarkable document and shall help establish the innocence of Don Juan.

January 1602
San Gabriel, N.M.

My Good Friend Gaspar,

It has now been over a year since you left our unfortunate enterprise. How I miss your companionship on the hunt and your soldier's eye in this land of never-ending surprises. And your poem. Have you finished it? The old Roman is sure to be jealous.

Salazar is carrying this letter for me, as you must know by now. He is returning to Mexico to report on the tragic events of the past year and to settle, hopefully forever, the evil lies being spread about the capitol by the deserters. Why does the viceroy believe them or even give them a hearing? They have deserted and should be executed as Don Juan has ordered. Things are bad enough here but at least we are all of a mind to make this settlement work. The deserters have fled like cowards and shall never receive the rewards of this great expedition.

I will try as best I can to explain the events which prompted your letter to me. You said that while in San Gabriel, Doña Perez accused the governor of forcing her to have intimate relations with him. How absurd. Have you seen this woman? She is a camp follower of the worst sort and was on the expedition, as you will remember, in that capacity. Her later marriage to Herrera notwithstanding, she is but a common whore. But one needs not take my word for it, as those in Mexico seem unable to do. I have enclosed a sworn statement from thirty seven men who swear they have experienced Madam Perez's delights. If the governor did partake of the flesh of this plump bitch, she should be flattered. Instead . . . ah, but you already know.

As for the other women laying down those same charges, they are trying to discredit the governor in the eyes of the Council. I believe nothing will come of this.

The desertion came about after you left for Mexico with the Acoman females. The governor set out for the plains of Quivira, leaving San Gabriel in the hands of Peñalosa. Everyone was smarting from the executions of Aguilar and Alonzo de Sosa, which I will explain later. I fear that these executions were a mistake since they helped to prompt the desertions. Yet, one can blame Peñalosa's lack of control over the situation. But let me start at the beginning.

It was the trial that set everything off. We would have been better off to have burned Acoma and been finished with it. Nothing incites our enemies more than to put bound natives on display in a courtroom, reliving the thing again and again through each witness. We warned the governor that his purpose would be ill-served by this trial and so it was. The punishment, as even you admitted, was unusually severe. And twelve of the Acoman men who had their feet cut off died during the execution or developed blackend flesh later and died.

After the remaining Acomans were given to us as slaves, we set their old people free. But they just stayed in San Gabriel and sat day and night in the streets, wailing in that strange way and slowly starved to death. Though we carried them out of the village every day, they would return and sit and stare, refusing to eat, their eyes getting big and glassy and then, dying, they would remain upright and rigid like the dried branches of a dead cork tree. Every day several died, and as there were many, it seemed that the more that died, the more there were until finally the constant presence of death overwhelmed us. We called a gathering and agreed to set the other Acomans free to take their old people and leave. At first, they refused saying that they preferred to die. Life in San Gabriel became more bitter and dark. We were now seen only as agents of death.

Nothing was being done. Food became scarce, the Indians refused to work, arguments flared and bloody fights broke out between our men. The colony was losing spirit and Don Juan remained out of sight, since the priests and men were constantly plaguing him with petitions to return to Mexico, which he would not grant.

It was at this point that Captains Aguilar and de Sosa petitioned

the governor to leave and while he steadfastly refused all petitions, these two brazenly announced their departure and offered
to escort all others who wanted to leave. The governor was
furious. I was not present at the incidents which followed, but
Marquez was there and has told me what I believe to be true. But
before I do this. I have copied down here part of a letter to the
viceroy describing Aguilar's murder through the twisted tongue
of Fray Escalona:

   ... The governor went to this affair (meeting with Aguilar) with a deceitful
purpose. After greeting him, the governor entered Aguilar's quarters, asking a
secretary he had along to admit secretly into the room a Negro and an Indian
with butchering knives and some servants with swords. And, in my presence
and that of many others, they seized him by his arms, the governor himself
giving him a push knocking him over some boxes, and right there they stabbed
him. The governor himself thrust a sword through his body. And even though
the poor man begged for mercy, saying that he was a married man and though
he asked for a confession since he was in a state of sin, they granted him
nothing. When Fray Francisco de San Miguel came to confess him, Captain
Aguilar was already breathless and in convulsions, his teeth set, his eyes star-
ing at the governor. They cut off his head, not satisfied with the mortal
wounds that covered his body. Your Lordship may surmise whether we were
all afraid, seeing that a man who had served so faithfully was given such
a reward.

A copy of this letter came to me from the scribe, Fray Urriba,
who does not believe it is true. As I said, Marquez was there and
the following is his written account:

   Captain Villagrá's investigation of the missing goods has yielded good
results. After the Acoma trials, we searched Bautista's apartment and found
that the scoundrel had forged the lists of inventory. The forged lists tallied
with the existing counts and he forged the signatures of all three signatories.
This is what made us all believe that the material on hand was what we
originally had left with. He has a most excellent hand for forgery. One cannot
tell the false from the original. He would not have been caught had he not kept
the originals. Vanity, I suppose.

   With some effort, we beat the truth out of this scoundrel. He was working
for Captains Aguilar and de Sosa who claimed they 'owned' all the goods
anyway. Since the great delay at Minas de Casco these gentlemen had agitated
for a change in the contract. They were no longer interested in the colony, but
only in searching for silver.

   In any event, Aguilar denied knowing about the forged documents. Bautista
suffered under the full accusation alone. He was furious at Aguilar for not
supporting his story. Thus, when the governor heard of Aguilar's intention to

leave, Bautista volunteered to assist in his arrest. The governor first warned Aguilar to desist and told him that any attempt to leave would be considered desertion punishable by death. Aguilar, headstrong as usual, ignored the governor's warning and continued to agitate the colonists to leave. The governor was furious and went with Bautista and an Indian servant to arrest Aguilar in his apartment. He asked me to act as witness. When we arrived, the governor ordered Aguilar arrested for desertion in the following manner as closely as I can recall:

'Captain Aguilar, you have sorely tried my patience beyond any hope for remedy. I have asked, nay, warned you, to desist and that further pursuit of this treasonous act would force me to take strong action. Here, we all can see that you have willfully disobeyed my order.' The governor was in a rage. He could not forbear disobedience in a soldier.

'As you can see, Don Juan, I have friends here who will vouch for my loyalty and obedience," Aguilar insisted, impertinent, as usual. There were several men in the room friendly to Aguilar. 'But we have all agreed to give up this godforsaken venture and return to Mexico. Nothing you can do will stop us.' Aguilar spat out his defiance in a rage. Clearly, he could not be reasoned with.

'I sentence you to death for treason. Don Juan shouted. 'Seize him. If you others assist him you too shall be equal in guilt.'

Aguilar looked at his friends. 'We must stand fast men,' he said. 'Draw your swords now and die or live like the dogs in this room.'

The thought of open mutiny proved so repulsive for the others that they stood fast. Aguilar drew his sword and lashed out at Bautista who was now almost upon him. The Indian servant circled around behind and knocked Aguilar down with a club; Bautista then stabbed him several times.

'Son of Satan," he screamed at the black fury hovering over him and getting to his feet, he lashed out at the two men, cutting a gash in Bautista's arm. He then lunged for a pistol on his desk which he had made ready for the occasion. At that point Don Juan entered the fray and ran him through before he could fire the pistol.

'Die, you whoreson,' Don Juan cried, enraged that Aguilar had brought circumstance to this dire conclusion. Aguilar fell across some boxes he had prepared for travel, his life's blood staining the floor around him. He looked up at Don Juan who hovered over him, 'You will . . . pay for this crime. I am . . . dying. You must bring a priest.'

Don Juan threw his sword down and ordered the servants to put down their arms. He told me to fetch a priest.

I brought Father San Miguel to confess Aguilar; he arrived too late. Aguilar died of his wounds before he was beheaded. This is what happened, as I personally witnessed the above events.

Aguilar, as you well know was always reckless and without proper respect for the governor's authority. Had he been more prudent, he would be alive today. The governor did what he had to do which was legal and justified.

As I have told you, these are Marquez's own words. And, as the events at Aguilar's apartment were taking place, Alonzo de Sosa had already deserted the village. Vincente de Zaldivar later tracked him down and executed him as a deserter under the governor's authority. Such was the nature of these "murders." Stories, such as the one put out by Escalona are untruths, serving only to make heroes of the cowards who have fled this place. You must help us to make the truth known to the viceroy.

After the executions, those who would have fled with Aguilar and de Sosa ceased their clamor although they plied the weakness of the priests. In particular, Father Escalona, as you can see, is now an enemy of the governor and this expedition, swearing he will have all of us tried for murder and cruelty.

Thus it was that our settlement divided into two hostile camps surrounded by hostile savages. Those that would leave hated the governor for refusing them permission and did what they could to create unrest. The Indians, sensing this, became even less tractable and both corn and clothing were in short supply. We were reduced to wearing rags and hunger stalked us with the spectre of death.

At this point the governor decided something must be done and he formed an expedition to Quivira. In close council he said that if they should discover gold or silver, it would reunite the colony.

I must admit that I disagreed with the governor. I pointed out that those who would abandon the settlement were now more a burden than a help, that our only need for them was defense against the Indians who now left us alone and that should an attack occur, they may only take the occasion to flee. An expedition to Quivira would take many months and if nothing was found, would lead to the end of community.

The governor disagreed, claiming that God and the law were on his side. As difficult as it is for me to say, the governor fails to understand his people. We are of two kinds here: those who are soldiers or tradesmen, and landsmen who have come here for cause and to secure some measure of benefits. We left little in Mexico and have nothing to go back to. Rather, we look forward to building anew for ourselves out of this wilderness.

Those who would leave, for the most part, are from the upper classes. They left estates behind for what they considered an adventure and a gamble, to become titled and more powerful in the eyes of the king. From the beginning, they were prepared to abandon this project should it not serve this purpose. Privation and danger beyond that of the exploration were never part of their plan. They have brought clothes of Holland cloth and silk, fine furniture, carriages and servants, perfumes, wigs and oils, and now find no use for these things here. Yea, this is not Mexico and will not yield its wealth so easily. Such individuals should be allowed to leave. We need sturdier folk.

When he left we were still in the old Indian Pueblo. The governor had tried to build a strong community, to seed plots and raise sheep and cattle. The great start we saw fell to pieces with the drought of '99 and the terrible winter which followed. The cattle were gone and as for foodstuffs, we needed Indian stores for every *fanega* of maize we ate. The Indians themselves were suffering from a great famine in the land and we could do naught but add to their woes. Thus, the governor was of the opinion that unless new discoveries were made, all would be lost.

Because he was unable to produce wealth in silver and gold, support for this enterprise was nonexistent. The viceroy did not, perhaps could not, supply the needed goods or soldiers to stay us over, although Don Juan pleaded constantly. Perhaps there were still those in Mexico that would see us fail.

After the governor set out, there was a great outcry from the colonist and in particular, the friars, who preached that all was lost. Captains Zubia and Velasco labored diligently for the abandoment of this land, and went about with a petition gaining signatures to do such. They incited those who were peaceful farmers and ranchers to leave, stating that their farms and ranches would be of no value if the colony did not exist. In such a manner, both the friars and these cowardly captains did great harm and convinced the majority to leave.

And so it was that San Gabriel was abandoned. Only the Royal Ensign, Fr. Escalona and a handful of soldiers remained behind to greet the governor upon his return many months later.

You know the rest of this story, so I will not bore you any further. Salutations.   J. Rodriguez

3

And so it was that the camp became divided. The friars had been unsuccessful in their attempts to convert the savages and they vented their frustrations on Don Juan and the loyal soldiers. It was as Father Oroz had surmised and perhaps the Indian, Pedro Oroz, would have been of great help. But then, he had died before we reached New Mexico. These Pueblo Indians were determined to pursue their idolatrous ways. The friars had never met people such as these. They listened to all the friars said but as soon as the Religious turned their backs, the Indians turned to their pagan gods. They feared neither punishment nor death and could not be coerced by fire nor sword as Father Oroz had suspected.

Throughout Don Juan steadfastly maintained his faith in God and was always the soldier, disciplined, ruthless and singleminded. He believed that faith and strength were needed to combat the adversity he found at every turn and could not tolerate the weaknesses. His every move had been challenged by friend and foe alike and against all these odds he perservered and established this fledgling colony. It is true that he was not tolerant and showed great cruelty to those who would destroy this dream, whether Indian or Spaniard. But the cruelty was limited to swift and terrible punishments and never meted out without sufficient cause, contrary to reports written by Father Escalona and Captain Velasco.

Don Juan lived alone in San Gabriel with his son and daughter and often invited me to his house. He was always preoccupied and missed his wife sorely. In front of her portrait he always had a vase of fresh red flowers and sometimes we sat late into the night while he reminisced of times when they were together. He longed to return to the land of his father's birth but would not entertain one thought of leaving New Mexico, which he insisted would soon be greater than any existing colony of the Spanish crown.

Without Don Juan, there would now be no colony of New Mexico from which His Majesty now derives great satisfaction. Don Juan was a man with a dream. Without such men, the world would be a lesser place for God and our country.

But the deaths of Aguilar and de Sosa and the desertion of the colony might not have happened if the great and terrible events at Acoma had not taken place.

BOOK IX

"A just war is wont to be described as one
that avenges wrongs, when a nation or state
has to be punished for refusing to make amends
for the injuries done by its people . . ."

St. Augustine

1

At the governor's camp in Hiwaku, I continued to recover from my bout with hunger and close brush with death and prepared for the journey to Santa Barbara. I would return to San Gabriel first. I missed Inez and my absence on this journey would be long. But my plans were rudely thwarted. One morning, before cock-crow, the camp was astir with wild rumors.

"Don Gaspar," I heard a voice call out in the darkness. "Don Gaspar, wake up, man." It was Rodriguez at my tent flap. I heard men and horse moving about in the darkness.

"What ails you?" I asked, irritated at the rude awakening. I fumbled for my clothes in the darkness. I pulled the tent flap open and he spoke to me from the darkness.

"Barnaby de las Casas is with the governor. Something has happened at Acoma. Something to make him look like death itself."

"What is it?"

"He would not speak to us. Said he must talk with the governor first."

Suddenly, a great cry was heard in the governor's quarters. We ran to find what caused this, my heart pounding with fear.

"It's the Maese de Campo," someone shouted. "They have killed him!"

"What's this?" I cried. I could not believe my ears. "You can't mean . . ."

"It's true The Maese de Campo, and all his men! The butchers of Acoma have spilled our comrades' blood . . . "

Through the uproar in every quarter, the message became clear. Juan de Zaldivar and twelve brave soldiers were dead, slain and brutally mutilated by the Indians of Acoma. Here was first blood and we became insane with grief. These men had been brothers to us and their loss was an unspeakable tragedy. The camp reeled with grief, dazed with these woeful tidings. On that bleak day we were unable to effect even the simplest task. We went about unclean. The animals went unfed. The governor secluded himself in his tent in prayer.

But pangs of agony must pass quickly for soldiers. Don Juan, bleary-eyes and gaunt, gathered us about the fire that evening.

"Gentlemen, first let us all pray to God almighty for their salvation." He raised his sad face to heaven and with powerful emotion evoked God's forgiveness for their sins and ours and recited a passionate Pater Noster. We all wept with grief at these words. Then Father Escalona said mass at which he mournfully sang the Te Deum. We were awash with tears.

"Courage, men," Don Juan mumbled. "We must gather our wits and strength for we are now in grave danger. Our people in San Juan are in great peril. We must prepare ourselves for battle and return quickly. Suit your armor to leave tomorrow at cockcrow."

We were poorly prepared for battle, having no heavy weapons or armor. The men who had reported the news remained secluded, unable to bring themselves to talk about the tragedy.

The next morning we turned our mounts toward San Juan. We rode quickly and in silence. Within two days the dreaded rock of Acoma loomed into sight, but we passed to the north at a great distance. We wanted to turn our swords on the place but the greater fear for our people made us press forward. A growing concern for Inez consumed my every thought.

Suddenly I heard a great commotion from the rear of the column. I turned my horse back to see and found Francisco Sanchez, torn with grief and rage, breaking ranks and riding fullhead towards Acoma. Immediately two men pursued him and within a league they had subdued the half-crazed man and brought him back.

"We must try," he cried out.

"It is no use, man. They are all dead. We could only get ourselves and our loved ones killed," Barnaby de la Casas spoke.

At that moment Don Juan rode up. "What is this?" he demanded.

"Sanchez rode for the rock," Barnaby de las Casas said.

"I gave strict orders not to break formation. Sanchez, we must get back to San Juan. All of us. We will return soon enough and right this terrible wrong. I promise it. Now, one more move like that I will have you flogged for disobedience. Do you understand?"

The blood drained from his face and he was about to say something that I knew he would regret but he fell silent and looked at the ground.

"Do you understand!" demanded Don Juan.

"Yes, sire," came the barely audible reply.

Don Juan rode back to the head of the column. In passing, he told me in a whisper to keep an eye out for mischief. I nooded.

The sight of Acoma laid a great gloom over the company and as we moved on, all was silent except for the creak of leather, the soft clatter of armored joints and the occasional snort of a tired horse. It was as if to speak would reveal the depth of our grief to our enemies and only furtive glances were shot at the rocky summit which gradually disappeared into the dying sun.

We continued eastward then northward until reaching the Rio del Norte when heavy snows began. Our band struggled valiantly against the bitter cold and the horses sank up to their bellies and I recalled the words of Castaño de Sosa. As we approached San Juan, a black depression and renewed grief filled my heart. I did not know then how deep my grief would be.

The tragic details of the massacre were sorted out as we traveled.

"It wasn't long after you set out that Don Vicente returned from The wild cattle hunt," de las Casas said to us one night. "The Maese de Campo was much relieved to see his brother again, ever fearful for his life."

"Were his fortunes on the hunt good?" I asked.

"No," he replied. "They were unable to secure much more than a few carcasses and skins. Vincente wanted to capture some of the those beasts alive but could not. The Maese de Campo was anxious to join the governor. He left San Juan in the hands of Vincente and with fifteen men set out on the governor's trail. I was with them.

"We had almost no provisions. We took little from San Juan as the stores were almost empty. We decided to provision from Acoma." He fell silent for some time, unable to continue. We knew that the Maese de Campo had a particular dislike for the Acomans ever since their appearance at our first ceremony in San Juan.

"We camped at the base of the rock," he continued, "and were well received, at first, by a band of unarmed Indians. They descended to the plain to discern our motive. Zaldivar told them he was on a mission and needed provisions. We had no satisfactory interpreter with us and they understood little. Yet, they seemed to agree after much talk amongst themselves. They left and returned to the summit.

"The next day they returned bringing only a few baskets of meal. Through signs they made it known that this was all they would provide." He stirred the fire sending a blaze of sparks overhead. "We didn't know then that they had just provisioned the governor's army," he continued.

Zaldivar had little faith in the word of these Acomans. When they continued to deny his request, he called them 'barbaric and obstreperous violators of Christian faith and charity.' A great commotion broke out amongst the savages as they could feel the great displeasure of the Maese de Campo. But, again they seemed to agree to our demands. They returned to the summit and shortly thereafter reappeared with but two more baskets. They now seemed very agitated and made it clear that we should depart. Then they returned to the rock.

"Zaldivar was furious and ordered a party to climb up and seize the provisions. He ordered me and several others to stay below and guard the horses. He ordered them not to draw blood under any circumstances without his order."

At that point the Caudillo, Francisco Sanchez, continued the story. "Zaldivar made a fatal move and gambled that the Indians would not resist. We were armed with pistol and musket, enough it seemed, at least at the time.

"We reached the top without any commotion, but once there, they surrounded us. Zaldivar again demanded provisions but the savages made it clear that we should leave.

"The Maese de Campo was now very angry. He ordered Bibero and Munuera to search one street and for me and others to search another. Before I could make my move, Bibero was stopped by a woman who barred his entrance to the street. He pushed her out of the way and she stumbled and fell. Suddenly a hail of stones rained down on him from the rooftops, knocking him to the ground. Before we could do anything, Indians swarmed over him and smashed his head to pulp. Then the entire pueblo erupted and they swarmed over us like angry bees. We got off a single volley before we had to use sword and knife as the fighting was so close." His voice began to shake and he stoped talking. Juan de Olague continued:

"It was bitter fighting. I've never been in combat like that before. So close to death and seeing it march at you like that.

"The savages were like the very devil himself. We killed several with the first volley and wounded many more but to no avail. They cut us down before we knew what was up. Their war clubs are like an ax. They'd fall on a man and in an instant would hack his body to pieces. We raced around like madmen, defending ourselves, trying to help our comrades. But it was no use.

"Zaldivar fought like a madman with knife and sword, killing a score. Cut one of them right in half, he did." Olague's eyes glazed as he recounted this warrior's tale. "He shouted at us to take courage just before he fell. They smashed his body to pieces with rocks and clubs until only a bloody mass filled his uniform."

"While they gloated over their bloody prize, we backed to the cliff's edge where we hoped to make a last stand. In no time they turned on us and we being only four against hundreds, decided to leap to our fate. By the Grace of God we landed on sand dunes and three of us survived. Poor Antonio smashed his head on a rock. Rotten luck, for he'd killed two with his own sword!'" He finished the tale and we sat silent trying to picture the bloody events.

To a man, they extolled the virtue of the Maese de Campo and none would accuse Zaldivar of making an error in judgement. His blood was still fresh and desire for revenge was great. Never would they tell these things, they said, except to their comrades.

As the embers glowed in that vast darkness and I mulled over the events, it was clear that we had misjudged the determination and strength of the Indians against our arms. The cost of tribute was now known. This bloody lesson set in motion events which would cost us dearly, destroying our dream of success.

Inez had been right.

2

I was alarmed to find that Inez was not amongst the colonists at San Juan. My fear grew to black despair as I lurched like a mad dog from house to house, seeking news but finding nothing.

How miserable we humans are, forced to exist in this cruel world. We endure this false existence filled with dangers so covered by deceit that we can neither fathom nor understand them. Ungrateful world. Festerous cancer, what poison reeks within your bloody fangs? You swallowed the love of my life and sit bloated with your prize, laughing. Little could I imagine how deceitful fate would be.

While I conducted my futile search, Don Juan formed a company of stalwart men to subdue the dogs of Acoma. He appointed Vincente de Zaldivar to lead the avenging army. Mercy would not be part of this mission. I was ordered by Don Juan to join the force and I readily consented.

Meanwhile, not knowing where to turn in my search for Inez. I went wearily from pueblo to pueblo while waiting word from San Juan. I encountered more and more hostility from the savages. News of the massacre at Acoma had spread and the Indians no longer feared our arms. They were recalcitrant and at times would not let me enter the village. This only increased my despair and I, too, began lusting for blood to avenge my countrymen.

Finally we were told at San Juan that the army would be leaving for Acoma within three days. I had returned to the colony to get ready for the march. The weather was bitter but the group was somewhat recovered and eager to get underway. It was a welcome relief from the melancholia that had invaded the little community. The task of preparing for the march broke my somber mood and I was relieved to be again preparing for battle. The soldiers, especially were glad to be going about soldier's business. Juan Rodriguez wanted nothing so much as to be soldiering and subduing the enemy. Captain Aguilar, always eager for adventure, was boasting about the trophies he would gain. Most of the men were of the same temperament, the usual euphoria before a battle. Soldiers brag of prowess to smother gnawing fears of the deaths they know may await them.

To forget my woes, I threw myself into preparation hoping to ease my fear for Inez. I oiled my steel as black rust was a plague in those parts. I selected "El Zaqal' for my mount and groomed the excited steed for the march. On the morning of the third day, we fell to, in military fashion, before the outskirts of San Juan.

Mounted and in full armor, the army was formidable as the red morning sun raked off the helmets and pikes. My command was a small squadrom of musketeers.

Vicente stood out from the rest. He was not so old as I, indeed, was not much more than a youth, but had battled as many savage foes as I and was often boastful about these deeds. He was heavily armed and straddled a large grey warhorse, his sword long and heavy and his armor, though battered, looked impressive. He was not a big man, but in his armor and mounted, he made an impressive sight. We were eager to set off under his command.

The governor, splendid in black full dress armor, reviewed our small band and with words of encouragement, ordered us to do battle with a foe who threatened our very existence. He longed to join us in battle but said it was the duty of his office to safeguard the colony. He made it clear that the Acomans had to surrender and accept punishment or be destroyed if we were to survive.

A mass was conducted by Father Martinez and he blessed the group before we set out. He begged for the Lord's guidance and urged us to spare the innocent. Both he and Father Escalona would be with us.

We turned south, riding in silence amidst the clatter of wagons and cannon, each man lost in his own thoughts. It then occurred to me that we had no clear plan for this expedition. This bothered me to such an extent that I spoke to Aguilar who rode beside me.

"Have you thought how we are to proceed on this mission?" I asked.

"I have discussed a plan with Vicente." he replied. "The rock is irregular so any firm plan can be thwarted by unforeseen obstacles. What is almost certain is that a seige would be useless. The Indians are well supplied and protected in their aerie."

Aguilar's armor was spectacular. Although I was not impressed by such things, I couldn't help but admire the burnished and scrolled silver plating covering him and his horse. I wondered what kind of soldier this man would make who seemed so keen on appearance.

"We must scale the rock and bring up the cannon," he continued. "That will put an end to them quickly." He laughed and said that the only problem was moving the cannon up to the summit.

We marched through deep snow until reaching the river. From that point, the ground was bare and the cold less bitter.

The night found us camped by a grove of large trees on the rivar bank. We dined on mutton stew and bread. The men enjoyed this rare treat as we were all sick of Indian corn and beans and the tough flesh of rabbits and the leathery tortilla which made us long for Spanish wheat bread. While the army rested in this grove, I was ordered to secure provisions from the nearby Tzia pueblo. We needed supplies for at least ten days.

Once again I faced the peril of making demand for tribute. To provision an army of seventy men for ten days would require several wagon loads Of food. I left the grove with a small guard, two carretas and an interpreter. Tzia lay several leagues to the west.

Fortunately this pueblo readily supplied us with the needed goods. It was, I suspect, because they were ancient enemies of the Acoman people and knew of our mission. They said that word of our expedition had spread rapidly before us and it was likely to arrive at Acoma before we did. No one, Castillo or Indian, had ever defeated the Acomans or scaled the rock in an open assault they said.

The Indians carried many buckets of corn, squash, beans and dried fruits and meats to our carretas and seemed eager to have us on our way. Well supplied, we rejoined the main army on the river bank and Vicente began to outline a plan for scaling the fortress. The plan was bold, even rash and there were many who disagreed. But I thought back to what the Tzia Indians had said: It had never been done by anyone. Would we be the first succeed or were our bones destined to bleach on the barren plain?

BOOK X

*". . . That the passion of inflicting harm,
the cruel thirst for vengeance, a plundering
and implacable spirit . . . all these are
justly condemned in war."*

St. Augustine

1

For several days, the Indians of Acoma had been preparing for our assault. We learned this from prisoners friendly to us and a spy we had planted amongst them. They offered the following accounts:

Shortly after the killing of the Maese de Campo and his men, there was great consternation amongst the Acoman people. The war chief Gicombo and the venerable leader Chumpo had been absent during the massacre and were appalled when they learned of it. They called the people together and demanded to know who was responsible.

"I am," a warrior called Zutacapan spoke boldly. "I, and all the people you see around you. We defended our honor against outrages from these Castillos."

"You have caused the death of many Castillos," Gicombo said. "We Acomans now feed their bones to the vultures. The Castillos now will come for more blood. You have brought much harm to us, Zutacapan."

"He will be our death," cried Chumpo. "He has killed without cause. This is our shame."

"Without cause? Shame? This Gicombo fears old women and this old man Chumpo is not fit for crow bait." Zutacapan spit out these bitter words. "We fight for survival. The Castillos would have us all slaughtered like rabbits to feed their wives and dogs. They steal our food and our blankets and leave us to die in the snow. Why should we let them do these things to us?" he paused.

"Is it wrong to kill your torturer?" he continued. "Your tormentor? Is it wrong for the hare to kill the fox? Or the deer to kill the mountain lion? No, I say. The Castillos act as if we are hares or deer for their taking. It is time to fight back. Do not listen to this council of old women."

Then Zetancalpo spoke. He was not in league with his father. "We are not hares or deer. They do not kill for pleasure like we did. It is we who have drawn first blood, not the Castillos. Chumpo is right. Gicombo is right. We must listen to their council."

Zutacapan was angry with these remarks. He pointed at his son and shouted, "Does this man seek to join the mice in the field who are trod upon by all? Who scurry about in dark holes because they fear the world? Is he afraid? We Acomans, we killed those who would have killed us. Yes, we drew blood first, but only to defend ourselves against these outsiders, these aliens who would destroy us. If we wait for their good will, we shall all perish. Their God, their cross, of which they are so proud and claim to be so good, is our burden, our death." He stopped speaking as many shouted encouragement to him.

"I ask you, who killed the Castillos? Did not all of us join in this blood-letting? Who are these that would deny such? Cowards, I say. Rabbits! Hares! Deer! Mice! There are no men amongst them."

Gicombo lunged at Zutacapan but was held back by friends. The crowd cheered wildly for Zutacapan and refused to listen to Gicombo or his followers. Seeing this defeat, Gicombo left the tumult and the field to Zutacapan.

The crowd called on Zutacapan to lead their defense against the Castillos. Gicombo and Chumpo had counciled to use help from Apache warriors who would attack from below. Zutacapan would not hear of this.

"We have no need for these Apache vermin. We can defend ourselves," he spoke to the crowd again. "But, as for every great battle, my people, we must prepare to die. This rock may turn red with our blood but it will forever be part of us, built from our bones.

"First, we must celebrate this death and prepare for victory over the Castillos. We will no longer be slaves but will, in our struggle to the death, destroy the hated Castillos. Our victory will be certain! Out of our blood will spring a new freedom for Acoman people."

For days after this fiery speech the Indians celebrated and determined to celebrate until we arrived. Warriors and women stripped naked and painted their bodies with demon symbols unconcerned about the bitter cold in their fortress heights. They performed many depraved and bestial acts to appease their gods and prepare for death. They stacked missiles of all kinds at the edge of the precipice. The drums beat continuously on that pinnacle and they danced around the devil's own fire until they dropped from exhaustion.

Zutacapan became worried as days went by with no sign of us to be seen. The unified will which he had so carefully constructed to struggle and die together would evaporate soon unless the hated enemy showed their faces.

2

It was then that we arrived, knowing nothing of these plans and schemes. We approached our destination through a deep canyon several leagues to the southeast of the fortress. Emerging from between the dark walls of the canyon, we passed into a large arroyo which led into the surrounding plain, keeping the rock hidden from view. Leaving the arroyo, we climbed onto the plateau and the black rock loomed over us like a demon. It was a sobering sight at that distance, as now it was seen with the eyes of those who would dare assault such a bastion.

It is an extraordinary natural fortress, rising in sheer vertical structures of rock to terrifying heights. There are two rock formations split by a yawning chasm at one end. As we drew closer, we could make out figures of the Acomans who were now astir at our presence, jumping about wildly on the southern summit.

"Do you hear the noise?" I asked Rodriguez as we drew nearer. It was a faint hum, like the buzzing of distant bees. As we drew nearer, the hum turned into a roar and finally into a terrible din as if Satan were leading a crazed choir from hell.

"They have been waiting for us," he replied. "Shortly we shall give them something to howl about."

We marched closer until we reached a grove of trees just out of bow shot. Here the cannon and other heavy guns were hauled to a placement with a field of view to the summit. As we approached I noticed the strange misshappen rocks I had seen on my earlier journey. Next to the grove of twisted trees were dry and dusty fields now with only a few dead stalks of corn. Nearby at the base of the rock, were pens made of sticks laced together with thick grass. They were empty. We estimated that it was possible to set a cannon ball into the pueblo from that point although the range was great.

After much argument we set on a plan to open a mock assault from the southeast. The main entrance to the fortress was well in the northwestern quadrant and would be the most heavily fortified. We deigned to draw the savages to the opposite side at which time an assault team would scale the main entrance. A real assault launched from the southeast was foolhardy as the savages commanded every field of view covering an approach. It was hoped that the Acomans would be taken in by our "blunder" while the cannon were hauled up the main entrance. This tactic had been used successfuly by the great Gonsalvo in 1500 against the Turks at St. George in Cephalonia.

Once we were in place and ready to carry out our plans, the surrounding bleak winter landscape made our prospects seem dim and a gloomy depression settled on the troops. We saw each other as if for the last time, knowing that our enemy greatly outnumbered us and remembering how modern weapons had failed to save the maese de campo.

We prepared our souls for battle as Father Escalona and Father Martinez moved amongst us to hear confession. I noticed that the rays of the weak winter sun shining on the kneeling men were almost obscured by brown dust kicked up by our horses. How dry. How barren. How I longed for spring and a fresh sea breeze, to be away from the infernal dust blotting out the sun. This dust that would soak up our blood as if it had never existed and bury us forever in this godforsaken place.

It was odd that at this point, with death looking down at us and howling down our throats, one of us should refuse confession. Lorenzo Salado struggled with Father Escalona and then retreated to a bush where he hid himself. This man was no coward and had always been a staunch fellow during all encounters. Yet something had blackened his soul, for he refused to make his peace with God. We thought this an evil sign and many of the men petitioned me and Vincente to leave this fellow behind.

I sought out Father Escalona in an attempt to solve the matter.

"Ay, the wretch is of bad blood," he said. "All attempts to bring him into the fold have failed."

I was puzzled by this. While many fellow soldiers showed weakness in their profession of faith, they were always eager to be first in confession or mass. My puzzlement turned to suspicion.

"What of his family? I don't recall relatives," I asked.

"Family? None, I suppose, although he is so closelipped that not much is known about him. He irritates me greatly and I have not pursued any particular interest in his affairs."

Asencio de Archuleta then joined our conversation. "I would speak to you about Lorenzo Salado," he said in hushed tones. "I have suspected for some time that this man is tainted. I know for certain he has Latin texts with him."

I trembled at this charge. But then I knew that this man had joined the expedition at Casco replacing those who left and for that reason had not been properly investigated. I decided to pay him a visit.

I went to the wretch and saw great fear in his face. I had seen this man only seldom, but now it struck me that I had seen him somewhere else.

"Why have you refused confession?" I demanded.

"What business is it of yours, Captain," came his surly reply. "I am not in your troop." He was greatly agitated by my presence. "I have come to fight, not to pray."

"You have stained this expedition by refusing confession." I watched his expression closely and suddenly felt the presence of Luis de Carvajal. "Are you a secret Jew?" I blurted out, startled by my own accusation.

"Captain, I say again, I am here but to fight. For God's sake, leave me be and let me fight. Now is not the time to pursue this matter. I will 'confess' in due time."

I left him and spoke to Archuleta. "I believe he is a Jew," he said. "Why else would he refuse confession? Why does he have forbidden texts? God will punish us if we allow this vermin to fight with us. Arrest him now and let the Holy Office decide."

I thought of Luis Carvajal and decided not to be stampeded by suspicion. "We have no grounds for this accusation. This man is an able fighter and if he chooses to risk his life in sin, we can then but pray for him. But, for now, we need every man in camp. Hold your tongue for now."

"Aye, Captain, but I don't like it. And neither do my comrades. It would be best if he didn't join us."

"Hold your tongue. Be off with you and stop this agitation. Save your bile for the dogs above." I returned to my battle preparations.

Firebrands now rained down close to us and as the sun began to lower in the west, these flaming missiles became more spectacular. All fell short of their mark except for a few which fell amongst us but did no harm.

As evening approached, bitter arguments broke out again. We were not yet of one mind on how to proceed. Vicente still found much resistance to his assault plan. There were those who had changed their strategy upon seeing the fortress for the first time. They argued for a siege.

"We can wait them out," said Muñuera, sergeant of the cannoneers. "When they run out of victuals we can drive them off the rock with a bombardment from the culverins." Several men gathered around Munera in silent agreement.

"We don't have the provisions or ammunition to lay a siege." The sergent's voice was sharp in retort. "we must attack. The sooner, the better."

"You best call for their surrender first," said Father Martinez, who had been monitoring the debate.

"That I will, but look above, Father. Do you believe that mob will surrender?"

As the sun had dipped to the horizon, Vicente decided to make his first move. Splended in his armor he mounted his horse and, calling the notary, made his way toward the base of the precipice. He told us all to stand well back and should they kill him, we were to fire the leveled cannon into their midst. Muñuera stood by the touch-holes with a flaming faggot.

As Vicente and the notary proceeded to the base, a barrage of missiles was hurled down on them but they were both well armored and remained undaunted. Vicente raised his spear arm to the crowd and then threw the spear in the dust. At this, the howling ceased and it was with much awe that we watched the silent figures above.

The notary lifted his trumpet and sent a discordant blast towards the summit. He then read a proclamation from Don Juan, calling for the sur— render of those responsible for the murders of the Maese de Campo and his men. This proclamation was long-winded, and before he could finish the Indians again took up their howling and hooting. Vicente called the notary to fall back to the troop and standing up in his saddle he shouted, "People of Acoma," his strong voice echoed amongst the rocks as the crowd quieted once more to hear this new voice, "we have come in peace. But there are some amongst you who have spilled Spanish blood." He said the words slowly, hoping that somehow they would understand. "You must come down and face justice." He gestured with his hand, motioning for them to come down. "This is our demand." His voice boomed off the silent rocks and died in the sandhills at the bottom of the cliff.

When they realized he had finished speaking, a new hail of missiles rain-ed down and the terrible din resumed. Amidst flying debris and rocks, Vicente calmly retrieved his spear from the dust and slowly rode back to where we stood. He was spattered with the filth hurled from above.

"Tomorrow, at cock-crow. We attack as planned," he said.

3

Huge fires blazed on the dark precipice, sending hot sparks skyward. The savages danced, wild and naked in the firelight. I had made a small camp under a tree and brushed Zaqal until his coat gleamed. The sound of the monotonous drum was maddening, repeating the same devilish beat over and over. I found myself brushing my mount too hard and he squeal-ed in pain. We were all on edge and I was besieged by thoughts of my beloved Inez. Where could she be? I thought I might never see her again should I find death my companion on this expedition.

As the night deepened and the drums continued their maddening beat, a small fear I had carried with me began to demand attention. This fear had loitered in my mind, much as a hidden flea under the skin. It irritated me greatly, yet do what I might, it would not go away. It was there, I could feel it. Then as my melancholy deepened, new images of Inez slipped into my mind. At first, she drifted in and out, like whisps of fog, but then, I clearly saw her — on top of the rock. It was but a fleeting vision but it had been clear and my heart leapt like a wounded deer. Had she returned to her people?

My mind reeled with wild thoughts but then I knew that if she were really there, it was to prevent bloodshed, to serve Father Oroz.

Inez. So foolish in her simple faith. But then the vision vanished. Yet some force beyond my understanding drove me, I had to scale the rock and search for her. I went to Father Martinez.

"You are mad", he said. "Even if she is up there, you will only manage to cause her death as well as your own. Forget this and wait till morning."

I reminded him about the robe, how it had saved me before and that I believe it would do so again.

"Let me tell you something", he said. "The robe will indeed protect you. But we all have much to lose. I believe Brother Leo is up there with the heathen. When none would go amonst these Acomans, he insisted on moving amongst them. I did not tell Don Juan this. I knew he would refuse."

I was shocked. I had forgotten Brother Leo, since he had been tended by the other Franciscans during the long journey. "But he is blind. The savages have surely killed him by now."

"That would be a blessing for Brother Leo. But his prayer was to avoid this confrontation. It seems this is not to be. I regret that Inez was involved. She was to lead him to the rock fortress and then return." He looked furtively toward the summit.

"If they are up there, we must try to bring them down. Father, why didn't you tell me? Why? Why? Oh Lord! If she is really up there!"

"Forgive me. I never thought until now that she would go up there with Brother Leo. But there was no stopping those two." He paused for a moment and then said. "I will go with you. We will both go to the top."

I changed into the robe and we moved quickly out of the encampment. We moved along the base of the wall without being seen, out of sight of those above. The moonlight shifted as thick patches of clouds passed over the pinnacle. With this light, we found our way through a small, narrow canyon. The broken white rock loomed up in the darkness and seemed a gateway to death and impossible to scale. After praying to God for help and salvation, I searched for handholds in the rock but found none.

"Let me go first." the friar said, and within a short time I saw him moving up the wall like a fly. I followed his lead and we climbed in the fearful darkness where all was silent except for the drumbeat. Broken rock fell and clattered down the wall. At what seemed to be the halfway point, the friar ceased moving and clung to the surface. I waited and then in a low voice asked him what was wrong.

"I don't know." he rasped. "I am unable to move. I can't find another handhold."

A light wind had sprung up. I hung below the friar, listening to the wind whistle amongst the rocks. His form above was black, I could see only his robe moving in the breeze. For a terrifying moment, I felt I was pitching headlong into the fearful abyss. I too, froze to the surface of the rock. Feeling as if eternity were slipping by, I grasped desperately at the crumbly surface. When I looked up again the friar had disappeared. I had not heard any cry or sound of falling. With God's help, I overcame my fear and moved up to where the friar had been and held onto the wall until my body screamed in pain. I was sure the void would swallow me and I prayed for Father Martinez and Inez and the others below. Suddenly, I heard a call from above: "Move to the left, Don Gaspar. There you will find what you need."

With a sigh I moved to the left and found an indentation in the rock large enough to support my foot. With some difficulty. I swung over to the new position on the wall. On the verge of plunging into the abyss, I found another foothold and then another. I realized we had come upon a ladder cut into the stone.

"The Indians have made this," he said when I reached the top. "It must be one of their entrances. God be praised."

It had been a miracle. I had been sure, on that wall in the dark of night, that we were doomed. But now that we had gained the top, I had no plan, no mind as to the whereabouts of Inez. if indeed she were up there at all.

"Follow me," he said. The drums were now much louder and I could see the glow of fires in the sky. We proceeded along an area of flat rock, but remained hidden from view by large boulders that loomed like small mountains into the sky. Finally we reached the outskirts of the village where multistoried houses made of stone stood over us. Dogs barked, but there seemed little else. We moved cautiously, Father Martinez always in the lead, seeming to know a destination. From a side door we heard a cry. We froze and listened. Again we heard the cry. It sounded like the crackled voice of Brother Leo.

We moved in the direction of the cry and were suddenly pulled into a room by strong hands. We were captured. They shoved us roughly to the floor and held torches close to our faces.

"Castillos!" they cried and then murmured in their own tongue. Shortly, a fierce-looking savage with a war-club moved towards us. Father Martinez began praying and I cried out the name of Inez. They lifted us from the floor and through signs, they indicated that we must leave the rock for our own good. I pleaded for information about Inez but there was no response. Even though we resisted, they took us down a steep incline and led us out onto the plain below where they melted into the darkness. With difficulty, we found our way back to the encampment. In despair, I changed back into my uniform and armor.

4

Unable to sleep, we waited for the thin light of dawn. Before cock-crow the message was passed to move out into assault teams. Twelve of us were to scale the entrance to the west while the main group carried a mock assault on the southeast. We waited, hidden, while the main group formed into squadrons. They formed three squadrons of fifteen men each, armed with harquebus and musket. A high pinnacle was sited as the staging point around which two squadrons would flank while the third would lead a frontal assault. While the main intent of this tactic was diversionary, it was important for this group to maintain direct contact with the enemy without being overrun. If the savages elected to attack rather than defend it would go badly for them. The two cannon would be with us.

While the first group circled south, we waited with the cannon to which we had hitched ourselves by ropes. When the drums ceased and a loud howl again came from the top, we heard the sound of gunfire from the south. This was our signal to move out.

Vincente led one squad and Aguilar led the other. We circled around the base without being detected. Muñuera and his men moved a heavy wagon of ball and shot behind us. We reached what we took to be a pathway to the top and immediately set to the climb. Each of us filled a leather pack with cannon ball and so burdened we pulled and hauled this armory to the summit.

The tactic worked. While the main body carried the mock assault against the southern ramparts, infuriating the savages, we gained the western most summit by sunrise. Positioning the cannon for an initial assault, Vicente sent a messenger to the main body. In the meantime, we found the craggy surface difficult to negotiate and were almost trapped when a footbridge gave out. As we progressed we surprised a large group of Indians waiting in reserve, it seemed. We were outnumbered ten to one and stood between our cannon and this group. Without hesitation, Aguilar led a savage attack with pistol and musket that so startled the savages they turned and fled as they watched their comrades drop around them. They retreated several hundred yards up the narrow ledge on which we were also perched. Finally they overcame their fear and turning, they launched a hail of arrows at us and bunched together to attack. When they were within a hundred yards, Vicente signaled to Muñuera and we dropped into the dust. At that moment the cannon fired one after the other into their ranks. The grapeshot did much damage and again they fled in terror. But they bravely turned and launched their arrows, one pierced Valesco through the thigh. We again fired the muskets and pistols while Muñuera prepared the cannon for a second volley.

Clearly the Indians were surprised and terrorized by our weapons. At each volley they would lose many and retreat, allowing us time to reload. At the same time they watched most of their arrows bounce harmlessly off our armor. They were confused and did not know how to deal with this except by direct attack, grouping together for protection against the sticks that spit death. But this made them fine targets for both musket and cannon and they kept coming at us in this manner until they all were dead or dying.

The irony of the ordeal was that our great advantage was the rock fortress itself. The Indians threw themselves at us over the rocky ledges, exposing themselves to an open field of fire.

Some of our second group now arrived climbing the same path and then more savages in great numbers appeared on the ledges in front of us. In the meantime Muñuera moved the cannon up to higher ground. It was now a furious battle as the spirited savages kept coming at us. Some survived the hail of gunfire and reached our quarter where we had to fight with sword and ax. We all fought under the charge of Aguilar and the sergeant major. Both these men led every foray, firing pistols, slashing with knife and sword until they were covered with the gore of the slain enemy.

Muñuera brought the cannon to bear again and the rear ranks of the savages were quickly destroyed. Finally, seeing the bodies of their comrades falling everywhere, the Indians retreated into their rock fortress, allowing us time to gain the uppermost summit. By that time, the battle had consumed the day and we prepared to fortify for the upcoming darkness.

Although we had hardly more than a foothold on this rocky perch, we already smelled the blood of victory. Our main force held the highest summit now bristling with cannon and harquebus. One squadron still harassed the southeast corner keeping half the Indians occupied.

I did a headcount as ordered by Vincente and found that it appeared we had lost three, with twenty wounded but still ablebodied. Two of the slain men died courageously under the savage blows of the war club.

The third man to die was Lorenzo Salado. Because of the trouble be had caused amongst the troops, I brought him with us on the assault, an assignment he eagerly accepted. He labored with us to haul the cannon up that slope and made many a bone-wearying trip to bring up the ammunition. He had been in the forefront of every foray. I saw him run through several with his sword and split open the belly of another who was about to bring his war club down on the valiant Aguilar. After one of the battles when the savages had retreated and he gave chase, I called on him to fall back to our position and as he turned a musket ball caught him in the face, tearing a great hole through his head. The force of the blow knocked him over the edge of the cliff. Archuleta had fired the shot, claiming an accident as he was aiming at the savages beyond.

The Indians had lost many warriors, by all counts greater than two hundred. It had been a serious defeat for them although they still greatly outnumbered us.

I reported our condition to Vicente and he was clearly pleased. "On the morrow we shall deal them the death blow they so richly deserve. Then we will fire the town."

"But," replied Father Martinez, who had climbed the summit to join us, "we must still give them a chance to surrender. Remember the opinion given in San Juan?" When Vicente clucked at these words Father Martinez frowned and drew out a parchment from his pouch. "Here, I will read the last paragraph again:

"If war be waged, the wrongs done which merit punishment should be dealt with and righted as the situtation requires. The innocent who have done no wrong should always be protected. Bloodshed and death should be avoided as much as possible, for death is most distasteful to Almighty God. So much does He abhor it that David, because he was a murderer, was not permitted to complete the temple he planned to build to God. Also it should be considered that those who die in an evil cause, such as is found now amongst these savages, are certain of damnation."

He stopped reading and lifted his head. he eyed us steadily, "Don't you see? These words have great import and should not be taken lightly. Those scattered corpses lying yonder are all lost souls. There is no chance for them now. Their souls will burn in hell forever. And who has been the cause? Will God blame us? Is our lust for blood so great that we ignore our Christian duty to God? Gentlemen, hear me when I call for protection of the innocent. But here, let me finish this opinion:

". . . many of these souls might well be saved and converted. Those who merit death can be properly proceeded against by civil authorities, and they, in inflicting death, do so because the penalty is deserved and under virtue of both civil and divine authority.

"That is the opinion of the friars and the commissary." He looked now at Vicente.

The sergeant major was upset by these words. That very day he had killed a savage wearing his brother's coat. This set him into bitter lamentations and the wounds of grief ran with fresh blood.

"I will obey your opinion," he said dryly. "As for God, I doubt if he holds with you or with these murderous dogs." He jumped to his feet. "Would you save the wolf that tears the throat out of your mother? Is God really angry with us because we destroy these vermin who blasphemy His Holy Name? Is it not God's justice that these miserable wretches suffer eternal damnation?" He glared at the priest.

"Yes," he continued, "I will protect the innocent. But as far as I can see there is not a single innocent soul on this miserable rock. They have all soaked their hands in innocent blood."

5

As the morning light lifted the dark veil on the eastern horizon, we formed into squadrons to move across the village to the southeast where we would join our men battling from below. Muñuera stood by the cannons to start the first fusilades which would open the way for us.

Before we could carry out this plan we were astonished to see through the dim light a great force of savages leading the attack in our direction. A hail of arrows greeted us as we quickly cleared the way for Muñuera and he fired the first round. The savages flung themselves though the morning darkness into this fiery maw without hesitation and gave us little time to reload before they were on us with club and stones.

The cannon's incessant fire illuminated the battle scene with a hellish glow and took a terrific toll on the savages as we beat off those who had penetrated our ranks. In short order the streets were filled with confused masses of the dead and dying and still the cannons flayed until their barrels were too hot to touch. Finally, the decimated savages fled back into the now smoking village. The battle ceased at that point and we rested and treated our wounds with glad hearts as it was almost certain victory was in our hands. We were thankful that we had suffered no fatal casualties.

But the slaughter before us was appalling. The streets were awash with blood and cluttered with broken naked bodies. An uncanny quiet settled over the grisly scene. Here and there a dog could be seen slinking in the shadows, nose seeking the street. Large black birds circled overhead riding the high wind, attracted by the smell of death. The confines of the rock did not allow us to withdraw from that ghastly sight and we saw the birds alight and pluck at the glazed eyes.

Several captains and the priest held council and then demanded that we call for surrender.

"And how, may I ask, can I do that," Vicente replied, "when there isn't a live savage in sight?"

Nevertheless, he sent several soldiers and the notary into the town to officially demand surrender. Finding no one, the surrender team returned and Vicente ordered two soldiers to a nearby house where we were certain several Indians had taken refuge. Upon demands for surrender they were greeted by a hail of stones from the rooftop and before we could react, the savages escaped through the labyrinth of rooms and alleyways.

"We cannot sit here and wait for them to surrender." And with that Vicente ordered the siege balls brought up to the deadly instruments.

But there were many who opposed this and at least I could no longer contain my suspicion concerning Inez.

"I don't believe she is here," he said when I told him of my fears. "I will give you and the men two hours to search for her or to get these vermin to surrender. Two hours."

We were in control of a high rocky ledge overlooking the entire pueblo. The top of the first cliff is covered by a series of shallow, rocky ledges falling away to the south. A cannonade at that point would bring every house in the pueblo under fire. I noticed that the houses were built of small stone and some were three stories high. The cannonballs would splinter these stones and turn them into deadly missiles. To our left was a large natural rock cistern filled with clear water. This was their water supply. It was now in our hands.

If I could find Chumpo, a man of great honesty whom I had met once though Inez, he could help us and tell me if Inez was amongst them. And so with Marquez, de las Casas and Rodriguez we imperiled our lives by entering the quarter still held by the savages. We moved from door to door, arms at the ready. Not a soul stirred as we walked the streets in the cold, glaring sun. We soon reached the northern precipice where a house stood balanced precariously on the ledge looking as if it would slide into the deep abyss at any moment. We were at the limit of our excursion. At any time we could be cut off from the main troop. Suddenly the wrinkled old Chumpo emerged from that perch and we made signs for him to join us.

We walked back to where Vicente stood and the old man, with tears in his eyes, told us the tale of woe that had befallen his people. We understood little of his words but most of the meaning was clear. *It was enough killing. It would be best if the killing stopped. They would be obedient to the governor.*

After he finished his plea I spoke. "We must stop the bloodshed," I told him. "Bring us those responsible for the deaths of the Castillos. We will punish those and your people will be free." I then asked for Inez but he seemed not to understand my meaning.

He motioned for us to follow him. shortly we came to a place darkened with gore. He made us understand that this was where Juan de Zaldivar had been killed. Vicente threw himself to the ground and wept. Then he rose and swelling with rage said, "Tell him to bring them to me. Tell him."

Chumpo was startled but motioned for us to be silent and wait for him. He left, his cotton blanket flapping like the wings of a white butterfly and disappeared down the street. After a while we heard a great commotion coming from the direction in which Chumpo had disappeared. Because the noise sounded threatening, we returned quickly to the main troop.

Some time later, Chumpo reappeared leading a large group of women who were carrying baskets of corn and herding turkeys. They tethered the turkeys and silently laid the corn at our feet. They then stripped themselves of the cotton and deerskin blankets they wore and piled them at our feet. We understood that they were giving us the original tribute the Maese de Campo had demanded."

After much talk, little of which was understood, the women were taken into custody and Vicente spoke to Chumpo. "You old fool. This will not do. We must have the surrender of the vermin who committed the crimes against the Castillos."

Vicente then ordered the turkeys released and he ordered the corn and blankets dumped over the precipice. Chumpo stood by, puzzled at such wanton behavior.

We made signs to show him that he was to bring those responsible for the murders to that spot. Chumpo listened quietly and watched our signs with glazed eyes that seemed to sink into the back of his skull. We thought he indicated that he understood. When we finished, he left us and disappeared down the street. He never returned.

Vicente would wait no longer. He ordered the cannons loaded and started firing at the nearby buildings. The hot balls crushed the rock walls into splinters and in no time the buildings fell into smoking, blackened ruins and caught fire. Soldiers stood by with muskets and harquebuses and as the Indians emerged from the smoke-filled ruins, they were blasted into hell. Although there were attempts to spare women and children it was not always possible. For several hours this cannonade went on and by nightfall much of the town had been destroyed and many more had been killed. The entire rock was now drenched with blood and smelled of the gases of death and a dense pall of smoke and ash covered the sky.

Again the carnage was appalling. Too much blood had been spilled and the sight of those dead and dying brought despair to our hearts. Here was everything that Inez and Father Oroz had feared. We were prisoners of our own fear and our outrageous need to be victorious in battle. And here was a foe so determined not to surrender that they flung themselves into the waiting bullets with glee. Now as the day faded and another hellish night faced us, I determined to search through the smouldering ruins, compelled once more by something I did not understand.

I walked the rubbled remnants of the streets, stumbling over stones and corpses, trying to close my ears to the groans of the dying. I had never been in a place where the smell of death was so strong. Finally, when darkness was about to rescue me from this vile scene, I heard a moan that I knew immediately was Inez. And then it came to me clearly why I had been searching and what my visions had meant.

I rushed to a building where only the roof had fallen in and found a woman amongst the smouldering rubble. She had been badly crushed by the falling rocks and burned and a missile had ripped through her shoulder. I rushed through the gloom and smoke to help her.

"Castillo," she gasped when I went to her. I called her name and tried to remove her from the rubble but she motioned for me to desist with a free hand.

"Castillo," she rasped again through her bloodied teeth and I detected a bitter hate in this rattling sound.

"Inez." I cried again, trying to revive her from this death stupor.

"Castillo," and I saw the flash of a knife in the darkness. With a cry of bewilderment, I knocked the knife from her hand and recoiled in horror from the dying figure. This could not be Inez.

I rushed from the place with terror in my heart but then I ran back and again knelt over the dying women.

"Inez. Inez. It's me, Gaspar," I cried.

Her dazed eyes slowly opened and in that gloom and smoke I saw a flash of recognition.

"Gaspar," she whispered. "Gaspar, My love." She reached out feebly with the hand that had held the knife. "Forgive me."

I cradled her in my arms, crying her name over and over. In my grief I died there with her.

6

There is no worse punishment that man can endure. How I survived that night is more than I can explain. When I heard the cannon start firing at daybreak, I rushed out and up into the mouth of death. But I was spared and when my men saw me they loudly cheered.

I called out to Vicente to cease the cannonade and he sharply pointed behind me. I turned and saw a large body of warriors, fully armed, advancing on our part with Gicombo and Zutacapan in front. It was a final bold maneuver and the guns and cannon blasted the savages into a mass of unrecognizable flesh and blood. When the smoke cleared, there was no one left.

This final futile effort by the savages had had its effect. They died, as men are wont to die, defending their homeland. With those cannonballs and bullets tearing flesh and smashing bone the hate was finally dissipated and Vicente called for a cease-fire.

There was no need for futher killing. The Acomans were defeated and my Inez was dead, killed by our lust for arms and victory. As the smoke began to thin Chumpo, his face streaked with smoke and tears, led the last of his people to our line. It was over.

7

That was long ago. Brother Leo was never found. Later, there was a legend amongst the tribes of a beautiful woman in a brown robe and an old blind monk who visited them from time to time preaching the truth of the Gospel. I was forever a few days behind the legend, searching the lonely sands and rocks, praying that I was wrong. I grieved for Inez until black despair forced me to leave those regions forever.

EPILOGUE

As I reread these lines, I am appalled at how much I have revealed. There will have to be serious editing if this document is to be used to prove our innocence. I may hide these papers forever lest too much be known. My epic poem has another kind of truth and it is much better if historians use the poem to write their tomes.

My sister's husband told me that my freedom is at hand. Proceeds from my poem will be used by the Council of the Indies to pay court costs in Mexico. They are now willing to entertain new testimonies from myself and Don Juan. The edited version of these pages will no doubt serve us well. Yet, I cannot say that we will be exonerated. It is a matter of pride that I claim our innocence is proven by these words, but this new king will not be easily convinced. I have been informed that he has taken a particular dislike to all involved in the Conquest. Yet, this same king proudly boasts of his new empire now represented by the village of Villa de Santa Fe.

Still, I feel my freedom is at hand and my purpose is done. The final story of the three friars is now included in the works of Father Oroz which is soon to be printed in memory of the Franciscans of New Spain.

Don Juan is here now and pleased that the commission has agreed to hear our relation. He is fit and looking well for such an advanced age. The sight of our beloved country has caused him to shed many years. He has told me that Marquez and Rodriquez are in New Mexico and have fared well. I shall write to them soon.

As I bring these pages to a close, my mind wanders back to the beginning, to those first glorious nights in Zacatecas when I met Inez. So long ago. If I could only relive them once again.

GLOSSARY

This glossary explains special or archaic terms of the 16th C. appearing in this book. It does not cover common usage words.

Adelantado: The title given to the first conqueror and colonizer of a frontier province. This title was held in great esteem.

Ako: Pueblo word for Acoma.

Arroba: Weight measure; about 25 pounds.

Bagre: Large scaleless fish, probably related to the catfish family. There seems to be nothing like this fish in the Rio Grande today.

Cacique: Word of Indian origin meaning leader. The Cacique held little power and the title changed hands often.

Carreta: Two-wheeled cart, usually with solid wheels and pulled by oxen. Large carretas were pulled by mule teams and were used to haul ore and quicksilver. The larger carts were also called carros.

Castillo: Pueblo Indian name for Spaniard. Castilla was used also.

Chaiani: Pueblo word for Indian spirit men capable of interpreting signs.

Chichimecas: Wild, nomadic groups of Indians living north of Mexico City. From all reports, these people were the most primitive of all North American aborigines.

Converso: A Jew who had been converted into Christianity. This was supposedly voluntary, but Jews who did not convert were expelled from the country or otherwise eliminated.

Colegio: Franciscan school. The Colegio de Santa Cruz de Tlatelolco was a large college and friary founded in Mexico City in the 16th C., known for its outsanding academic achievements.

Criollo: Person of pure Spanish ancestry either born or brought up in the Americas.

Culverin: Small cannon, usually about a 15 to 20 pounder. These cannon were devastating against the pueblos.

Entrada: Frist penetrations by explorers of an unexplored territory.

Estancia: Large horse-breeding or cattle ranch. Breeding was carefully controled and some of the finest horses and bulls in the world have come from the Estancias in the region of Seville.

Estufas: Spanish word for stove or oven applied to what is now known as a kiva; a pueblo ceremonial fireplace usually in a small, dome shaped room with an entry in the roof.

Falcon: Small cannon usually made of brass; about a 25 pounder.

Fanega: Dry measure; approximately equal to 1.5 bushels.

Guachichiles: A particularly fierce tribe of Chichimecas centered around San Luis Potosi. Also spelled Huachichiles.

Hamper: A travelling case made of wicker; the forerunner of the modern valise.

Harquebus: Firearm of large caliber designed in the 15th C. It was usually held with a tripod or forked rod at the end of the barrel. It was heavy and unwieldly but could fire a pod of musket balls or grapeshot a great distance. A squad of well-trained harquebusiers could lay down a sustained, deadly hail of fire.

Maese de Campo: Commander of the field. There is no equivalent rank in translation.

Marrano: Derogatory term used to describe converted Jews: It literally means 'pig'.

Moriscanos: Another fierce tribe of Chichimecas particularly troublesome in the region around Zacatecas.

Morrion: Half-moon shaped helmets worn by 15th C. soldiers.

Oficium: Small room to conduct interviews or meetings in a friary.

Presidio: Small military post on the frontier designed to protect settlers from marauding Indians and outlaws.

Refectory: Dining hall in a monastary or friary.

Quemadero: Literally means the burning ground. This was an area set aside for burning victims of the Inquisition. It was usually stage with special seats for dignitaries and viewing stands for the public. The entire affair was called an auto-da-fe.

Sanbenito: Black robe with demonic symbols in red. Used by those condemned to die by the Inquisition. Another version was a yellow robe with crosses worn by those who were penitent.

Santiago: War cry used by Spanish soldiers envoking the aid of Saint James, the patron said of Spanish victory.

Vaquero: Cowboy, in the 16th C. this was usually an Indian from one of the sedentary tribes.

Virreina: Title of the wife of the Viceroy.

Zambo: 16th C. term for a person of mixed race - half negro, half Indian.